One Loose String

Christine Scarpa

FIRST EDITION
www.christinescarpa.com

Book Cover, Editing, and Interior
Design by: Michelle Morrow
www.chellreads.com

Front Book Cover Art by:
Katie Seliger

Author Notes and Acknowledgments

I grew up in Rio Grande, NJ just over the bridge from the Wild-woods, a popular shore community known for its beaches and boardwalks, and its amusement piers and back bays. My family owned a motel, The Sans Souci Motel on 21st Street in North Wildwood. Sadly, the motel is no longer there, as the island has become inundated with modern condo buildings. While this book is fiction, many memories of my youth went into the story of Anni and Michael. Arcades, namely Ed's Funcade in North Wildwood where I spent many days playing the Phantom of the Opera pinball game, and Hassles Ice Cream Parlor and Mini Golf which has the greatest waffles and ice cream you will ever have. Other memories include Morey's Piers, The Sea Serpent roller coaster, Raging Waters and The Kite Shop. All of those places are still there!

The ideas from this book came from a collaboration of stories told to me by people who grew up on the barrier islands of Cape May County, including my husband, Kevin who grew up in Avalon. And, of course, some of my own experiences are thrown in there, but I'll never tell which ones!

I want to make special mention to some really amazing people:

My parents, Lois and Richard - for love and support

My husband, Kevin - who critiqued the sex scenes! And, he didn't really complain all that much when I went missing during the editing phases. I love you so much!

My 3 awesome children - who were essentially motherless for

the last month before I published this book!

Chris C.- without her friendship and support I would have given up on the first draft! I love you!

Nancy L. - who spent hours and hours helping me edit, I questioned whether I actually knew English or not after reading her edit suggestions!

Cindy C. Thank you for your round of edits! And sparking some great Facebook conversations on "hooking up"

Chell (my book doula) - Chell Reads Publishing - a special thanks for coaching me, counseling me, talking me down from the ledge!

My Book Club - or should I say my fan club! I love you ladies! And yes, we do read books!

Jennifer, Kelly, Jackie, Elizabeth, Stephanie, Melissa, Christine and Nancy - for reading my pre-edited story and giving me the confidence to keep going.

Katie Seliger - I told Katie to make me a cover for a beachy book and she did not disappoint! She hand paint each draft!

Hayley Scull - for the photo shoot on the beach in February!

All my friends who have cheered me on and gave me the courage to move forward and publish, I love you all!

Contents

Chapter 1: The Scoop

Anni

I lean against the cream-colored wall in my walk-in closet and stare at the row of clothing draped over the hangers. Wow, I own a lot of black stretch pants. A red pencil skirt catches my eye and I wonder if it still fits. It's been a while since I had an occasion to wear something other than yoga pants.

I glance in the mirror and slide my hands down the side of the skirt and over my belly. But, I decide it is too formal. I unzip the side of the skirt and let it fall to the floor, then pull the blouse over my head and drop it on top of the skirt. A basket of clean laundry sits on my bed, and I rummage through and pull out a pair of skinny jeans and a purple t-shirt. I remember he likes purple. I hold my breath and suck in my stomach as I slide the pants on and zip them up. I slip on a pair of black flats, the one with the white checkered bows, and check my hair in the mirror.

A sigh escapes at the sight of myself. Thirty-nine years old. Is that a gray hair? I pluck it out. My make-up drawer overflows with expired products, so I pick through it, pulling out some of the bottles. I put a bottle up to my nose and take a whiff and it seems OK. I rub moisturizer on my face first, followed by some foundation, a little blush, and some black eyeliner. Is this how women still wear their makeup? The last thing I want is to appear too eager.

Being a local in Beacon meant you couldn't leave town from Memorial Day to Labor Day. When school was out and tourists were on vacation, Beacon came alive and the island residents capitalized on tourism as their livelihood. That meant that all your friends' parents owned a seasonal business or worked all summer waitressing at seafood restaurants, bar tending at a club or cleaning the houses of rich summer residents. When you were old enough, you worked. Sometimes two or three jobs. Most of the time, you'd get around by bike, and your parents hardly ever knew where you were because they were so busy working. Come winter, the unemployment lines would be long as employers close for the season.

The drive is short, but road construction has detoured traffic around a newly paved road. It's about time. This road with its potholes has needed repairing for a decade. I recall one morning when I spilled my coffee after leaving The Scoop in a rush to a doctor's appointment. My attention wanes from the orange traffic cones and flashing lights of police vehicles directing traffic and my senses take in the morning.

Old stone buildings house real estate offices and insurance companies on Main Street of Fairway, just a few miles across the bridge from Beacon. The new building being erected will contain many new medical offices. The municipal buildings fill the block in the center of town. I stop at the crosswalk in front of the courthouse to let pedestrians cross the streets in their business suits. A briefcase in one hand and coffee in the other.

The mid-September morning is sticky already, as the humidity rises. The sun in the eastern sky attempts to peek out of the dark clouds. The damp air is so uncomfortable. I adjust the air conditioning in the car so that the vents blow toward my face to avoid my make-up running. A thunderstorm threatens on the western horizon, as it has been oppressive all week.

The gravel parking lot of The Scoop crunches beneath my tires. The Scoop is a family-owned coffee shop in a small, old strip of stores flanked on either side by a thrift shop and a fabric store. Some days I get a cup of coffee and browse for cute patterns or a new treasure from the thrift shop. The last store in the strip is empty. It used to house a fancy, upscale frozen yogurt shop, but Fairway is not upscale. Many residents in Fairway work seasonal jobs in the summers. Others are construction workers, and nurses and school teachers and small business owners. Not the type that would spend ten dollars on a cup of frozen yogurt with real fruit. But you can be sure to wait in line at the Dairy Queen any day.

I take a deep breath as I sit in the car, contemplating calling it off. *Anni, you are crazy. I'll admit he caught me off guard, but it was my fault.*

I check the visor mirror once more and frizz has begun to set into my long brown hair. So, after carefully straightening it this morning, I throw it in a messy bun and re-apply my eyeliner. I take my glasses off and glance in the mirror once again but put them on. Perhaps they will hide some of the regret and deception. I open the camera on my phone, change it to selfie mode and take a picture. And another, and another. I won't post the selfies, but I use them to examine my imperfections, the wrinkle between my eyes and the frown lines in the corner of my lips. I take note to keep my head tilted slightly down while making eye contact. That's my best angle. I should have applied something to the dark circles under my eyes. I hope I don't give the impression of the tiredness I feel. I shut the car off and the thick, damp air seeps through, as I try to make it into the coffee shop before the sweat beads on my forehead.

It is early, but I wanted to settle in and appear "cool and collected." I also want to be sure to get a seat in the back away from the bustle of the morning crowd.

The inside of The Scoop is old brick painted yellow which brightens up the cafe. The black chalkboard sign on the wall reads "The heart wants what it wants - Woody Allen." Oh, The irony. The long counter is made of old dark wood with several stools in a line, occupied by customers enjoying a cup of fresh coffee, chatting about the weather. Behind the counter is a variety of bagels and pastries.

"Good morning, Anni," Miranda says.

"Good morning, Miranda."

"Vanilla latte?"

"Yes, please. And Miranda, can you put in an extra shot of espresso? I will need it." Miranda gives me a sideways glance on her way to the espresso machine. The cafe smells of fresh-baked blueberry muffins combined with the robust aroma of coffee brewing. On a normal day, those smells would welcome me, muffins begging to be warmed and buttered. But this morning they make my stomach turn. I chew on my fingernail while waiting for my coffee... like caffeine will calm these nerves.

I find a seat in the back of the coffee shop. The black table is old Formica and wobbles slightly, but it has two chairs out of view from the front entrance. I glance at my phone. It is 9:05 and my nerves are buzzing. My face burns as my heart pounds out of my chest. I can't sit still. I need to get up. I walk to the bathroom, pee, then recheck my face and my hair. I run my finger over the wrinkle in my forehead. There are quite a few more freckles peeking out this summer and I make a mental note to call the dermatologist to schedule a spot check. After I let out the breath I've been holding, I return to my table.

By 9:15 I am nauseous with anticipation. I tap my fingers on the table, glancing towards the door. It's been so long, over twenty years. I admit I was surprised at Michael's 1 am Facebook IM. I would have probably said no if I wasn't drowsy with sleep. Oh, who am I kidding, I've never been able to say no. Eight hours doesn't give me much time to dwell upon how terrible of an idea this is. Will it feel familiar? So much has changed in twenty years. My hair is straighter. My skin looser, I definitely dress better.

The past seems more like a novel I have read rather than my story. Many memories have faded and seem so unfamiliar. Are my recollections accurate or am I making things up in my head?

I rethink my decision as I contemplate running out the door. If he doesn't come in the next 5 minutes, I will walk out and pretend this never happened. I glance up and make eye contact.

"Anni, is something wrong?"
"No. No. I'm fine. Just meeting a client for coffee," I lie.
Miranda gives me an expression of confusion. I shrug.

Over Miranda's shoulder, I spot him. I sense my pulse quicken as a lump rises again in my throat. I have imagined this moment so many times, but I never thought it would come. I quickly glance down, trying to slow my breathing. I have pictured running into each other's arms like a movie – slow motion, reuniting long lost lovers following a war or some contentious separation. A dramatic piece of music playing in the background, maybe "A Thousand Years." But I am too smart. This is Michael. You have to play his game. *Never let down your guard, I remind myself.* He walks in the coffee shop tall and confident, like a dandruff shampoo commercial. Michael looks familiar, a childhood movie you have watched repeatedly until you have memorized all of its parts. The one where you know the characters inside and out. I hadn't realized that I had memorized his smile, the way he moves. He doesn't see me yet. I try not to appear too fervent, so I stare down at my phone to appear relaxed. My thoughts were broken by a voice I haven't heard in over two decades.

"Anni."
Without thought, my body rises, "Michael." Michael hesitates, then takes a step towards me, as I lean in. We don't know whether to hug, shake hands or passionately embrace or press our lips together and kiss away 20 years of separation. Get a hold of yourself, Anni. We stare at each other for what seemed like an eternity, taking in the newness and familiarity. Michael barely resembles the twenty-one-year-old guy I last saw. Yet, his smile is the same. The crooked smile that melted me every time. His hair is darker and receding slightly. His face is full and

his shoulders are broader. He has a 5 o'clock shadow I never would have imagined him allowing. He looks amazing. I wonder how I will keep myself together. My heart flutters slightly. He is wearing khaki pants that hang low on his hips, which is a stark change from the mesh basketball shorts he wore too frequently. How did I ever find basketball shorts attractive?

So many feelings... fear, love, anger, longing. Then, Michael moves closer and kisses my cheek and embraces me in a hug. I forget to breathe and; I realize I need air. I inhale the scent of him, and the deepest memories flood my mind. His presence fills my thoughts with the trace of the cigarettes, the beer and the rubber smell of condoms.

"Would you like coffee?" I ask, desperate to find something to say.
"That would be great."

I walk to the counter and Miranda puts her hand on mine. Her eyes narrow, her eyebrows making a V. "Anni," she says. I know she doesn't believe Michael is a client.
Miranda makes Michael a coffee and we settle in our seats. We stare in silence not knowing where to start.

"So, how are you?" I ask.
"I'm well," he replies as he laces his long fingers around his coffee cup.
"I have thought of you now and then." That's a lie, though. I think of Michael often. In my dreams, in my nightmares. Smells and places bring back memories, some fond, some not so much.
"As have I." He sounds so serious, not like the Michael I knew at all.
"Have you?" I cock my head to the side, resting my elbow on the table.
"Anni." Michael looks at me as if there are 100 unsaid things in that word. I smile.
"I graduated college," I laugh to break the tension and revel in the absurdity of the simple conversation. It is similar to talking

about the weather. But, I did not come to this coffee shop to talk weather. Plus, I graduated from college 15 years ago.

"I did not," he chuckles back. "I am an electrician. I own my business."

"That is surprising."

Michael chuckles, "Why?"

"Well, I don't know. You never seemed the labor worker, that's all." Michael never had to work in the summer like other teen-agers on the island. He always had brand new cars and seemed to have an endless supply of cash.

"How about you, Anni? What are you doing?"

"I am between jobs at the moment." Michael stares at me for an eternity. I try to stare back but divert my attention to my coffee cup, uncomfortable with his gaze.

"Anni, you look great. You haven't changed much."

"Thank you."

After I got Michael's message last night, I set two goals for meeting here. My first goal was to get out everything I have been holding in for the past 20 years and the other was to prove to myself I am over him. With the way this conversation is going, there's not enough time. And, I don't want to come across as crazy jumping right into a heated discussion that would bring up emotions I haven't dealt with.

"Do you still come to the island in the summer?" I ask.

"No, my business keeps me busy all year. How about you?"

"No, I moved just inland to Fairway a while ago. I don't come back much." The truth is, it 's hard to go back to the island. There is so much hurt and confusion and anger. When I pass by the places we used to go, it reminds me of happy, playful times; laying on the beach, laughing and the promises for the future. But those places: the arcade, the ice cream parlor, mini-golf, motels, they all remind me of tumultuous times, too. The trials and tribulations of being on the cusp caught us between need-ing the security of childhood and the freedom of adulthood. We longed to hold on to innocence yet made bad decisions. I craved Michael's attention at any cost. I lacked confidence. I couldn't go back to the island. I needed so badly to leave that life behind, to bury the memories and the heartache in the sand. If I stay away, it doesn't find me. I wanted to find love, proper love. If I returned home to the island after college it would be the same as ripping a Band-Aid off a wound and I couldn't. I settled in Fairway, and I don't cross the bridge much anymore.

Chapter 2: Summer 1990

Anni

T he air was oppressive and beads of sweat glistened on my face. I pulled my long brown hair in a ponytail and headed into the ocean feeling the cool, wet sand beneath my feet. The waves rolled lightly to shore now that the storm had drifted to sea. The tide was going out, which means we didn't have to worry about our things being swept away by the current. Holly and I came down here practically every day this week. Few tourists crowded the beach with their large beach umbrellas and boom boxes. Children screamed loud noises while they threw Frisbees back and forth. Come Friday, however, Beacon would be jammed with Shoobies, tourists that visit the shore in the summer. Traffic would flow steadily on the island, and our family's motel would be busy with people leaving and new guests coming to start their vacations. Restaurants would have long waits, pedestrians with baby strollers would take their time crossing the streets and the line at the Dustin's Ice Cream and Mini-Golf would be out the door. Parking would be impossible and cars would swerve to avoid colliding with bicycles.

When Holly and I met for the first time, her parents sat at the table on the patio with a deck of cards and a few beers. My parents across from them.

"This is Holly, she moved next door," my mom said. "Why don't you take her to the pool?"

My parents and Holly's parents played cards and talked while Holly and I got to know each other playing Marco Polo. I guessed Holly moved into the beach house Amy lived in. Friends came and went in Beacon. Come Memorial Day, you figured out who was returning and who wasn't. If you were lucky, you'd get a letter. I didn't get a letter from Amy, and she never came back. Instead, Holly's family moved into the house. I liked Holly because she was 10 years old, like me.

This summer, Holly and I were both 13. The nice part about being 13 was the freedom that came with it. I could go to the beach or the arcade or ride my bike around town.
"Anni, should we go to the beach later?" she asked, as I helped restock toilet paper on the shelves in the utility room.
"Sure" I answered. Holly reached for rolls of toilet paper and handed them to me as I stood on the step stool. "I need to vacuum the balcony and then we can go." My mom walked into the utility room with her rubber gloves on and grabs a new bottle of all-purpose cleaner.
"Go ahead, Anni, I can do the rest," she said.
"Thanks, Mom."
Holly wore her red and black bikini. Her long blond hair makes her Irish skin appear even paler. Her type of skin needs to be slathered in sunscreen so you don't turn into a lobster on the beach. I hid behind my pink one-piece bathing suit and a pair of shorts, aware my body still resembled a 12-year-old boy. Holly looked older than 13. She made it through puberty early than me. Many times older boys turned their heads and whistled at her. Holly and I didn't like boys though. Don't talk to anyone, my mom lectured us each time we ventured alone, especially the older boys. There's only one thing on their mind. Holly and I shrugged. I did not understand what they had on

their mind. But Mom was right.

"Holly, that boy is staring at you," I would say.

"Creepy," Holly would add.

"Yeah."

Sometimes boys threw Frisbees in our direction.

"Oh, sorry about that," they said. Holly and I rolled our eyes. We like to lie on our towels and read or gossip about our friends. Our favorite subject to talk about was the future. We planned to get our driver's licenses and I would drive to the city and visit. I knew my father would never allow me to drive to the city when I got my driver's license.

Holly and I set up our towels close to a family with children, another bit of advice from my mom. My flip-flops held down the corners of my towel as I sat and dug my toes in the warm sand. Holly and I turned every once in a while, to even our sun exposure so we get just as tan on our backs as we do our fronts. A few feet down from us, a little boy cried as a seagull makes off with his lunch. Flying rats. That's what we called them.

"Do you think we will be in each other's wedding one day?" I asked Holly.

"You will be my maid of honor and I will be yours!"

"How many kids do you think you'll have?"

"I want three kids, two boys and one girl named Vivienne."

"Me too..." I said as we both closed our eyes as the sun warmed our skin.

"I'm going home next week." Holly sat up on her towel to glance at me.

"Why?" I asked, surprised she was leaving before the end of the summer. I know I'd be bored and lonely once she is gone.

"Some company barbecue thing for my dad's work." She frowned her face. "You're lucky, you get to stay here all year long. This is a common myth among tourists.

"Yeah, I guess."

∞∞∞∞

The tips we got from cleaning rooms at the motel were ours to keep. My brother, Justin, and I usually walked to the end of the block for ice cream or spent our money in the arcade. He liked to play race car games, but I liked to play pinball. My favorite game, The Earthquake, was filled with volcanoes and caves. The object was to get the silver ball into the small hole that will set off the earthquake. The game would blare warning signals while your ball hit one obstacle after another, elevating the score. I was great at carefully catching the ball with the flipper and letting it come to a stop in its elbow. Then, slowly releasing my finger off the button, the ball would slide to the tip of the flipper. Then I hit it and the ball would land it right in the earthquake trigger. The bright red siren screeched a warning: "Caution, Earthquake! Caution, Earthquake!" People in the arcade turned to see what was happening as if someone had hit the jackpot on one of the slot machines that pay arcade tokens instead of real money. I was fantastic at pinball. Considering the amount of tip money that had gone into The Earthquake, it is no wonder my name was right there in the Highest Scorer position: ANT123.

"Anni, stop daydreaming and pull the sheets off the bed. There are 12 checkouts to complete by noon," Mom demanded. The motel was a bright yellow and blue L-shaped building three stories high. Each room faced the pool, but the sun deck stuck out farther on the end of the second floor for an unobstructed view of the beach. The sun deck lined with lounge chairs and a small table. A metal railing lined the walkway of each level. Large blue curtains hung in the large over-sized window of each room.

Motel guests crowded the pool today, jumping and splashing

around. The fake palm trees swayed in the warm ocean breeze, and towels lined the fence surrounding the patio. I stared out of the motel room disappointed we spent our summers cleaning up after people having fun on vacation. Vacuuming, fresh towels, sandy bedding. Children laughed and swam while parents relaxed on the pool deck. I imagined they were school-teachers and bankers and lawyers down from the city, escaping the heat and the stresses of their jobs. The weather was always cooler on the island which makes it attractive to visitors, not to mention the ocean and the bay which provided many opportunities for water activities. Jet Skiing, boating, fishing, jumping waves. The ocean met the bay on the north and south sides of the island at the inlets.

I mindlessly pulled the sheets off the bed, shook the pillows of their cases and piled the dirty bedding outside the room. Two girls splashed in the pool, and I hoped they would still be there later so I can splash along with them.

"You live here? That's so cool," they would say. I'd smile a fake grin and pretend I loved not being able to go anywhere in the summer unless I can walk or ride my bike. My parents were so busy they either made me work or were oblivious to my existence. I'd pretend I loved having my little brother as my only friend for 2 1/2 months because I'd have to watch after him. Justin wasn't so bad though. He liked to jump waves and swim. He didn't have to work yet because he's 11.

"Carry these towels down to the laundry room and bring up another box of trash bags," my mother ordered. I grabbed the dirty towels, many sandy from the beach, and carried them down the stairs. The laundry room smelled of bleach and soap and dryer lint. The dryers running make the space stifling, so I moved quickly. I stood on the step stool to reach the box of trash bags and headed back up the stairs to Room 14.

"Anni, Room 12 and 13 need vacuuming," she said. I grabbed the vacuum cleaner and head back down the deck. At noon, my mom gave me my tips.

"We are heading up to the arcade," I said, with sandy, soggy dollar bills in my hand.

"OK, Anni, have fun." She didn't give me a time to return or details to check in or ask me to stay within a certain distance. Close supervision didn't exist on the island.

Justin and I walked along the sidewalk past condos and Dustin's Ice Cream Parlor and Mini Golf and up the old wooden ramp of the boardwalk to the arcade. I could hear the sound of bells and music and kids pushing buttons throughout the store. Children laughed and begged for more money to throw coins into the claw machine hoping a toy drops into the dispenser. I didn't waste my money trying to win prizes.

Chapter 3: Summer 1990

Michael

"Seriously? Who is ANT123? He is going *down*." Anthony? Andrew T? 123? I try to imagine what ANT could mean. You're an ant? You can't think of anything more clever? I considered myself to be quite the expert pinballer, yet every time I came here, someone had knocked me down to second highest scorer. It was so boring down here on the island with no friends. Since my father worked so much, my mother and I spent the summers in a rented beach house. He joined us on the weekends.

"Go make friends, Michael," my mother said, as I annoyed her with my presence. "Or get a job, you're 16. When I was your age I had a job."

This was the third summer we had rented this beach house on Tide Street. The old wooden staircase rose up the back of the house leading to a small deck to the second-floor unit. Two bedrooms and a living room occupied the cramped space beyond the kitchen. Most days I sat on the couch watching TV or spending money playing pinball at the arcade. I guess I should have considered myself lucky, spending summer vacations at the beach, but I would have much rathered be home playing soccer with my friends. Or driving to the movies hoping we can meet girls and hang out in the parking lot of the school. Most of my friends worked summer jobs back home at the mall or sub shops and spent the evenings sneaking beer and picking up chicks. I suppose I could have gotten a summer job on the island, but what would have been the point. I preferred to be on my own schedule. So, my only excitement that summer was to compete with the mysterious ANT123 for the high score on a pinball game and maybe pick up girls and bring them back to the beach house while my mother was out. But I had had little luck there. The summer was such a drag. Girls in bikinis everywhere, but I was stuck here with the old lady.

"YES!" Several heads turned to stare at me. I hung my head but indulged in the satisfaction I, once again, claimed the highest score. I got bored with pinball and made small talk with the coin attendant, Scott. Scott is about my age, I never bothered to ask. He was local and forced to get a job he hated. His dad knew the owner which is apparently how local kids got jobs around here. My interactions with Scott revolved around the exchange of dollar bills for coins.

"Still at the pinball game, huh?" Scott asked.

"Well, you can only spend so many hours driving up and down the island, swimming in the ocean, and hanging with your mom. Where are all the girls?" I handed Scott a $5 bill, and he clicked his change dispenser 5 times, 4 quarters for each time. He dropped the quarters in my hand.

"Some of my friends are getting together for a soccer game tonight if you are interested? I'm sure there will be girls there."

"Yeah, that would be great!" Scott knew his way around here and so I took advantage of the invitation.

"What? Oh my God!"

The squeal of a young girl was heard above the bells and clangs in the arcade. Scott and I turned in the direction of the pinball game. She seemed to gawk at the backboard of the game wide-eyed, incredulously. I peeked to see my name, MICCAR, still in the first place and I smirked impishly. Scott and I waited as she puts quarters into the machine and drew back the black knob to send the silver marble flying. I know my high score was not threatened by this girl. She was hardly tall enough to see above the pinball table. I returned to my conversation with Scott to get details about the soccer game.

"Caution, Earthquake" the machine roared. The little girl giggled, and I peered in her direction. I saw her entering her name into my previously held #1 spot. I watched in horror as she spells out A...N...T..1...2...3. Scott and I exchanged a glance, and he shrugged as I approached her.

"Excuse me, what?! *You* are ANT123?"

"Um, yes," she said, shy and quiet.

"You can't be. You can't be ANT123. You're a little girl," I said in disbelief at this girl no more than 12 years old. I held my hand out towards her and turned my head in Scott's direction. He shook his head and tried to stifle a laugh. She said nothing. I realized my breathing was quick, and I took a few deep breaths to calm myself down. *It's just a stupid pinball game.*

"I am MICCAR." I pronounced it Mick-car realizing it sounded ridiculous. "I mean, I am Michael. Hi."

We stood facing each other at the pinball machine for a few seconds. She seemed alarmed by me and reluctant to talk. She was so small, and I had to look down to her.

"Hi," she finally spoke.

"Hi," I replied. This is not how I imagined my encounter with ANT123 would go. In my head, I imagined ANT123 to be a big giant man child similar to adults who play teenagers in the movies. I wanted to take ANT123 down, make him feel my wrath, all 120 pounds of my 16-year-old, fresh out of puberty boy body. But, she was so young. I hung my shoulders in defeat.

"Actually, most people call me Mike." I put out my hand to shake hers.

"Antonia." She placed her hand in her pocket. She probably thought boys have cooties. "But people call me Anni," she added.

"So, you're good at this," I said, gesturing towards the pinball game.

"I guess," she shrugged.

"So, you want to play again?" I put a coin in the slot, "You go first."

Anni pulled back the lever, and we watched the ball fly, hitting the targets. I gave her a high five.

"So, how'd you get so good at pinball?"

"I play a lot. My parents own a motel down the street. I get bored by myself."

"You want to meet tomorrow? We can play more."

"I have to clean rooms," she pouted, "maybe after?"

"Yeah, I'll come by and get you," I said, thrilled to have a new friend, even if she was a little girl. Anni told me the address to the motel and I looked forward to seeing her the next day.

"Sorry man, I didn't want to tell you," Scott said after Anni had gone.

"You knew?" I replied, amazed. "You asshole!"

"She comes here all the time with her brother, been coming for years. I think she goes to Beacon Prep Middle School. I've seen her around." I sunk down on my stool, sulking I lost to a middle school girl.

Over the next week, Anni and I became good friends. I loved her spirit of competition and I looked forward to picking her up after she finished helping her parents. Anni was sweet and quiet, and friendly. I enjoyed her company. Some days her brother, Justin, tagged along.

"Anni, it's your turn," I declared. She giggled and slid off the stool she was barely big enough to get up on. She gave me an evil look before she pulled the smooth black handle back as far as it could go. The silver ball ricocheted around the machine setting off bells and dings and a racket of noise. She set off the earthquake and turned to me. I gave her a high five. Anni and I took turns playing while we laughed and jabbed at each other.

"Do you like rollercoasters?" I asked.

"Yeah, do you?"

"Yes. Have you been on The Beast yet? My mother and I were going to go this afternoon, but I want you to come with me."

The Beast was brand new and just opened. Three loops and a corkscrew. We walked down the boardwalk laughing and nudging one another. I thought about holding her hand, but I decided against that. Not holding her hand like a girlfriend, but more of like a parent holds a child's hand. Her long brown hair tied up in a neat ponytail, separated from her bangs made her appear younger than she was. When she walked, her hair swung back and forth. Anni and I seemed like an unlikely pair. She was not even in high school yet, and I had a car. She felt like the little sister I didn't have.

"Two tickets for The Beast," I said to the kid in the ticket booth. He couldn't have been over 16 years old himself. He was probably the son of a local business owner, made to get a job. I said a silent prayer thanking God I did not have to show up for work somewhere every day. Anni and I got in line for The Beast.

"Anni, are you nervous?" I asked her.

"No, are you?" she answered. I stood behind her with my hands on her shoulders, thinking about how petite she was.

"No way." The train roared back into the loading area and we climbed in the last car. This was my favorite place to sit because it is the fastest. Anni was so tiny I wondered if I should hold on to her so she doesn't fall out of the coaster. The train climbed the ramp to the top, bumping and pulling all the way up. I looked at Anni to make sure she was OK. Once the train cleared the top of the hill, it screamed through the corkscrews and loops, all while it swung us behind. Anni and I put our hands in the air as the force of the forward motion pinned us to our seats. The wind whipped through our hair and we were jolted back and forth before coming to rest back at the station. I glanced at Anni and smiled, happy to have her here with me.

Anni and I walked back to her parents' motel. We laid on the pool deck taking in the hot sun. The plastic straps of the lounge chair stuck to my sweaty skin. During the mid-day, the pool was not crowded. Families and vacationers headed to the beach. They packed up their wagons full of beach toys and towels and boogie boards. It seemed exhausting. Anni wasn't like the other girls in my high school classes. I could be myself around her, one of the guys. We didn't always play pinball. Sometimes we hung at Pizza Palace or had ice cream at Dustin's Ice Cream Parlor and Mini Golf down the street. Some days Anni and I caught a few waves in the ocean.

"Anni, I am leaving to go back home at the end of the week."
"Ugh, that sucks," she declared as she slouched in the chair by the pool. Anni always made new friends in the summer. They always had to leave. Sometimes they would come back year after year to the motel, and sometimes they would say they would keep in touch, but they didn't. I guess Anni didn't know if we would ever see each other again after this summer and neither did I.
"Will you write?" Anni asked.
"Of course, I will." I had never been much of a writer, but I wanted to keep in touch. Every summer I came here and was alone because my mom sat on the porch and reading book after book. This summer had been so much fun because of Anni. I looked at her and smiled. She smiled back at me.

9/30/90

Dear Michael,

Wish we could play pinball right now. I guess we will have to wait until the summer. How is high school? Eighth grade is OK. I hang out with my friends a lot and we go to football games. I can't wait until summer again.

Love, Anni

She included her school picture, and I put it in my wallet.

10/2/90

Dear Anni,

      I am glad we got to become friends. High school is good. My mom got me a new car. It's a convertible. I can't wait to show you and take you for a ride. If your mom lets you that is. Thank you for sending your school picture. I put mine in here but it's terrible. Talk to you soon.
Love, Michael

Chapter 4: Present

Anni

"Let's go," I yell upstairs. "You will miss the bus!" I distribute all the lunch boxes on the cold granite counter top and carefully pack each lunch for the day. Peanut butter and jelly, an apple and a few Oreos in a Ziploc bag for Maisie, turkey, and cheese, hold the mayo for Ivy and no sandwich for Ricky.

"I can't just pack snacks. You need to have something of substance," I say to Ricky almost every day.

"I don't like sandwiches," he says every day. Fine. I take a deep breath, exhale. Pick your battles, I remind myself. I gather a plastic container of strawberries and grapes, a pack of crackers and cheese and a bag of chips, hoping it keeps him full for the rest of the day.

"I can't find socks," Ivy says.

"Look in the dryer."

"I need $12 for the school trip," Maisie tells me.

"Get my purse."

"Can you sign this permission slip?" Ricky asks.

"Find me a pen."

"Maisie has a boyfriend," Ivy sings.

"What?"

"Shut up, Ivy," Maisie yells.

"Shut up, Ivy," squawks Juliette.

"The bus is here," I cry, "Go, go, go!"

"Love you all! Have a great day!" I shout as I give the bus driver a wave. She is a hero that shows up every morning and brings me some peace and quiet. Like your best mom friend that says, "You look stressed, let me come pick up the kids and keep them for the whole day." I breathe for a moment and then put my cold coffee in the microwave. I plop on the couch next to Juliette who is busy watching cartoons on the iPad.

Jack comes downstairs freshly showered and dressed, oblivious to the chaos that just ensued. Excellent timing, Jack. His khaki pants and a white-collared shirt mean he will work in the office seeing patients rather than performing in surgery. Jack is tall and lean. All the hours at the hospital gym show in the way his belt buckle lays just right across his waistline, with his shirt tucked in. Dr. Evans embroidered across the left upper chest. His short light brown hair is gelled to the side and his face freshly shaved.

I inhale his scent of sandalwood and leather. I feel lucky to have this handsome man as my own, but most of the time he is emotionally unavailable. Some days I wish he would get up early and sit and enjoy a cup of coffee with me while we talk about our plans for the day, the children's activities, politics, weather... anything.
"Did you know Maisie has a boyfriend?"
"No, that's great," he says.
"You think it's great our 16-year-old daughter has a boyfriend? What were you doing at 16 years old, Jack?"
"You're right, this is not good." He pours a cup of coffee into his thermos.
"Don't forget I have an important meeting this evening." Of course I don't remember. I am certain he did not tell me about this meeting before, but I know how this will go. After his meeting, he will continue to the bar and have a few beers with the guys. He'll miss homework time and dinnertime and bath time and bedtime. I will check my phone at midnight when I get up

to go to the bathroom and find he isn't home yet. I text him to ask when he will be home. It will presumably be tomorrow by the time I get to ask him how his day was and by then he will shuffle out the door once more.

"OK," I say. Jack always has to do something in the evening which prevents him from helping with the kids' busy schedules. I haven't even been able to catch him up on all the trouble Ivy has been having in school and the phone calls from the teacher regarding her struggles with learning.

My last conversation with her teacher left me feeling frustrated and worried."Mrs. Evans, Ivy seems to struggle and I think it would be a wise idea to get her tested by the child study team to rule out a learning disability and to provide her with needed support." Jack won't be thrilled about Ivy's trouble in school. "She needs to apply herself more," he will say. "She needs to try harder. She needs to turn off the electronics."

Jack leaves without so much as a kiss goodbye. He has never been one for formal goodbyes or unnecessary affection. Even after 17 years of marriage, I still crave a kiss goodbye as my husband leaves for the day. I look around my over-sized Victorian home, all the lavish furniture and window treatments and photos of the kids in Mexico and Jamaica and I remind myself to be grateful.

Juliette snuggles up with me while I sip my coffee and open my laptop to check what's what. Articles of shootings, protests, obituaries, natural disasters and foreign affairs crowd the screen. I click on an article:School Enforces Dress Code for Parents at School Drop Off.

Facebook opens and I scroll through my news feed, catching up on friends and family. A few years ago I reconnected with Holly. We spent several summers together on the island like so many other friends that have come and gone. She moved to California and now edits newspaper articles for a living. Her profile picture is of her teenage daughter. If I didn't know better, I would assume I was looking at an old picture of Holly. Tall, slim, and pale.

Facebook memories show me pictures of my children as babies. Before Maisie went through puberty, before Ivy struggled with reading and writing back when Ricky wanted a "spiky haircut dyed blue." Many pictures are from before Juliette was born. We never intended on having a fourth child, but accidents still happen, even at 36 years old. Today's memories are from five years ago on our trip to Disney World: Ivy crying with her Mickey ears on, Ricky sticking out his tongue, blue from cotton candy: and Maisie smiling her great big toothy smile, before braces.

I take a sip of my coffee again, which has gone cold for the third time this morning.

"Oh, Juliette, another creepy cat selfie," I tell her referring to Susan from 10th grade homeroom and her obsession with Snapchat filters. Juliette doesn't acknowledge me as she continues watching videos on YouTube. Maisie likes to take selfies and post them on her Instagram. "Facebook is for old people, Mom" she says.

My mind roams back to 10th grade. What a turbulent year of high school. I amuse myself with thoughts of how I imagined my life would be then. Ben, my high school boyfriend, and I would be married with 2 children, a boy and a girl. We would run the family business and our children would experience the same summers on the island as I had. We would own an ice cream parlor and mini-golf and our children would grow up running barefoot on the beach every day. In the winter we would travel to the mountains and ski. Funny how the high school adolescent mind is so egocentric you don't think of what the world is like beyond those walls and this coastal town. Ben isn't on Facebook, but I heard he sells used cars up the road. I take a moment to imagine myself as the wife of a used car salesman. Perhaps I might be a successful psychologist as I had planned, making a good living and supporting my two children and my car-selling husband. I could live with that. I shake my head to erase that theory. Ben and I could be good friends if he ever joined Facebook. Thinking of him makes me smile.

Facebook has a sinister side though. It makes it possible to locate people instantly without contemplating the consequences. It's like a Pandora's box that can alter everything. Spontaneously, my fingers move over the keyboard, pushing letters in the search box.

I have dreamed of doing this before. The possibility of one search could bring me together with the past is terrifying and exhilarating. I know the perils that will occur from typing his name. That has saved me from doing it. I don't trust myself. Don't, Anni. Even thinking of him, which I have done often, makes me sick to my stomach. I marvel at the power, social media has to change your world with one click. Did I want that? Why would I want that? I know why. Because I haven't been able to get him out of my head for 20 years. Would finding him mean I would have to relive the pain and the heartache and the betrayal? Or could I break out of this emotional prison I have been living in for two decades? Some things are safer in the past. I know this search could cause a reunion like no other. It would dig up old wounds, relishing the possibilities.

I stare at the white, rectangular box with the cursor blinking and my fingers danced across the keyboard. I don't know what I was looking for. Maybe vindication, closure, validation? I type in the name Michael Carter. I click on the search button and hold my breath. In an instant I feel regret and I pray that I see "No Matches" appear on the screen and I can resume my incredibly normal and predictable life. I prefer to be in command of my destiny. Clicking this button could mean losing control. In my memories, I have frozen Michael in time. Still a teenager, a heartbreaker, still obscure.

"Come on," I beg aloud to my dinosaur of a computer as it loads at a turtle's pace. My pulse races, my palms are sweaty. I push "enter" a few times even though I know it won't speed up the process. All at once, time stands still. Before me on the screen is Michael. That face, that smile, his name on the screen. All right here in front of me. In my living room. I slam the laptop shut.

"Juliette, do you want me to read you a book?" Juliette prances to the bookcase and pulls out her favorite book and crawls in to my lap. Her wispy hair tickles my cheek as she props her head against my shoulder. I open the book and recite a well-read story about a princess and a horse. My mind wanders back to my search. My hands are shaking and clammy and my throat feels parched. The same sensation you get when you're expecting bad news. I can't wait to get back to the laptop again. But it's a terrible idea, Anni.

I fix myself another cup of coffee and settle back down on the couch. I fold my cold hands around the warm mug that says "World's Best Mom" as I consider what to do. My laptop is impossibly slow today, or is it trying to tell me something? I aimlessly trace the concentric pattern on the arm of the sofa as I contemplate this juncture of uncertainty. My pulse beats in my throat and I plead with myself not to look.

I never thought I would see this face again. The pictures stored in the attic of my parents' home is all the tangible memories I have. The box hasn't been opened in 20 years, but I've memorized its contents: Arcade tickets, stuffed animals, photo booth pictures, the ring. And now, at this moment, Facebook, or better yet, my search, has brought the world in to a stuffy space making it arduous to breathe. Michael Carter. Married. Well, I already knew that. Michael, more good looking than ever before, his face fuller, jaw more square. I had fixed him in time in my fantasies as a 21-year-old, but he was a grown man. A flat smile on his face, his eyes dark. And those lips. I was not prepared for that. I battle to keep down the unsettled feeling in my stomach, but it creeps up and burns my throat.

A million emotions race at me all at once. Emotions I wasn't ready for. Five minutes ago, Michael Carter was in my imagination, not here in my life. The possibilities swim in my mind. My heart swells and I smile at the computer screen, until the next emotion makes me feel sick and heartbroken, followed by jealousy and guilt and anger. I knew this would happen. I knew

I was not capable of handling this open wound. Oh, Michael. Why do you still hold this power over me? This is no good.

I close my laptop again and carry Juliette to the bedroom where I can hear her play. I turn on the water in the shower and wait until it warms up, glimpsing myself in the mirror. What happened to you? There are creases in the corner of my eyes, a wrinkle in my forehead and gray roots in my hair. For a moment I see an ephemeral image of the girl I once was, a teenager. A perfect figure, great hair, a sense of style. A teen so intelligent and full of promise, destined to shatter goals and boundaries. But this body has birthed four children, given up on dreams, dependent on a man. I abandon my clothes to the floor and get in the hot shower and try to scrub myself back to sensibility.

I need a distraction, so I pull out my phone to see if there are any new messages.

"Jack, Ivy's teacher wants to test her for a learning disability," I text. In my head I beg for a response. An acknowledgement. But minutes go by, then hours and finally a response.

"OK". Jack responds. I grimace at the phone, disappointed. Jack and I have been married for 17 years with 4 wonderful children. Jack is an OR surgeon. He provides a wonderful life for us. When I first met Jack at Rosie's Tavern, he was in medical school. His intelligence attracted me to him. And he was good looking with icy blue eyes. Eyes I swear I had seen before.

Jack and I connected, and I knew we would spend our lives together. Jack was good for me. We had similar backgrounds, values and ambitions. He wanted to be a doctor; I wanted to be a psychologist. We were both hard workers moving along a path to success. Jack was everything I wanted and needed. Life with Jack would be simple, uncomplicated, normal. For a moment, I imagine how things would have been different had Michael not hurt me, left a gaping hole in my heart that no other man could ever fill.

I sit Juliette in her chair and slice apples on a plate. I open the laptop again, for the third time, to look at his face once more.

He's an electrician, which is surprising. I don't know what I was expecting, but I never took Michael to be a hard worker. All the summers spent together riding up and down the island in the Jeep, lying around the beach. He never had a summer job like the other teenagers. Michael always had fancy cars and beach house rentals. He seemed to come and go as he pleased, even at 16 years old. I met his mom only once and never his dad.

I curse Facebook's existence for a moment. Damn you Mark Zucker-whatever. Michael, why couldn't you have had your privacy settings on? I need protection from myself. As I flip through his family pictures, I analyze every detail, every facial expression, his words, his statuses.

I haven't seen Michael since that night at college. It's seared into my brain like a flashbulb memory that, at any moment, I can reach in and pull it up into consciousness and feel as sick as I did that day.

I search through Michael's Facebook page. There are no pictures of children. His wife is tall, thin, black wavy hair. I don't like her. She has a cute round face and her eyes squint when she smiles. I don't want to admit to myself that it seems adorable when she does that. She is thinner than me. I wonder what Michael would think of a body that has birthed a bunch of kids. Of breasts that nursed for a straight decade. My finger moves over the mouse pad and I snoop on his friends list. Some names I recognize like Doug, and Scott. I close the laptop. I've already given too much time to stalking his Facebook page.

Feeling guilty, I text Jack again. "I will see if your parents are interested in babysitting tomorrow night. Maybe we could have a date night. It has been a while." As usual, hours go by. I'm not sure if he is busy or ignoring my texts, but I can't help speculating he doesn't want me to bother him with stupid trivial things right now.

"Whatever you want," he replies. I sigh. Typical Jack response. No emotion, no excitement, nothing. "What were you expecting, Anni? Want me to jump up and down?" he would say if I complained.

Juliette and I head for the coffee shop before heading to the park.

"Hi Miranda, can I have a vanilla latte and a blueberry muffin. Oh, and a chocolate milk."

"Cocat milk," Juliette requests. Today Miranda's hair is purple. She looks adorable with her apron around her waist and a t-shirt that says, "Smash the Patriarchy".

"Hi Juliette! You are getting so big!" Miranda says.

"I'm trrrhee," Juliette tells her.

Miranda is our favorite barista. She looks about twenty, but I suspect she is at least 40. I don't know how she doesn't age, but I am slightly jealous. Many times I have come to this coffee shop after I drop Juliette off at daycare. I feel awful taking her to daycare when I am a stay at home mom, but I need time alone to run errands and clean and have child-free time. Some days I meet friends here at the cafe, and other days Miranda and I engage in deep conversations about Love Languages and politics and women's rights.

"How is it going today, Anni?"

"Miranda, have you ever snooped on profiles of people from your past?"

"All the time. I snoop on ex-boyfriends, ex-girlfriends, friends of my kids. Bad tippers. It's easy to get lost down that rabbit hole." Miranda replies. "Tell me who you've been snooping on?" She puts her elbows on the counter and her head in her hands.

"Just an old summer friend. It's nothing." I want to drop it now. I regret bringing it up. Saying it aloud makes me feel guilty.

"Oh, I see. Was this a boy?"

"Yes, but just a friend. Someone I really cared about. Seems like a lifetime ago."

"Did you make contact?"

"No. And I am not going to. There is too much unresolved. I can't face it again."

"You should. It could bring you some closure on whatever it is. Maybe you'll rekindle passion!" She winks her eye.

"Miranda, I'm married!" I bark. She shrugs her shoulders and turns back to her machine. She might be right about closure, but no. I am a married mother of 4. I can't go digging up my past. I immediately feel ashamed for not appreciating the life I've been blessed with. For bringing the past into my home. For the temptation to explore. Some things are better left in the past.

"Thank you for the coffee." I sweep up Juliette and head to the car.

Juliette and I head to the park for a play group. I unbuckle the straps of her car seat, wipe her chocolatey-face and fix her little brown pigtails. I rub sunscreen on her nose and her forehead and lead her to the playground. I join the other moms at the bench. The weather is warm and sunny with little humidity. My favorite kind of weather to be outside.

"Hey Anni, did you talk to Jack about our girls' weekend in the mountains yet?" Lily asks. Lily is a tall, thin mom with short brown hair. She is wearing yoga pants and a pullover and likely just came from the gym while Callie sat in the child care center. She sips a large bottle of water and checks her steps on her pedometer. She promptly marches in place.

"No, not yet. I really haven't had time to talk to him," I respond. "Jack is so busy at work with meetings nearly every evening. I can't even talk to him about Ivy needed help in school." I hate complaining about Jack, and I will myself to be grateful.

"I can't imagine having a husband who works so much," adds Jennifer. "Anni, you're practically a single mom."

"Jack works hard to take care of his family." That is always my go-to line. It is true, he takes care of his family. Sometimes I feel like a burden to his career. Jack always works a long, stressful day and comes home to a chaotic household with messes everywhere. There is homework to be finished, dinner to be cleaned up, children to be put in bed.

"I worked all day, Anni," he says as he puts his feet up and turns on the TV with the remote.

I do unpaid work; I remind myself. The discipline and meal planning and homework and shopping and parent-teacher conferences.

Going away on a girls-weekend seems like a great way to unplug from the stress. If only there was a way I could magically disappear and all my responsibilities can be cared for by someone else in my place.

My phone vibrates in my pocket and I reach in and pull it out.

"Hello?" I answer.

"Mom, I need my clarinet," Maisie says.

"Maisie, I asked you to be sure you bring everything you need this morning."

"I know, Mom, I'm sorry. Can you please drop it off? Thanks!"

"Well, I need to run. Maisie needs her clarinet," I say to our playgroup moms. "Juliette, let's go honey." Juliette promptly protests.

"I'm not going!"

"Yes, sweetie, we need to bring Maisie her clarinet." Juliette drops to the pile of woodchips under the playground equipment and refuses to move. Lily stares.

"Get up, Juliette." I crouch down to her level and whisper through my teeth. Leaving the playground is always hard for kids. But, this is one of those times where I need to scoop up the 3-year-old and carry her like a wet noodle to the car while she screams and kicks. All while hoping that no one thinks I am kidnapping her.

"Sorry ladies." I break a sweat buckling this sweet girl into her car seat and fall down into the driver's seat forcing the air conditioning on as high as the blower will go. I lean my head against the steering wheel and my eyes fill. I realize I need this vacation now more than ever. I plan to talk to Jack this evening.

Chapter 5: Summer 1992

Anni

Dear Anni,

I hope your first year of high school was great. I will be in town soon, and I will come over and get you and we can drive around town. I got a new car. It is a Jeep. I can't wait to see you.

Love, Michael

Dear Michael,

I will work this summer at the ice cream parlor. Come in when you get in town. I want to introduce you to my boyfriend Ben. We met shortly after I started school in Sept. I think you will like him.

Love, Anni

"Anni, don't look, but that guy is staring at you," Sarah said while we watched Beacon Prep vs Beacon High football game. The night was cold and dry, a perfect night for football under the bright stadium lights at Beacon Prep Memorial Field. The bleachers were crammed with cheering parents, students, and the marching band. The band spontaneously played "We Will Rock You" while the crowd stomped their feet on the bleachers. The cheerleaders danced to the music twirling with their blue and white pompoms.

I spun around to see who she was talking about and she rolled her eyes at me. Not too obvious, Anni. I was blinded by the ridiculously loud lights they use for night football games, but my eyes slowly adjusted. There were so many people. The crowd was getting even more excited. I looked back at the game and Beacon Prep was set up to score around the five-yard line. I noticed a group of BP soccer players sitting in a group wearing their blue and white varsity letter jackets, fresh off a win against Beacon High earlier in the day. The cheerleaders broke into a new cheer to get the crowd on their feet and I lost sight of the group. "Touchdown, BP!" the announcer beamed into the sound system and the crowd, now on their feet, high fived and the sound of cheering was deafening. The players celebrated their TD on the field, hugging, and pumping their fists. Sarah and I made our way out of the bleachers to roam around.

"Hey," I felt a tap on my shoulder and twisted around to see a blue varsity jacket. "I'm Ben," he said, holding out his hand. "I saw you looking at me." My cheeks flushed with embarrassment, but I made some words. Ben's mouth formed a toothy smile, and I realized he is smirking.

"Hi, uh, I'm Antonia, I mean, call me Anni,"

"Hi, Just Anni" he quipped. Ben was very attractive, not like other scrawny high school boys. He had broad shoulder and dark brown hair, cut short. I couldn't help noticing the dimples on his round face when he smiled.

"Do you go to Beacon Prep?"

"Yeah, I'm a freshman."

"Cool, um, do you want to hang out sometime?"

"Yeah, OK," I said calmly, though my heart was doing cartwheels. I offered him my phone number and he would call me the next day. We talked for hours, unlike middle school boys.

"Hey Anni," Ben said, leaning on my locker in between history and gym.

"Hi Ben," I repeated, shuffling around the books.

"What are you doing after school? I'd love for you to come to my soccer game."

"Yeah, that would be great, I'll ask Sarah to come with me." Ben smiles and I shut my locker.

"Gym, right?" he asked.

"What?"

"You're going to gym next, right?" he asked.

"Yeah."

"Mind if I walk with you?"

"No, not at all." I arranged my books in my arm, resting them on my hip and walked side by side towards the gym. We stopped in front of the double doors and had an awkward moment.

"So, see you at the game?"

"Yeah."

It was very warm and sticky at the soccer game, and we arrived as the teams were warming up. The fresh-cut grass made my allergies flare up, but I endured it as I pulled a tissue out of my pocket. Beacon Prep, in their blue and white shirts and white bottoms and Fairway in red and black occupied opposite ends of the field, practicing passing and shooting. Sarah and I sat on the bleachers, choosing a spot in the shade to cheer on BP.

"What's with you and Ben?"

"Not much." We talked on the phone a lot, but I don't know how to describe it other than friendly. Sarah frowned. Ben looked really hot in his soccer jersey. He hung in the back while his teammates took a shot on the goal. Then he looked over at me. Our eyes connected and his mouth widened, and his smile grew. Oh, those dimples.

"Oh, Anni, the boy likes you!" Sarah beamed at me.

"Well, maybe as a friend."

"No way, you need to make a move."

"Do you know me at all?"

I tried to follow the game, but my eyes only followed Ben.

Parents yelled from the stands as the ball get passed from one player to the other and back again.

"Off sides, Ref!" a parent screamed.

"What's off sides?" I whispered to Sarah.

"I do not understand," she shrugged, and we both laughed. Too bad I didn't pay attention to the rules in gym class. Instead, I settled in the field in my awkward PE uniform praying the ball didn't come and I chatted with Sarah about boys.

The crowd was on their feet as the ball got close to Fairway's goalkeeper. Number 5 passed the ball inside to Number 17 and then back out to Ben who took a shot, and it was in! Anni and I jumped up and down, cheering. I at least know what a goal is. Beacon Prep celebrated their win over Fairway and the coach pulled them in for a debriefing. They yelled something indecipherable on the count of three and dispersed. Ben grabbed his soccer bag and started his way towards me.

"Anni, hey," he grinned. "Meet me by the gym." He was sweaty and his face red as he tried to calm down his breathing. Sarah gave me a devilish expression. Ben made his way back to the gym to collect his things and emerged with his backpack on his back, and his soccer bag. He slid it to the ground as he approached me.

"I'll be right back," Sarah said, "forgot something in my locker". She entered the school building.

"Anni, do you want to go to Homecoming?" Ben asked, nervously.

"Yes!" I said, excited. He smiled. I had never been asked to a dance before, and it had slipped my mind people do that in high school.

"Oh, and one more thing," he said. "I like you. Do you want to be like, together?"

"Oh, like, your girlfriend?" I asked, surprised, but stupidly excited.

"Yeah."

"Yes!" I said, throwing myself at his sweaty body. He put

his arms around me and hugged me tight. My first real boy-friend.

Ben met me at the gate of the football field for the Home-coming Pep Rally. The night was dark, but the flames of the bon-fire illuminated the area. The scent of burning wood permeated the air, as it crackled and sent red-hot embers high into the sky. He took my hand and led me towards his soccer team. I reveled in being on Ben's arm in front of his soccer buddies.

"Hey, Ben," another varsity jacket called out. Ben shook his hand.

"Yo! What's up?" he answered.

"This is my girlfriend, Anni," he said. He introduced me to many people, and it never got old hearing him call me his girlfriend. The marching band played the Notre Dame Fight Song while the cheerleaders jumped around with their blue and white pom-poms. The football team charges through a paper thin banner that said "Go Beacon" held by two cheerleaders. The students cheered, and the band continued to play and we moved in closer to the bonfire to keep warm. Late September in Beacon can be very hot during the day and chilly at night.

"Let's hear the Seniors make some noise!" the MC roared over the speakers set atop of the bleachers. The Senior class screamed and pushed and shoved each other in a playful display of camaraderie.

"Class of 93!" yelled a girl into a megaphone. Ben put his arm around me, his varsity jacket thick and scratchy, and pulled me close. I gazed at his face, illuminated by the roaring glow of the bonfire and he smiled.

"Let's go, Anni," he said, taking my hand and leading me away from the crowd. We headed behind the bleachers, but there were teachers there.

"Move along," the teacher demanded to all the students walking through.

"No making out under the bleachers," Ben sneered, peer-ing at me. I giggled nervously. Coming out the other side of the bleachers, Ben stopped in the dark shadow of the concession stand, faced me and pulled me in close to him. He smelled like hair gel and fake leather from his varsity jacket. Ben would try to kiss me and my heart pounded in my chest. I was eager and nervous as he leaned in and our lips touch. I held my breath. I had never had a boy kiss me before although I have had fantasies about it. Ben looked down at me and smiled and my heart melted. He kissed me again, opening his mouth this time. I was awkwardly unprepared, but my heart swelled at the warmth of Ben's lips on mine.

"That's enough," said Mr. White, interrupting my moment of induction. Ben smiled and took my hand. I was grateful for the dark of night to hide how red my face was.

That was ten months ago. A lifetime in high school relationships. I guess I had not considered how having a boyfriend would alter my summers with Michael. Even Sarah and I had difficulty navigating our friendship through my relationship with Ben.

"What are we doing tonight?" she would ask.

"I'm going to the movies with Ben," I'd reply.

"Oh, cool, I'll go," she suggested. Ben would get annoyed. "Just tell her we want to be alone so we can make out," he'd joke. Other times we would hang with his soccer teammates and Sarah happily tagged along.

The waffle machine sizzled as I poured the thick batter on to the hot iron. The aroma of fresh hot waffles filled the air at Dustin's Ice Cream and Mini Golf. I closed the lid and set the timer and punched the price into the register.

"Do you want whip cream?" I asked the customer. Turning back to the iron, I flipped the lid open, and plopped the hot waffle onto a plate. I don't care how many waffles I made, the smell always made my mouth water. Three scoops of vanilla bean ice cream and some hot fudge, whip cream and a cherry, I handed it to the customer. My stomach growled and I glance at the clock. Only an hour and a half left to go on this shift. I grabbed a wet rag and wipe up the counter space.

"Is Anni here?" I heard a recognizable voice ask my co-worker. Looking up, I saw Michael in basketball shorts and a t-shirt, hair combed to the side, standing on the other side of the freezer. He smiled, and I ran around the counter and threw my arms around him, breathing in the smell of soap and cologne. I realized I missed this so much over the winter. He'd grown into his body and looked so much more mature than that scrawny body from last summer. Michael held me at arm's length and studied me.

"So, this is what Anni, the High School girl, looks like," he joked.

"I missed you, too," I said.

"Come over after you're done work."

"OK!" I hugged him again before returning to work behind the counter of ice cream flavors.

After work, I changed my clothes and combed my hair into a neat ponytail before I raced over to Michael's house. His new, yellow Jeep is parked in the driveway with the doors and top removed. Of course, yellow! Michael always has to stand out. I walked up the old wooden steps and knocked on the door, peeking through the curtains in the window.

"Anni," he said, kissing my cheek and pulling me close. It made me feel special when he kisses my cheek. My other friends didn't do that. Maybe because Michael is 18, or maybe that's a city thing, but it's new. He held the door open and I duck in under his arm, though I don't have to bend much, since he is taller than me.

Gesturing to the couch, "Sit down," he said. He turned down the music playing from his boom box before sitting next to me. Rap music. I hate that.

"How about a back scratch?" Michael loved back scratches. I remember the first time he asked me to scratch his back.

Grabbing my hand, he said, "Anni, look at these fingernails!"

"I give great back scratches," I joked.

He pulled his shirt over his head and turned away from me. "Let's see."

I ran my fingernails up and down making red marks like zebra stripes on his back.

"How was school?" he asked.

"OK, I guess." Being friends with Michael seemed so easy and effortless. That's why it would be so hard to talk to him about Ben. "I have a boyfriend." I add.

"So you said in your letter," he turned to face me with his legs crossed on the couch.

"Is that going to be weird?"

"Probably," he answered.

"Why?" I asked, even though I had given it a lot of thought. I didn't think Ben would understand my relationship with Michael.

"Because, look at me," he teased. "Bob is going to be so jealous!"

"It's Ben," I snickered at Michael's cockiness and punched him casually in the arm. "I'm serious! I haven't told Ben anything about you."

"Why not?"

"I don't know, I didn't know what to say. I mean, when would it come up?"

"Don't you have my picture in your wallet?" I stared at him.

"You took it out?" He frowned and reached in his back pocket and showed me he still had my picture in his wallet.

"I'm sorry, Michael, it's just.... I don't know," I said, unable to put my thoughts into words without it sounding hurtful.

"We must see how it goes." He shrugged his shoulders. I tried to read his thoughts, but he his lips are straight, and his eyes stared at me, giving away nothing.

"Well, I don't know. Like, we would never hook up, but Ben might think...," I said.

"Ben sounds like a jerk" he scoffed. I smack his leg and he got serious again. "Why do you think we'd never hook up?" he added. This surprised me. It's not something I had given any thought to. He was Michael, my best friend in the entire world.

"Michael!" I said, in confusion. "We're best friends."

"Whatever you think Anni," he said. "I don't see why you can't have other friends."

"It's not just other friends, it's you. We spend so much time together in the summers, I.... I don't know what to think." Michael seemed thoroughly annoyed now, and I gnawed on my bottom lip. I leaned back on the sofa and stared up at the ceiling, hoping for an answer to this dilemma.

Michael shrugged and rested his head on my shoulder. We sat quietly for a little while. I thought of nothing, and just enjoyed feeling the warmth of his head on my shoulder. I closed my eyes and breathed in my favorite smell.

"I really hate this music, Michael," I said.

"How about the beach tomorrow," Michael asked as I rested in the doorway of the beach house, ready to leave.

"I can't," I say, disappointed. "I have to work."

"After work?" I stared down at my feet. It was starting already. I didn't want to tell him I had plans to go to the beach with Ben after work tomorrow.

"I have plans," I said.

"With the boyfriend," he added matter-of-factly. I didn't answer, but he could read me well. "I'll join you."

I cocked my head to the side.

"Ok, fine," he said in resignation.

"I'll call you, ok?"

I haven't seen Michael in a few weeks and I guessed the lack of time I had to give him was disappointing. Ben and I spent more time together, and I worked at Dustin's Ice Cream Parlor to pass the time and to have extra spending money. I missed seeing Michael. Growing up on this island, friends come and go with the seasons, but I didn't want him to be one of those.

After work one day I headed up to the arcade, hoping to run into him. I checked the Top Score board of Earthquake but there was no ANI123 or MICCAR.

"Hey Anni." It was Scott. He was watching me check the Earthquake Scoreboard. Scott worked at the arcade every summer. Giddy children, and sometimes giddy adults, line up to get coins from him. Some arcades had coin machines you can feed a dollar in and get quarters, but this arcade still employed coin attendants, lucky for Scott.

"Scott!" I gave him a hug. "Good to see you are still here! I've been working a lot and haven't gotten up to play much. Have you seen Michael?"

"Yeah, we've been hanging. Cruising around, picking up chicks," Scott said.

"Oh." Hearing this made me feel different. My cheeks flushed, and I thought of Scott and Michael having fun without me. Michael had been around yet avoiding me, but I suppose I deserved that. Boy/girl friendships were complicated. Perhaps I should call him.

My hands were sweaty as I dialed Michael's number into the telephone. "Hi Mrs. Carter, it's Anni. Is Michael home?"

"No Anni, I'm sorry, he's not here but I can have him call you when he gets back." I waited several days. Michael did not call.

A few weeks later I purposely walked past Michael's house on my way home from work. His jeep was parked in the grass. I stared at the house as I tried to find the nerve. I took a deep breath and walked towards the stairs. For some reason, I made my steps as quiet as I could. I knocked on the door and I peeked through the curtain. Michael's shoes were lined against the wall and his wallet was on the kitchen table. His mom answered the door after I knocked once more. "Michael's not here, Anni." she said.

I turned and walked down the stairs, my head hung low and my eyes burning and wet. It's over, Anni.

I tried calling again several days later and got his answering machine. "Michael, please call me, I miss you so much." I pleaded. I hung up the phone, and a tear fell down my cheek. My heart ached so badly to see him or hear his voice.

One Loose String

The air was so hot on the mid-August day I threw on my dark blue one-piece bathing suit and a pair of cut-off jeans and put my hair in a ponytail. Ben leaned over and kissed my lips and we headed to the south end of Beacon near the beach.

"Ready for some beach volleyball?" he asked.

"Ready!" I answered.

We walked to the beach where several teams had gathered, some from the city, but many locals. An island tradition. Tom, from chemistry class approached with a clipboard. He was wearing a wide-brimmed hat, sunglasses and thick sunscreen on his nose.

"What's your team name?" he asked. I looked at Ben for a response.

"The Bennies," he answered. I put my hands to my mouth and laughed. "Benny" is a term the locals used to describe obnoxious tourists, which is why it was so clever.

"Ben and Anni," he winked. I hadn't even thought of that!

"Brilliant!" I clapped my hands.

"OK, The Bennies," Tom repeated, scratching down on his clipboard. He disappeared to sign up more teams.

"Anni, Ben... hey," I heard in the distance. I strained my neck to see and spotted Sarah waving and running our way.

"Hey, Sarah, you playing?"

"No, I'll watch." Sarah looked cute in her blue beach cover up. Her big brown eyes, round face and perfect brown hair attracted a lot of attention wherever we go.

"First match, The Bennies," Tom peered in our direction, "And the Pearls". Two girls walked up and shook our hands. Girl 1 was tall and lanky in her black bikini top and a pair of shorts. Girl 2 was not as tall, but equally fit in her yellow bikini top and blue tennis skirt. We headed for opposite sides of the net. I adjusted my sunglasses and Ben and I took our positions in the hot sand. Tom handed Ben the ball, and he tossed it in the air, striking it over the net. Girl 1 bumped the ball, and girl 2 sent it flying over. I dove to bump the ball and quickly got up in time for Ben to pass it back for a spike. I spiked the ball over the net and girl 2 missed. Ben ran and double high fived me before returning to our positions. After several rallies, Ben and I ultimately lost to Girl 1 and Girl 2. Ben puts his arm around me and squeezed.

"Good game, Anni! You were awesome!" He handed me a drink from the cooler and I chugged it down, sweating and sand sticking everywhere on my body.

"Let's go cool off," I said.
Hand in hand, Ben and I followed Sarah down to the ocean for a swim. I dropped my shorts on the sand and Sarah left her cover up next to them.

"Hey, Anni, isn't that your friend over there.... the one from the arcade?" Sarah said. I turned my head to see who she was pointing to and saw Michael in a group of local guys congregating near the volleyball games. He turned his head and spotted me, making eye contact and walked my way, followed by his friends. My heart pounded in my ears. He knew I saw him so I can't turn my back.

"Anni," he shouted when he drew closer. He was wearing board shorts and no shirt, his sun-kissed hair flattened from the surf. He smiled, and I forgot to breathe. I want to run from him and to him. I wanted to embrace him. I would have in any other circumstance. Thankfully, he doesn't hug me either.

"Hi Michael, um, this is Ben. Ben, this is my friend Michael."

"Michael," Ben said as he shook his hand. He put his arm around my waist, claiming me as his and I looked down at the sand feeling awkward. Michael's gaze is fixated on Ben's arm around me and my knees weaken. I wanted to push Ben's hand off my waist, which made me feel guilty. Michael turned his head looking to his friends for their reaction.

"Yeah, well, it was good to see you Anni" he said, backing away. I notice Doug and Brandon and someone else I have seen at the basketball courts. John or Jake or something. I don't recall his name but I remember his icy blue eyes.

"Yeah." He turned and walked back to the crowd. My face

flushed and my eyes burn hot.

"Michael," I called, "wait." I ran towards him not sure what I would do or say. Far enough away Ben couldn't hear me, but feeling his eyes on me, I approached Michael.

"I tried to call you," I said. Michael silently stared a hole in my heart.

"I left messages." He said nothing. "Say something, please."

"Like what, Anni?" Michael just looked at me and I didn't know what to say. Then he walked away. I knew I needed to do something. Summer was running out. I grabbed his arm, wow.... that muscle wasn't there before. Ben took a step forward, but Sarah held him back.

"I don't know," I whispered. I dug my foot in the sand.

"Life goes on." He nodded to Ben.

"That hurts." I said. He shrugged and turned his back.

"No, Michael, please," I begged, "Don't walk away."

I turned around, aware Ben and Sarah had been staring at me. I begged my eyes to take the tears back. Ben raised his eyebrows, and I ignored the need to give him an explanation.

I walked beside them and try to gain my composure. I felt Sarah's eyes on me, and I turned my head to look at her.

"You OK?" She mouthed silently. I shrugged my shoulders. I wasn't sure if I was OK. No, I was definitely not OK.

The pounding of the waves drowned the thoughts of Michael and how he had avoided me all summer. I dove under a wave and the cool ocean water refreshed my hot sweaty skin. Ben emerged from a wave and shook the water off his hair and pulled me close. His bare wet chest pushed against me. I felt nothing.

We spread our beach towels and laid down, absorbing the warm sand underneath. Ben grabbed my hand, and I closed my eyes trying to block the images of Michael. My feelings confused me, and I knew if he came back and told me to drop Ben for him, I would in a heartbeat.

Chapter 6: Present

Michael

"Oh, shit" I say. I run my fingers through my hair. The screen of the computer stares back at me. "Anni, now there is a name I haven't heard in a while." I picture Anni, wet purple bikini clinging to her body, splashing in the ocean. God, I wanted her so badly that day. She was talking to that fucking lifeguard and told me he invited her to a party. Those lifeguard parties were bad. Drunk guys, hot girls. Probably STD's on every surface. I felt hot jealousy that day, an emotion I was not used to.

"Anni, you are not going to that lifeguard party," I said to her.

"I am," She told me. I remember being upset with her for being so irresponsible, but really it was jealousy. It's funny now, the irony. "You will get hurt," I had told her.

Perfect fucking Anni. I honestly thought someday we would be together. She would have made a great partner. But at that time, there was no way I was giving up my summers for her. Anni was so complicated.

Danielle, my wife, squints in my direction. I wonder how my life would have been different if I married Anni instead. Smart, beautiful, ambitious, perfect. She would have wanted a big white wedding. She would talk me into having at least one child. If it was a boy, it would have been Michael Jr. We would call him Mikey until he got older. We would have coffee every morning and a glass of wine every evening after Mikey went to bed. We would make sweet, passionate love every night. Well, probably not every night because Anni would work so hard at her career. She would be exhausted. I would give her tired muscles a massage as she sipped her wine and told me about her day. I'd sit around all day playing Xbox and she wouldn't say anything because she'd be afraid I would leave her. I shake the thoughts. It wouldn't be like that at all because I am a fucking dickhead. Isn't that what I convinced myself of 20 years ago when I left her? I bet she has a perfect life. At least I hope she does.

I click on her name to accept her friend request. This should be interesting. I contemplate sending her a message, but I want to see if she strikes first. I'm not sure why I feel nervous, but I stare at the screen with anticipation, refreshing my browser frequently.

I glance at Danielle. Twenty-plus years of a pretty shitty marriage. On again, off again. Danielle has walked out and come back more times than I can count. I've been a terrible husband, too.

"Who's that?" she asks. "One of your summer girls?" Anni wasn't a summer girl, she was different. I don't even remember the names of the summer girls.

"Yes," I concede. "Don't worry, though. It was before I met you," I say sarcastically.

"One of many," she snaps. "Probably an island girl." She puts an island in air quotes.

Danielle throws her purse over her shoulder and grabs her keys. I am thankful she is leaving to go to work because I can't deal with her right now. It's not always bad, Danielle and I have some great times. She can hang with the guys and she's crazy in bed. I squirm in my seat thinking about it. She slams the door on her way out. I feel terrible for a moment, but I turn back to the computer.

You have a new message.
"Hi Michael! I came across your name. I hope you don't mind me sending you a friend request. You look great."

Ok, this is happening. I write back almost immediately. "Hey stranger, good to see your name on my screen this morning. I hope you are well." I erase that. Doesn't sound like me at all. I try again.

"Anni, wow! How the fuck are you?"

"I'm good Michael." I can tell Anni is guarding herself. I click through her Facebook profile. *Are all those kid hers? She'd have a bunch of kids. She is probably an awesome mom. She was always so caring and nurturing.* Once I stopped by her bedroom on my way home from a party and she cleaned up cuts on my hand from a fight. I loved how much she cared about me. I came and went as I pleased then, didn't answer to anyone. My parents checked out on me well before I graduated high school. They were older, raising a rebellious teen during their retirement. My mother usually gave me some money to keep me out of the house all day.

"It was nice chatting," she says, "Take care."

What? That's it? I can tell Anni is trying to protect herself. She always was. She will probably have to go to confession after contacting me on Facebook.

"Same Anni, don't be a stranger," I say. But she logged out already. Damn, I would like to see her again. The thought surprises me. I'm not the "feelings" type, but Anni almost had me 20 years ago, probably more than she knew. She was the only one that could affect me with her talks. She used to taunt me with her questions. "Michael, why can't we be more?" Penetrate the wall I put up to protect me from feeling. It was frustrating. The way her body teased me, the way she called me Michael when everyone else called me Mike. I remember telling her I needed space, and she was confused and crushed. But if there's anyone that could have made me settle it was her. We didn't make it because I fought it too hard.

Chapter 7: Summer 1993

Anni

"Prom?" Ben stood at my locker with a single yellow rose. I jumped up and down, squealing like a mouse. "Yes, yes!" I wrapped my arms around him. I knew Ben would ask me to the prom, as we had been a couple since freshman year began, nearly 18 months. When I met Michael at 13 years old, I always imagined him taking me to my prom. He would drive down from the city and rent a tux and my friends would gawk at him in surprise, wondering where he's been hiding all this time. "Did you see Anni's date?" they would all whisper. Funny how things change. Now at 16 years old, I miss his company so much my stomach gets tied in knots and my heart aches when I think about him. It's been over a year.

Ben leans in at my locker and kisses my lips.
"Move along," Mrs. Miller said. My cheeks flushed. I closed my locker and Ben grabbed some of my textbooks and we headed towards class. Me, geometry, Ben, biology. He kissed me before I headed into the classroom and Mr. Johnson gave me a glare. Ben didn't seem to care about public affection, but I was still getting used to it.

The last day of sophomore year at Beacon Prep was hot and humid as I walked to Ben's car.
"Anni, I think we should see other people."

"WHAT, why?" I felt like a wrecking ball knocked me in the heart.

"Anni, we're just different." I could barely breathe, and I felt like I might vomit. How different can we be? What is he talking about?

"Ben, please. Please don't leave me." I sobbed into his shirt. I have never had a breakup before, unless you count my friendship breakup with Michael, which hurt equally as bad.

"Anni, I will be a senior, you will be a junior, things will change eventually. You couldn't have thought this would be forever. It isn't how things work." he said, trying to rationalize this. I swear I never saw it coming. It felt like a deep cut washed with rubbing alcohol. I thought it would be forever.

"Is this because of prom night…. because I didn't want….." I stuttered, nervously, "Because you wanted to…"

"No, Anni. Well, not exactly, I think we are different, that's all."

On prom night, Ben put a flower corsage on my wrist. "Anni, you look amazing," I couldn't take my eyes off Ben in his tuxedo and admired how incredibly good he looked. It was a rainy spring day, dark and gloomy and cold. Ben stared at my strapless teal cocktail dress with wide eyes and a goofy grin. He twirled me around in my living room while the limo waited outside. Sarah and Robert arrived as we pose for pictures. Robert's girlfriend broke it off with him a week before prom and Sarah agreed to fill in.

"Shall we go?" Ben asked, as we made our way to the limo. He held an umbrella for Sarah and me and we settled down inside the car.

"I've never been in a limo before!" Sarah cried. There are sodas in the icebox. There is a red carpet and track lighting and plenty of room for the 4 of us inside the limo. We arrive at The Palace Hotel in Beacon. Loud music poured from the ballroom.

As we entered, the DJ announced our names, Anni Marino escorted by Ben Walker. I smiled at Ben and he held his arm out for me to take and we make our way down the grand staircase.

"Shall we dance?" he asked. A slow ballad played, and we made our way to the dance floor. Ben puts his arms around my waist and pulled me in close to him. Our bodies were flush against each other and I rested my head against his chest, matching my breathing with his.

After the prom we settled at Robert's family owned motel on 43rd street in South Beacon. The rain had stopped, yet; the air was still damp and cold. Ben, Robert, a few of their soccer buddies and their dates arrived and joined us in Room 104.

"Who wants a beer?" Robert asked. He held some beer cans from a duffle bag.

"No thank you," I said, holding my hand up.

"I'm good," Ben said, also declining a beer. I smiled at him, knowing he turned it down for me. He had snuck beer with his soccer team before so it's not that he didn't enjoy drinking. But I was grateful. Sarah downed a beer quickly and moved in close to Robert. He seemed to handle his heartache pretty well.

"Come with me," Ben whispered after a while. He took my hand and led me outside. A few doors down, he produced a key from his pocket. My muscles tensed. We were both virgins, but I wasn't ready that night.

Ben opened the door to the motel room and locked it behind us. It was dark in the room, illuminated only by the porch light of the balcony outside the room. Ben pulled me close to him and kissed my lips. My heart raced, and I pushed him back. It felt rushed and uncomfortable.

"Ben, I don't want to."

"Why?"

"I'm just not there yet. It's not the right time." Ben had been hinting to me that his friends on the soccer team have been pressuring him lately, making assumptions because Ben and I have had a long lasting relationship, sex is something that has happened.

"But, we love each other."

"So, then you'll wait."

"But, Anni..... OK," he resigned. He looked away. I knew it disappointed him. I worried that Ben won't want to wait for me, but I couldn't bring myself to give in. He pulled me close and kisses the top of my head. I was thankful he didn't press on any further. Awkward silence filled the room, and I tried to think of a reason to get out.

"Do you want a soda?"

"Sure," he said. I walked down the balcony to the stairs and down towards the office of the motel. Outside there was a soda machine, and I dug in my purse for some coins. I leaned my head back feeling the cool mist on my face as I sighed for turning Ben down. I returned to the room with the soda and Ben's face drooped with disappointment.

"I'm sorry," I said.

"It's fine, Anni, really." His voice was unconvincing. I knew it frustrates him.

"Do you want to go back to the others?" he asked. I wanted to stay and kiss Ben but I guessed I would complicate things by teasing. I didn't want to lead him on or frustrate him. I loved kissing him and being in his arms, but I was just not ready to go all the way. Was I scared? Was I saving myself for someone else? I ruined Ben's prom. No drinking, no sex.

"Sure," I said. We returned to the room a few doors down and Sarah gave me a confused look. I shook my head, letting her know nothing happened. She narrowed her eyes in disappointment.

For weeks after the break-up I couldn't eat or sleep. I cried. A lot. Ben and I had been together for nearly two years and all of my life revolved around him. Weekend football games, studying, walking the hallways, waiting by our lockers, driving to school, the beach. Unfortunately, summer is classic Beacon breakup season, made more tempting by the influx of new girls and guys to the island. Why would anyone want to be tied down in summer? I wondered if Ben would come back around in Sep-

Christine Scarpa

tember. Would I take him if he came back?

Chapter 8: Summer 1993

Michael

"Mike, it's going to rain," my mother said from the kitchen, "Your top is down on the Jeep!" I pulled on my sneakers and ran down the wooden stairs. A pink envelope sat on the seat of the driver's side. I immediately recognized the handwriting, and my heart skipped a beat. Anni. It's been about a year since she told me about Ben. I folded the envelope and stuck it in the pockets of my shorts and put the top back on the Jeep and ran back into the house.

Pink was Anni. Everything pink. What could she want to say? I became unaware of my surroundings as I held the pink envelope. The nerves in my hands tingled as I unfolded it, carefully removing the letter. Her handwriting was so familiar, the way she curled her letters and dotted the "i" in her name with a heart. I closed my eyes and saw her ponytail with a pink scrunchie, her big brown eyes lit up like the lights of the pinball machine. I imagined her smile and heard her sweet laugh. I fidgeted with the letter as the images caused my heart to pound. I did the math in my head and figured Anni is 16 now, going to be a junior in High School. I wondered if her relationship with Ben has changed her. At that thought, I opened my eyes. Ben, I didn't want to think about that. The letter...

Dear Michael,

It has been a while. I have not been a great friend. I am sorry. I know we haven't talked in a year but I wanted to let you know that Ben and I broke up. I miss you. I got a new job this summer working at the novelty shop on 21st Street. I want to talk. Please come by. I will be there by myself all day.
Love, Anni

I put my sneakers back on and checked my hair in the mirror.
"Where are you going so fast?" my mom asked.
"I'll be back soon." I threw the letter on my bed. I took the stairs two at a time and jogged up to the shop on 21st Street. The air was hot and damp and I felt sporadic raindrops. Anni was buried in a book when I got to the shop. I noticed the familiarity of her face and the scrunched up look she gets when she reads. After a moment of studying her, she looked up from her book. I couldn't help but smile when we made eye contact.
"Hey Anni." I put my hands in my pockets unsure of how to approach her.
"You're here?" Anni's hair was cut much shorter than the last time I saw her, tucked behind her ears. She looked different, older. Her black denim shorts were tight against her legs and a fitted crop top showed off her new curves. I tried not to stare. She ran into me, and I instinctively picked her up and swung her around. The shape of her body against mine was unexpected and new, and I could feel my skin flush. I put my hands on her shoulders and held her out to look in her eyes.
"I didn't know if you would come," she said. If I had given it any thought, I might have changed my mind, but I did the first thing I wanted to do after I read her note. I wanted to see her smile and hear her laugh.

"Ben was a jerk, huh?" I smirked. "I tried to tell you that."
"Not really, but…" she said, letting her sentence linger unfinished. I pulled her in close again.
"I missed you," I whispered.
   "I missed you too." She said.

"Are you working tonight?" I tried to come up with a reason to see her again.

"No, I'm not."

"Do you want to go to the jetty?" The newspaper on the kitchen table this morning announced a meteor shower for tonight.

"Yes, definitely," she answered quickly to my relief. I hoped she would let me kiss her, but I didn't think she would expect it. It's never been like that before.

I pulled slowly into the parking spot of Anni's parents' motel and she approached the Jeep. She was wearing a denim skirt and a fitted striped t-shirt, and she tucked her hair behind her ears.

"Anni, you look.... wow!"

"What?" she laughed, confused. I loved that about Anni. She didn't know how beautiful she was. She didn't know the effect she had on me, yet.

As we drove with the Jeep top down, Anni's hair became wild by the wind. I loved it, but she struggled to put it back into a scrunchie. I wished she would leave it down. Loud rap music with heavy bass vibrated through the speakers of the stereo.

"Why are you turning down my music?" I knew she hated rap.

"That's not music, it's awful" She really hated it.

It had been so long since Anni and I had been together. She was quiet, and I noticed her biting on her fingernails. The scenery distracted her as we drove by.

"Anni." As I got her attention, I turned the music louder and threw my hands in the air, my knee controlling the steering wheel, while I sang the lyrics. Anni shook her head and smiled. It was nice to see that smile again.

The air was damp and hot, but the sky was clear. The moon rose over the ocean in the eastern sky, as the sun set in the west.

It was such a beautiful sight of two horizons, one dark, illuminated by only the light of the moon, large and low. Across the island in the west, hues of purple and orange surrounded the sun as it sets. The temperature dropped as the sun faded away.

"This is my favorite part of the day," Anni said. The sunset glowed in her eyes. I put my hand over hers, resting on the Jeep's console as I parked. I helped her out of the Jeep, and we walked hand in hand to the jetty. At the far end, the ocean slammed into the side of the massive black and silver rock, creating a wave of salty water. The sun fully set, the night became dark quickly, and we were careful to keep our footing on the slippery surface. I took her hand and walked to the end where the waves were crashing. A sign says "Danger, Do Not Climb Jetty". I could hear Anni in my head saying, "It says not to climb, Michael." But she didn't protest.

On the jetty, I spread my sweatshirt out and Anni sat between my knees, leaning back into my chest. She smelled so good, like lavender and vanilla, different from the fruity watermelon body wash I remember from years ago. This lavender and vanilla scent was more calming, warming, grown-up. More like this Anni.

The waves crashed with a soothing rhythm against the jetty and we could taste the salt in the air. The conversation was easy and simple as Anni had been staying on safe subjects like school and friends and work. I could feel her body rise and fall against mine.

"I think Ben broke up with me because I didn't want to go all the way with him."

"What?" I said. The music from the deck bar lingered faintly in the background as couples walked the beach holding hands in the moonlight.

"I mean, I loved him and all but...."

"Please stop." I couldn't listen to her talk about this. I fixed my gaze towards the sky and pulled her back towards me, hoping she would drop it.

"What?"

"Anni, did you see that?" I pointed out a shooting star, grateful to change the subject. Thank God Anni and Ben broke up before he could steal her virginity. The thought of them together made my skin crawl.

"I'm sorry I was a terrible friend," she began, "It's just that I don't really know how to navigate dating and friendship with boys."

"Boys?" I nudged her playfully in the side until she giggled.

"Yes, boys. How come you've never had a girlfriend? Wouldn't that be weird?" she asked. "On second thought, why have you not had a girlfriend?"

"I don't know, I just like, hook up," I said, feeling awkward with her questions. I shrugged my shoulders.

"You do?" she said, her face falling.

"Well, yeah, Anni. I'm 19, you think I haven't kissed girls?"

"That's what I thought," she said. I squeezed her with my knees. I looked at Anni still sweet and naïve, yet different.

"You have changed," I said.

"You did too, Michael," she replied leaning back against me. I wrapped my arms around her and felt the warmth of her body. The air became cool and damp so we headed back towards the Jeep.

I had been thinking of kissing Anni all afternoon, but laying there with her against me, her back against my chest, and smelling her new scent, feeling her new curves, my pulse raced and I felt restless. She seemed so oblivious to my attraction to her, that is the innocence of Anni.

I stood up to help her to her feet, and I thought it might be a good time, but I can't bring myself to kiss her. I don't know what was making me so nervous. We left the jetty as the air turned cool and Anni shivered.

Anni

I settled on the couch with a book since it was a dreary

summer day. The salty smell of the beach permeated through the motel living quarters while a cool ocean breeze blew gently through the windows. I heard Michael's Jeep pull up outside with the bass thumping to some rap music. I always knew when he arrived. I got up off the couch and went outside.

"Hi, surprised to see you here."
"Hi Anni, was hoping you would be here."
"I am."
"I was just, I was thinking...."

Michael leaned against the jeep and put his arms around my waist, which felt much more intimate than usual. He pulled me closer to him. He was acting nervous, and I tilted my head to the side, trying to figure out what was different. Occasionally there was a playful punch in the arm or a shove. Our usual hugs were arms around each other's shoulders. Michael was serious though and his playful smile replaced by something I didn't recognize. It was something more mature, the way I had seen men look at women in the movies. His eyes were dark and mysterious, and they stared into mine. He leaned in and his closed lips met mine for what seemed like forever. Oh my God. It froze me and made me unsure what to do. I held my breath. The warmth of his lips lingered on mine. It was a sweet kiss but, our lips had never touched before. He acted surprised and held me out from him to look at me.

"Did you just kiss me?" He said with his usual crooked smile.

I opened my mouth to speak but no words come out. A million little firecrackers were exploding in my brain. He pulled me in and kisses me again, opening his mouth this time. I felt his tongue on mine. He was experienced at this. This was definitely a lot less clumsy and awkward than kissing Ben. He held me tighter and kissed me longer. I thought maybe my mind had checked out momentarily. He pushed me back, and I looked in his eyes confused and amazed by what just happened. And I realized I had never thought this might happen.

"Oh," was the only thing I can force from my voice.

"Speechless?" he asked.

"Yeah, I um, I just wasn't expecting....Michael, you are very good at that!" I blurted without thinking. How embarrassing, Anni. Oh my, what if I was not good at that!

"Anni, I have to go."

"No, not yet." I said, staring at his face. He smiled and pulled me close to him. My ear was on his chest and I could hear his heartbeat. "You smell good."

He leaned his chin on my head, then he pushed me against his Jeep and our lips touched once again. We parted, and he smiled and jumped in his Jeep, bass now pumping.

"Meeting up with Scott tonight." he said.

"Oh, ok." I said, disappointed he's leaving so soon.

"See you tomorrow?"

I said nothing. I shook my head in agreement.

Michael

My bedroom at the beach house was simple, a bed and an old dresser. I laid staring at the popcorn ceiling feeling the breeze from the blades of the ceiling fan. I followed them with my eyes. Ever since seeing her yesterday at the novelty shop, I couldn't get her out of my head. She had breasts and hips. And the way she wore her too-short cut-off jeans and fitted t-shirts made it difficult to think. She didn't know how hot she was. I loved that about her. I imagined taking her into the back of the store and pinning her with my body against the wall, meeting her lips with mine, sneaking my hands under her shirt. But, I know Anni. That would have been a sure way to kill the friendship. So, I invited her to jetty, hoping to make out with her. It would be romantic, quiet, serene. But I couldn't go through with it. I loved feeling her body laying on me, watching the stars and laughing. Why was she making me so nervous? I've kissed lots of girls.

I was getting restless as I laid thinking. I needed to go see her. I grabbed my keys to the Jeep as I ran out the door and down the stairs. The motel was only a few blocks, but I put on my music and turned up the volume. My mind was on how much I wanted Anni. I drove passed Waterford Bed and Breakfast, Shipwreck Island Ice Cream, Bait N Tackle Shop. Banner planes flew overhead, "Early Bird Specials at Beacon Bar." I stopped to let a family cross the street carrying their beach toys and a wagon full of tired children and coolers.

I parked my Jeep by the light post, the one that shines into her bedroom at night. I didn't have to call her from the pay phone because she came outside when she heard me pull up. Anni wrinkled her nose, confused why I was here. It wasn't like me to show up unannounced.

"I was hoping you would be here," I said. My hands sweated and my heart palpitated as I worked up the nerve to finally pull her close my hands around her waist. She was confused and her big brown eyes look up at me. I stuttered over my words and decided to just go for it.

I leaned against the Jeep. Anni's body tensed up when I pulled her in, and our lips met. Her lips were soft and warm, and I breathed in her lavender scent. She stared up at me waiting for me to say something.

"Did you just kiss me?" I took a step back and scanned her face for a reaction. Anni didn't respond. I needed more. I leaned against the Jeep and pulled her close again and cradled her face in my hands, kissing her with more passion than I've kissed girls in a while. Anni's fingers touched her lips and her eyes widen. I waited for her to say something, but for a moment, I thought she has gone catatonic on me. Her eyes fixed in a gaze, her breathing was shallow. Finally, she responded to my touch, standing up on her toes and wrapping her hands around my neck. I could taste the vanilla lip balm on her lips.

"I have to go."

"No," she said sharply, "not yet". She wanted more, so I pushed her gently against the Jeep and left her with one last kiss. A long, slow kiss to last until next time. I felt her knees buckle underneath her.

"See you tomorrow," I said as I hopped in my Jeep, turned up the bass and pulled away.

Chapter 9: Summer 1993

Michael

I pulled into the parking lot of our two-story beach house, which is on the corner with a small grass parking lot. Strollers and toys littered the front porch from the family who rents on the weekends. I sat in the Jeep for a few minutes, bass pumping through the speakers. My heart pounded to the beat. I knew it annoyed the neighbors but I didn't care. I shut the car off and headed upstairs.

"Michael, are we going cruising tonight?" Scott asked when I picked up the phone.

"Sure, I'll pick you up." I didn't ask what we are doing.

When Scott and I went cruising, it involved beer and girls and terrible decisions. Scott and his friends were locals, they lived in Beacon all year. During the summer, new girls came and went every weekend making it easy for us to meet some. Most city girls were eager to meet a local guy and willingly obliged to a night on the town, cruising around and drinking, local parties and pool hopping. Scott was not good looking, but being a local enticed girls to hang out. Beaches, the boardwalk, and parks were all good places to pick up chicks. Scott was a pro at starting a conversation, making girls feel like they are getting the inside-scoop of the island.

"Hey, some locals are getting together tonight," he would say to them. "I can pick you up and show you around town." It was a smooth line. They wouldn't be here in a few days and there was no commitment.

I pulled up to his modest two-story home, one of the few traditional looking homes on the island. Many homes were modern beach homes with large decks, cathedral ceilings and lots of open space and windows. I turned on the music in the Jeep and Scott came out of his house.

"Hey, you ready for some fun?" Scott rubbed his hands together.

"Where to?" I asked.

"Well, we have a real special treat tonight Mikey!" He beamed in an announcer voice, handing me a bottle of beer. I chugged it down before I pulled out of the driveway.

"I kissed Anni." No warning, I blurted it out and waited for his reaction.

"You're a fool!"

"I know. It was nothing." I regretted bringing it up. I expected Scott to react that way, but then I felt defensive. I've kissed many girls, but none like her. Scott wouldn't understand, so I dropped it. It definitely wasn't nothing.

"Now she will want a "Re-la-tion-ship," he drew out and in air quotes. He added a shudder as dramatic effect.

"Turn here," Scott said, and I pulled into a condo complex. Two beautiful girls were waiting near the parking garage. One girl, tall and thin with olive skin was wearing a tight black dress which immediately captured my attention. The other girl was a petite blond with cute dimples and a baby face. I glanced over at Scott and he shook his head up and down.

"Scott, you are a devil."

"Michael, this is ..." Scott held his hand up to the tallest girl of the two.

"Sophia," she said. He didn't even know her name.

"Sophia," Scott repeated, giving me a nod. She jumped in the passenger side of the Jeep while Scott hopped in the back. We drove down to the beach and parked. I jumped out of the Jeep and grabbed a cooler and I helped Sophia out. I wanted her friend, but Scott was already moving in on her, his mouth on hers and has his hand underneath her shirt. I grabbed Sophia's hand and walked down towards my usual spot. My usual ritual.

The sand had cooled down now that the sun had set. The moon lit up the night sky, and the air smelled salty. We walked over to a set of swings and sat down. Sophia and I swayed back and forth closer towards each other and then apart. I needed something to loosen this girl up, so I opened a can of cheap beer and I handed it to her. I opened another can for myself, and I held it up. Sophia touched her can to mine, and we sat in awkward silence.

"So, where are you from?" I asked.
"I live north of the city."
"How long are you here on the island?"
"Just for a week with my family and Janie"
Janie must be the friend in the Jeep with Scott.
"So, how did you meet Scott?" I was always amused to hear how clever he is. Sophia opened a pack of cigarettes and offered me one. I took it and lit it up.
"Um, on the beach today. We played volleyball." Her voice was soft and quiet and she looked young. She reminded me of Anni. The thought of Anni alone with a guy on the beach at night made me wonder where she was tonight.
"So, How Old Are You?" I asked, curious if this is even legal.
"Seventeen," she said.

We made more small talk until we have had a few beers each, and I felt buzzed and confident. "Do you want to go somewhere else?" I asked. "Sure," she whispered. Sophia didn't speak much. I wondered if I scared her, or nervous. I tried to picture her at a party, dancing and throwing back beers. I'm sure she knew what we were doing here. She had cigarettes and was drinking cheap beer, so I wouldn't exactly say she was corruptible. I didn't like to hook up with girls that didn't seem to have a clue what they were doing down the beach in the dark with a local-by-association. Briefly, I thought of Anni and how she would never touch a beer or a cigarette, and she would definitely tell you "no way" to making out on the beach with strangers. Good girl, Anni.

Under the boardwalk it was damp and dark, but the slices of moonlight sneaked through the planks of wood and illuminated Sophia's face. Her brown eyes were dark and mysterious. I had no idea what she was thinking, and she was clearly not going to make a move. I leaned towards her and brushed her light brown hair behind her ear. She didn't flinch. So, I met her lips with mine and she put her arms around my neck. We kissed many times until I got bored with kissing.

"So, um, so you come down often?" What a stupid thing to say, Mike. I had no idea what to say to Sophia.

"Yeah, my parents have a condo."

I leaned in to kiss her once more and slipped my hand under her shirt. She didn't protest.

I pulled her up on me and she threw her leg over so she was straddling me, her skirt hiking up. I pulled her closer against me, wrapping my arms around her body, kissing her neck. She was more experienced than I gave her credit for. I imagined how Anni would respond, awkward and nervous.

Well, ok, I thought. Let's get this party started. I rubbed my hands down her smooth legs. We heated things up when we hear soft footsteps in the sand. Perfect timing, dickhead. Sophia climbed off me and fixed her skirt. She brushed through her hair with her fingers when Scott and Janie approached.

"Janie and Sophia need to be home by 1:00," Scott said. I checked my watch and stood up. I brushed off my shorts.

"Let's go then," I said. Sophia hopped in the back with Janie and Scott got in the passenger seat. We dropped them off at their condo right around 1am, and I never saw Sophia again.

"Scott, please pick up girls that are at least 18. You will get me fucking arrested."

"Thanks, man," Scott said as I pulled into his driveway. Reaching in the back, he grabbed his cooler, and I'm grateful for another night of not getting caught with an open beer in my Jeep. I drove back to the beach house slowly, careful not catch the attention of any police. The streets were empty, except for a few stragglers making their way home from the bars. I walked up the stairs and quietly made my way around to my bedroom. Sophia reminded me so much of Anni, young, soft lips, shy, well, not that shy. If Scott and Janie hadn't arrived, I probably wouldn't still have that condom in my pocket.

∞∞∞∞

I picked up the phone and dialed Anni's number. I knew she was sleeping, but I hoped she'd be happy to hear from me.

"Anni... what are you doing?" She picked up after the 3rd ring. "Michael, it's 1:30 in the morning." I woke her up. She had that raspy voice.

"I'm sorry Anni". I said, not meaning it. "I just wanted to hear your voice." That I meant.

"Michael, are you drunk?"

"It is possible."

"Goodnight, Michael."

"Don't hang up," I blurted, but it was too late.

I looked out the window and Anni was walking towards my house. I pulled a shirt over my head and headed towards the door. Anni looked adorable in a pink sundress. She was showing more cleavage than usual, and I realized how amazed I am by her by her body. Her skirt was short and her legs tan. I wanted her. I wanted to pull her on my lap and put my hands underneath her dress. I made a silent deal with myself not to kiss her again, at least not all the time. At least not while I had these thoughts in my head. Even though I wanted to. Really wanted to. But, I didn't want to lead her on or give her the impression I was committed to her. It would be hard though, even to convince myself.

"Hi," she said. I wrap my arms around her shoulders and pulled her in for a hug. We sat at the table in the kitchen and I realized I was struggling for words. She stared at me saying nothing and I wondered what she was thinking. Hopefully she didn't want to talk about the kiss. It was a moment of weakness. Wasn't it? I didn't want it to be a big deal, but I knew it would for her.

"Hey Anni, I'm just on my way out but stay for a few minutes." As usual, we sat on the couch. I pulled my shirt off and backed up to her. Anni was great at giving back scratches and I couldn't resist one when she was here. Except this time, her back scratches felt more sensual than friendly. The touch of her fingers made my skin come alive. Was this my imagination or had Anni's back scratches changed too? What was happening?

"How was work?" I asked, trying to change my train of thought.

"Boring as usual. I stocked shelves all day. I need to find something new."

"You should quit that job."

"I can't. I need to buy a car." she said.

"Are you going anywhere tonight, Michael?"

"Out with Scott," I said, praying she doesn't ask anymore questions. Without a commitment, I shouldn't have felt guilty, but I did. I didn't understand my feelings anymore.

"Oh, to do what?" she asked.

"Stuff," I said, stone-faced.

"Drinking?"

"Probably."

"Were you drinking when you called me last night? You remember calling me, don't you?" she asked. I shrugged my shoulders, trying to get this conversation to the end. I don't need lectures from Miss Perfect.

"Anni, everyone drinks," I suddenly felt defensive. She doesn't live in the same world as me. She thinks the entire world is sunshine and rainbows and nobody ever gets hurt.

"Girls?" she asked.

"Possibly," Her eyes looked away. "Anni, stop, don't make this weird." I said with a hint of annoyance. We sat quietly for a while before she broke the silence. I could feel my face flushing and I was getting frustrated with her interrogation.

"I'm sorry," she said.

"I need to leave soon, Anni." I got up and took her hand to pull her to her feet. She knew I was upset with her now, and I made my way to the door. Why was I getting so bothered by this?

"Michael wait," she said, but I didn't wait to hear anything else. I walked Anni down to the street and kissed her cheek. She reached for a hug and I noticed her curves against me. I pulled her closer so her hips and breasts touched my body. This would be hard.

"Michael, come by tomorrow if you want to swim." She turned and walked away and I sighed in resignation. Why did she make me feel so fucking guilty?

Chapter 10: Present

Michael

My phone vibrates in the pocket of my jeans and I reach in. "Yo, Mikey!" Doug texts.

"Yo, Doug," I text back.

"Brandon's flying in from California this week. Why don't you and Danielle take a road trip! Scott's coming too."

"Yeah, maybe. Business is slow," I say. Business is always slow. I've lost my motivation to call anyone back.

"Awesome! You can stay with me. The wife won't mind."

"I'm good, Doug. We'll get a motel." I'll surprise Danielle with a motel that has an ocean view. We can sit on the deck and watch the sun rise and sip coffee. She will love that. Plus, I don't want to put Doug out for having to make us breakfast and whatnot.

"Well, ok, but if you change your mind, hit me up."

"Cool," I reply. I haven't been back to Beacon in so long. I took Danielle there once or twice when we were first married, but she didn't have the same emotional connection to this island as I did. We'd head down to Anchor Beach some summers when we had the time. It's been years since I saw the guys.

I flip through my phone for a local motel in Beacon, hoping to find one on the beach opened after Labor Day. I find an ocean-front motel open and the rooms are cheap this time of the year. I type in my information and my credit cards and book the room.

From the kitchen, I hear Danielle as she walks in the door of our narrow town home, throwing the mail on the hallway table. She moves down the hall and I brace myself for whatever mood she is in. I study the look on her face, and the tone of her voice. I try to remember if I did anything recently that pissed her off.

"Hey," she says, rather dull.

"Hey, how was your day?" I asked. I try to lighten the mood.

"Fine," she responds, "did you call the repairman for the washer?"

Damnit! I knew I forgot something.

"I forgot."

"What the hell did you do all day, Michael? You don't work, you don't do anything I ask!" I roll my eyes at the same story every day.

"Dani, we're taking a road trip," I try to change the subject to put an end to the daily misery.

"Where?" She asks as she leans in the fridge to grab a beer.

"Doug's brother is flying in from Cali and invited us down to Beacon." I answer. "I got us a room". I grab her around the waist and smack her ass hoping to break the tension. She jumps and pushes me away. Danielle isn't fond of my island days, although she enjoys hanging with Doug and Brandon and the guys.

"I don't know. I can't leave in the middle of the week, and I made plans with the girls Friday night. When are you going?"

"Oh, come on, Dani, it will be fun," I say. "We haven't seen the guys in a long time".

"Michael," she begins as she slouches in the leather recliner with her beer, "Just hang out with the guys. I have a lot of work to do and I have plans. You'll enjoy yourself more without me, anyway."

"You sure?" I ask, making sure this isn't a setup.

"Yea, no problem, have a good time."

"Thanks, babe," I say, disappointed to make the trip alone. I sit next to her, overlapping her body in the recliner and kiss the top of her brown hair. She pushes me off.

∞∞∞

Beacon looks different now. The old motels are gone, and large condos in their places. It doesn't have the small island charm anymore. The bed and breakfasts and small family owned shops have been replaced with high end boutiques and recognizable brand name stores. I drive up and down the streets where I spent many summers, trying to remember where all our hangouts were. I drive past my old summer house, but it is gone. The arcade where Scott worked is gone and the diner where Doug, Brandon and I used to go late at night has been replaced with fancy restaurants and outside seating. Even Anni's parents' motel is gone. I drive along the beach and remember sneaking under the boardwalk with girls. I couldn't remember a single girl's name or face. I headed across the island to the bayside and parked in front of Doug's house.

Doug was on the porch having a cigarette. He throws it in the tin can and meets me at the step.

"Mike!" Doug puts his hand out and pulls me in for a hug. "Man, it's been forever. How ya been?" Doug is shorter than average and slightly stocky. His thick blond hair is wavy and too long. It's as if he hasn't realized he is way past his surfing days. Girls used to dig him back in the day because he looked like an island guy, rather than a city boy with that surfer hair, board shorts, and tan skin.

"Wow Doug, you're eating well." I patted his belly. Doug fake punches me in the arm. It feels good to be back on the island with Doug. He, Scott and I tore this place up back in the day, scoping the chicks on the beach and inviting them out at night, drinking too much beer and hooking up if we were lucky... and we were very lucky. Danielle hates those stories. That is probably why she was too busy to come.

"Come inside," Doug says as he takes the case of beer from me.

His wife, Monica, makes her way to the foyer and leans in to my kiss. "Monica, you look great."

"Thanks, Mike. Danielle come?" she looks around.

"No, she's got work to do. Hard for her to get away during the week." I explain. Monica frowns as the back door flies open.

"Oh shit, don't tell me Mike, the Island Champion, Convertible King, is here!" Brandon says. We embrace, patting each other's back. He rubs the scruff on my face jokingly, "Nice touch, Michael. About time you grew some facial hair".

Brandon turns to his girl, "Maria, this is Mike. He's a legend on this island." He holds his hand out for a high five. I laugh at the legend comment. It was more of a team effort, Scott was good at picking up chicks, Doug got us the beer, and I was just luckier with girls. Brandon was the least lucky, he talked too much.

"Nice to meet you, Maria." Maria has small facial features, a tiny nose and tiny ears. She reminds me of an elf, though she is strikingly beautiful. Long dark flowing hair and a tiny framed body. Doug emerges from the kitchen with some beers and passes them out.

"Let me take your things, Brandon." He takes his bags and disappears up the stairs. "Mikey," he calls down, "You still got a motel room?"

"Yeah, man, I'm good with that."

"Ok, cause we got plenty of room here if you change your mind." he says.

"Holy Shit!" I cry. "It's got to have been 15 years." I embrace Scott as I see him enter the house. It feels good to be back here with these guys. I am an outsider, with all of them having grown up here on the island. Brandon and Scott moved away, but their families are still local.

We stand in the foyer of Doug's house and Monica emerges with two beers in each hand.

"That's a good wife," I joke to Doug, throwing an elbow to his side.

"Come on, guys, lets head out back." Doug motions for us to

follow him. It is late in the day and the sun has set over the bay behind the house. The orange and purple sky reminds me of so many summers here in Beacon.

"Do you need help?" I ask Doug as he carries firewood to the fire pit.

"Here," he hands me a log, "put this in the pit." Doug carefully stacks the wood and throws a fire starter and some newspaper underneath. Squatting down next to the pit, I pick up the matchbox and strike a match. Doug crouches, too.

"So," Doug begins, "Everything good with you and Danielle?" he whispers.

"Same old, you know."

"What are you going to do?" Doug asks.

"What can I do?" I shrug my shoulder.

"She still sneaking around?"

"I have no idea, Doug." I say "I don't even care. What am I going to do, leave her? My business is down, and I don't have the energy to go through a separation. It doesn't always suck. I can live with it." I stand and admire the fire.

This time of the year is so peaceful and quiet in Beacon. We settle outside on the back patio overlooking the bay. We sit in chairs arranged in a circle around the fire pit. Typically, the water would be filled with jet skiers and boats and loud music. Children screaming as they jump off the docks into the bay, careful to stay out of the way of watercraft. The houses are situated on a channel, facing other homes across the water. Doug never left the island and married a local girl, but Brandon joined the military and has been stationed in several areas from Alaska to New Jersey. Doug grabs some beers from the cooler and places them on the table, since we are nearly finished with the ones in our hands. Once the fire is going, beers are plenty, and we are settled in, we begin telling stories.

"Remember when Doug got so fucking drunk he dove off the deck of that motel in the pool?" Scott says. We roar at the memory. Doug holds his hand up while Scott returns his high five.

"That was Mike's fault, he double dog dared me," Doug says in defense, pointing his finger at me.

"You were trying to impress that Swedish girl," I jab.

"I think she was from North Carolina," Scott adds. We laugh and clink our beer bottles.

"Yeah, well, remember Mike picked up that girl and her dad followed us down to the beach? Man, you almost got us fucking killed, dude." Scott laughs.

"Yeah, I see why Danielle didn't come," Monica laughs, "Maria, do you want to help me put some food together in the kitchen." Monica throws Maria an escape.

"Sure," she excuses herself from a conversation she probably doesn't want to hear about.

The guys continue without noticing the girls leave.

"Scott, you convinced us to jump waves naked one night and the fucking cops came driving up. You're lucky Doug's dad was the police chief!" I point my finger at Scott.

"Yeah, man, we were all lucky Doug's dad was the fucking police chief!" Scott says. We sit in silence for a while, each one of us thinking about a summer memory and staring into the fire.

"Mike, what was that pinball girl's name? The one you booty-called each night after you got wasted." Doug asks.

"Anni, and I didn't booty-call her. I just visited." I held up my beer to him.

"Right! You racked up the points with her," Scott chimes in.

"No, I racked up the points, but not with her." I elbow him. We all laugh.

"I heard she wouldn't give it up for Mike," Brandon jabs. Doug looks at me and I recall the conversation we had the last night I saw Anni. "You're a fool," he had said.

"No, I was just a gentleman," I bark sarcastically. The guys die laughing. Gentleman was the polar opposite of what I was. Of course, Anni was different. She wasn't a point in Doug's stupid sex game, even though she always thought she was. But, having sex with Anni was different. There were many layers of feelings involved, and I cared about her. Anni's skin against me, her lavender scent. All of that felt different from with any of the casual girls. They were points.

"Oh, come on Mike, spill it on the ping pong girl!" Brandon eggs on, "Why is she such a secret."

"It wasn't ping pong!" I laughed. "Drop the fucking subject, I don't want to talk about Anni," I say.

"Uh Oh," Scott says, "You hit a nerve."

"She was local, I remember seeing her around at football games in the fall. She had that hot friend. I think she made out with Doug." Brandon chimes in. Doug pops his head up, "Who?" he asks.

"You made out with Ping Pong girl?" Scott jokes.

"Ping Pong girl was Mike's, off limits. Her parents had a motel, I think, right Mike?" Doug joins in. The guys laugh, and I try to laugh along with them but I feel my face flush. Of course she was off limits to them, I wouldn't want her near any one of these guys.

"Can we change the fucking subject," I beg. "What about you Scott, where's your girl?"

"Fuck that," he says.

The guys drop Anni, thankfully. I relax as the night goes on as we reminisce and laugh and drink beer.

"I should get back to the motel." I say around midnight.

"Mike, come by tomorrow, I'll take you out on the boat," Doug suggests.

"Cool, that sounds like fun" I answer. I kiss the girls goodbye and shake the guys' hands and make my way to the convertible.

I return to my motel room around 1am and stumble to the bed. I throw my clothes on the floor and get under the scratchy covers. I regret not taking Doug up on the offer of shacking up at his house, but at least no one will bother me in the morning. Maybe I'll take a run on the beach when I wake up. I rest my head on the pillow and my phone buzzes.

"Yo, man, you make it to the motel ok?" Doug texts.

"Ya, thanks for a great night! I had fun."

"Hit me up tomorrow."

Before I put my phone down I touch the blue Facebook app

square. It's been a few weeks since Anni sent me a message. I wanted to reach out to her again, but I didn't. And here I am in Beacon. I thought about her often since she made contact, but I had not thought about the possibility of being so close. I wonder if she still lives here or if she has moved. I type Anni into the search field and I touch her name when it appears. I scroll through her profile and it says lives in Fairway. If I wasn't intoxicated, I might have thought twice about sending her a message, but I touch the messenger picture and open a dialogue box.

"Hey Anni, I'm here on some business. Let's have coffee." I hit send. I wait a few minutes staring at the phone. I see she has read my message, and my heartbeat quickens. She doesn't reply. Disappointed, I toss the phone on the bed, roll over and close my eyes. I drift when my notification sound dings.

"Michael, that is really...unexpected." She writes back. I wonder what she is doing up at 1am, but I don't ask.

"Is that a yes?"

"I'm not sure that is a good idea," she replies.

"Of course it is." Several minutes go by, and I think maybe she has signed off. I stare at the phone for a while in anticipation but I don't see she is writing. I analyze every minute that goes by. Then a message pops up.

"I drop my daughter off at daycare at 8:30. There's a coffee shop on Main Street in Fairway. It's called The Scoop. I can meet you there."

"Perfect. I'll be the tall, handsome guy walking through the door. You may recognize me. I look forward to it."

"LOL Michael. See you then." She texts back.

That was easy. Anni was always so easy to give in, even when she didn't want to. When we were teenagers, I was careful not to put her in a position she would get hurt because I knew she would go along. But, there were times she would need some convincing. "That's not a good idea" she would say if I suggested taking a drive in the jeep, or heading out to the jetty, or down the beach at night. I could talk her into it though as long as it didn't violate her strong convictions. No drinking, no drugs, no smoking, no sex. Well, some of her convictions were violated, eventually.

"Michael, you will get in trouble," she would say. "The sign says 'Stay off the Jetty' Michael." I can still hear her voice in my head. But she would always follow me.

"What's your point, Anni?" I answered.

After nights of partying with the guys, I could convince her to let me in to hang out. I would call her from the payphone outside her window of the motel living quarters late at night, and I could see her peek through the curtains.

"Michael, go home," she would say.

"I really want to see you," I would beg. She would melt like butter. She liked to feel loved and wanted, no matter the circumstance. She would come outside and sit on the deck with me while I slurred my words telling her how much I loved her. I loved her.

Well, Anni was right, that was unexpected. I turned the alarm on since I know I will sleep right through 9:00. I put my phone on the table next to the bed and pulled the cover up. I hate sleeping in motels. I lay awake for a while before sleep comes. I play scenarios in my head of how our reunion will go tomorrow. I haven't given myself very much time to prepare. How will Anni receive me after more than two decades of no contact? I wonder if she is still bitter about the dorm incident. Or if she will run across the coffee shop and embrace me like old friends do. Or will she tell me how much she hates me, and how I ruined her life. I deserve whatever I get.

I rolled over in the uncomfortably springy motel bed. I took deep breaths to try to slow my breathing. I'm seeing Anni tomorrow.

Chapter 11: Summer 1994

Michael

"Michael, I met some girls on the beach today. They are staying at the Carousel Motel in Room 222. I told them we will swing by around 9:00." Scott said.

"Sweet, ok. I'll pick you up around 8:30." I hung up the phone.

I turned to Anni, who was standing in my bedroom. I felt guilty leading her on. I should have known better than to kiss her. Anni doesn't casually make out. Since the kiss, she had come around more often, showing up here in her little dresses which made me want her so bad. Did she know what she was doing? Was she flirting? Or was it just innocent Anni being herself? She didn't try to kiss me, and I doubt she would take any initiative, anyway. She turned my world upside down. I couldn't go out without feeling guilty. But, we had nothing in common anymore. She didn't fit into my crowd because we did all the things Anni hates: drinking, smoking, rap music, loud car stereos, promiscuity. God, did Anni hate rap music.

"Anni, I need to get in the shower, I'm picking Scott up at 8:30".

"OK," she said.

"Come with me?" I took a step towards her, putting my arm around her shoulder. I smiled my crooked smile at her because I knew she would melt.

"In the shower."

Ok." Her eyes darted around the room, probably looking for a way out.

"Really?" I asked, knowing she wouldn't. I only said it to watch her freak out. She was so adorable when she is nervous.

"No, Michael, are you being serious?" She laughed, nervous as hell.

"Come on, it will be fine," I said, my face close to hers. She squirmed to break free.

"You're being weird, I'm not going in the shower with you," she said, wrapping her arms across her body. I stuck my lip out, giving her puppy dog eyes in an attempt to make her feel guilty.

Anni laughed. I laugh. "I'll be right out." I said. I knew she wouldn't. I'm such a fucking dickhead for leading her to believe there's something more than there is. She doesn't believe me, anyway. Thank God she said no. As I scrubbed the ocean water from my hair, memories of Anni flood my mind.

The first time I took Anni for a ride in my Jeep was the summer she was going into high school. She was 14, and I was 17.

"Come on, Anni, I'll take you for a ride in the Jeep."

"I have to ask my mom," she answered. I picked her up with the top and doors off and she jumped, her ponytail was swinging back and forth. She could barely get in by herself. I helped her into the passenger seat and put her seatbelt on. She smiled ear to ear.

"I've never been in one of these before!" she squealed. I turned the music up in the jeep as we rode up and down the streets of the island and down to the inlet. I parked, and we climbed on the rocks of the jetty, watching the bridge open for the boats. Her hair was blowing in the warm ocean breeze, and she smiled at me. I loved seeing her so happy.

I snapped back into the present, under the stream of cold water and thought how complicated things are. My heart sank, and I wished I could change things for her, but I couldn't. Or at least I didn't want to right now. I turned off the water and wrapped a towel around my waist. Anni was sitting on the bed and lowered her eyes when she saw me return in a towel.

"You're going to be shy?" I asked.

"You're weird." I loved when she called me weird. It was her word. I shrugged, admitting I was acting weird. I'm not sure why I was acting weird because I wouldn't know what to do if she took my teasing seriously.

"I want to go out with you one night," she said.

"Why?"

"Because, I want to."

"Anni, it's not your scene. You wouldn't be comfortable, and you'd get hurt."

"You're embarrassed by me?"

"No, I'm not embarrassed by you, I'm embarrassed by my friends."

"Come on, Michael, just once."

"Maybe one night," I conceded, hoping she will stop asking. I pulled her close my body still damp from the shower and put my arms around her, holding her against me. She tensed up.

Anni stood and walked to my dresser and pointed to a photo stuck in the slots of the mirror frame. Two photos, one half of a strip of photo booth pictures. Black and white. She pulled the picture out and turned. Several more pictures fell to the floor. She bent down to pick them up, glancing at me when she stood. One photo strip for each year. 1990 when we met in the arcade, 1991, 1992, and 1994, and this year, 1995. A kiss. Each strip of 4 pictures, torn in half, two for Anni and two for me.

"Look how young we were, Michael?" she said, turning the torn strips of photos in my direction. She read the back, "Summer of 91." Anni looked at me.

"Ninety-three is missing." Anni frowned at me. Ninety-three, the year of the fucking boyfriend.

After I got dressed, we walked down to the Jeep. I pulled her close and kissed the top of her head which nestled just under my chin.

"Do you want me to drive you home on my way to Scott's?"

"Sure."

I pulled up in front of the motel and leaned over to kiss her cheek.

"Michael." I raised my eyebrows. "Please don't drunk dial me tonight."

"You don't mean that." She tried not to smile, and I pulled her over and kissed her lips. She slid out, and I watched her walk in as I pulled away.

∞∞∞∞

I got to Scott's at 8:30, as promised and he delivered his promise, two girls. These two looked like college girls and I was optimistic for tonight. Olivia and Meghan. Scott and I paired off, as usual. I opened a beer and offered one to Olivia. She pulled vodka from her purse and we drank shots directly from the bottle.

"Do you want a cigarette?" I asked Olivia. She took a drag from my lit cigarette leaving bright pink lipstick stains on the filter. Olivia and I headed down the beach. We found a secluded spot and laid down in the warm sand. The mix of beer, vodka, sand and salt was the perfect recipe for sex. My lips met hers as I slipped my hand under her shirt. And so, another night began for me.

"Do you have a condom?" she asked. Fuck. She looked at my face and stood brushing off the sand. And that was that. No condom, no action. Nothing. We sat on the beach awkwardly for another half hour before Scott and Meghan appeared. Meghan stumbled while Scott steadied her. I finish the rest of my beer, crushed the can and threw it in the sand.

"Let's go," I said, walking to the parking lot.

∞∞∞

"Anni?" I asked through the telephone

"Michael, it's 2am."

"I know. I just wanted to hear your voice. Can you let me in?"

"What?"

"Look out your window." I stared at her window and saw her pull back the curtains. Neon lights from the ice cream parlor were flashing on the pay phone across the street as drunk teens staggered down the sidewalk, laughing and screaming.

Anni looked so sexy in her yellow nightgown and fuzzy pink slippers. The nightgown says something on it, but the words blurred at that moment. "Sweet Dreams?" I fell into her in a drunken bear hug. "I missed you".

"Let's sit outside, my parents will kill me if they hear us." Anni slipped outside and gently closed the door behind her. We moved to the upstairs deck overlooking the beach. We sat on a long lounge chair that reclined and I put my head on her shoulder.

The night was cool and damp, and the smell of the ocean lingered in the air. The deck was dark, aside from the streetlights. Occasionally there was a laugh somewhere in the distance or loud talking of stray people walking home from the bars. Couples emerged from the beach late at night.

"Michael, you stink!" she said, running her hands through my hair.

"Anni," I slurred.

"Michael."

I didn't lean in to kiss her because I knew she would not like the taste of beer and cigarettes. Instead, I grabbed her hand, and I kissed it over and over. I nuzzled my face in her hair and breathed in the trace of her shampoo. Kiwi Strawberry?

"Anni, you are my girl."

"I know, Michael."

"Anni, we will get married someday."

"Are you sure?"

"Yeah, where's your ring?" I took her hand and examined it, but it wasn't there.

The first summer after riding the rollercoaster, Anni and I stopped back at the arcade.

"Anni, I bet you can't beat me in skeeball." I had teased. I put one quarter in a skeeball lane and a second quarter in the other. Anni and I threw the smooth wooden skeeballs down the lane with enough force to make it over the hump, but not enough to reach the highest corner. Red tickets flowed steadily out of the machine. I don't recall who won that game of skeeball, but I grabbed the tickets and put them in my pocket.

"Close your eyes, Anni." I put my hands over them to be sure she was not peeking. "Put out your hand." I slipped a shiny tin ring, that cost 10 tickets, on her finger. She opened her eyes, and we both laughed.

"I will cherish it and wear it always," she joked. Except it turned her finger green after a few days.

∞∞∞

"It's in my jewelry box," she said.

"Really?"

"Yep."

I pushed Anni gently down on the lounge and I curled up next to her.

"I'm sorry," I said.

"For what?"

"For being stupid."

"Michael, let's not talk about this now."

"I want to kiss you," I admitted. I wrapped my arms around her.

"Not tonight," she said. I was thankful she said no because I was afraid of what I would try to do to her. I ran my hands along her stomach, over her nightgown and pulled her closer. God, I wanted her so bad.

She put her arm over me, holding me onto the lounge. "I love you," I said.

"I know," she answered. *She does know I love her. She's my best friend.*

Chapter 12: Present

Anni

"Anni, I should go." Michael stands up and throws out his trash. My eyes follow him. "I'm glad you agreed to meet me here. I've enjoyed catching up with you. Walk out to the parking lot with me." He takes my hand. Rather than noticing Michael waiting for my reply, I notice Miranda glaring at us from behind the counter. I feel like she's judging me. Is it my guilt?

It drizzled outside and thunder rolls in the distance. Michael and I stand on the sidewalk under the over-hang to shelter our goodbye. "You've changed." Looking in his eyes, I'm trying to memorize his new features, his grown in hair, the shadow of stubble on his face, the broadness of his chest. He seems more reserved, less reckless than I remember. I suppose I have changed too. I find myself somehow disappointed. It's better that way, Anni.

"Oh, Anni," Michael gives me a playful nudge and says slyly, "I haven't changed all that much." And then that smirk on his face. He hesitates and then kisses my cheek. I think I hear some of the old Michael in his voice. We linger for a few minutes before we have no real reason to stay. I watched Michael get in his electric blue convertible. A convertible, of course. Now that's not much of a change.

I can still feel his kiss on my cheek when I hear his voice call, "Anni" and I turn, "I love purple on you." I look down at my purple shirt and laugh. Well played.

∞∞∞

Pulling into my horseshoe driveway, I sigh at the list of housework I have to accomplish. I think about escaping to the beach for a while, but I know that is not a good idea. As I walk through the front door and into the kitchen, I take in the dirty dishes in the sink from breakfast, the dirty soccer uniform I need to throw in the wash, and Juliette's puzzles thrown about the floor, left there in a hurry this morning to get her ready and dropped off at daycare. I try to put Michael out of my mind and return to the tasks at hand. I roll my sleeves up and open the dishwasher to load the breakfast bowls and wipe down the countertops. I pick up the puzzle pieces, matching farm animal with farm animal, rewarding me with animal sounds as I match them. I resolve that I will tell Jack about my coffee with Michael.

I remember I am supposed to get a babysitter for this Saturday night so Jack and I can have a much-needed date night. I pick up my phone to call Sydney, our babysitter. I glance at the screen and it says Incoming Call from the school.

"Mrs. Evans, this is the school nurse. Ivy isn't feeling well. Can you come pick her up?" she says. Ivy isn't feeling well because she forgot to do her homework last night and doesn't want to get in trouble. I note the time on the screen of my smartphone: 1:00.

Yep, Ivy has math at 1:15. I sigh to myself and head to the school.
"Mom, it's not that," she says when I confront her about her homework. Ivy throws her backpack in the back seat and opens the passenger side door, taking a seat in the front. Her light blond hair, in a messy bun, makes her look younger than 13. She

is petite, nearly the same height as Ricky, at 9 years old.

∞∞∞

I make a mental plan for my afternoon. Pick up Maisie from after school band, and Juliette from day care, although she can technically stay until 5:00. Ricky has to be at soccer practice by 4:00. I map my route. At least Ivy is with me, one less kid I have to pick up and drop off. I pack a snack in my bag for Ricky so I can pick him up from school and head straight to soccer practice. Cleats, socks, snacks, a soccer ball. I think we are good to go. I am exhausted before it's begun.

"Ivy, let's get your homework done," I say, watching her text and play games on her phone.

"Now?"

"Yes," I admonish.

"Did you know Maisie has a boyfriend?" she blurts.

"Yes, you mentioned that this morning," I say.

"That football guy," she offers.

I have heard Maisie talking about a boy, I should have seen the signs. I cringe at her dating. I don't look forward to heartbreaks, and kissing and God forbid, sexually active teenagers. Maisie is 16, the same age I dated in high school. Ben, I think and smile to myself. Oh, God, that night at the motel after prom. And Michael.

On my way out, I open the refrigerator and see what I can make for dinner. It looks like a frozen ravioli and meatballs kind of night. The washing machine buzzes, and I throw the soccer uniform in the dryer for tomorrow's game.

"Let's go Ivy" I say.

"Can't I stay here?" she is lounging on the couch with her phone suddenly not sick anymore.

"No, let's go." She protests by flipping the blanket off of her in a dramatic fashion, sighing, and dragging her feet to the car.

I pull into the parking lot of the daycare to pick up Juliette.

Christine Scarpa

Warm sunflowers painted on white brick greet me as I enter the building.

"Mrs. Evans, Juliette's tuition is overdue. Can you please send that in tomorrow?" Miss Tanya, the director, asks.
"Oh, my, I completely forgot. Please let me write you a check now." I pull out my checkbook and scribble it. "I'm so sorry."
"How was school?" I ask Juliette as I buckle her into her car seat.
"Dumb," she says. I roll my eyes, get into the car and back out of the parking spot. I go through the kids schedule in my head to see who is next. Ricky gets picked up at the school and taken to soccer practice. Then I will return for Maisie.
"These aren't the right socks, Mom," Ricky protests. "I wanted the black ones."
"I'm sorry Ricky, these will have to do for today."
"But..." he starts. I hold up my hand and signal for him not to complain about it and he slumps in his seat, arms folded across his chest. We pull up to the soccer field and Ricky runs from the car to catch up with his team, already stretching. I pull away and race back to the school for Maisie.

"Mom, here's a fundraiser for the band trip." She hands me the form as she gets in the car. I sigh, deeply agitated by fundraisers. I flip through the pages and note chocolate and candles and wrapping paper. Perhaps a wine fundraiser would bring in more money.

"Jack, can you pick up Ricky on your way home from work? He's at soccer." I text.
No answer from Jack. A while later, I call his phone. It goes straight to voicemail. I suddenly remember his meeting after work. Crap!
"Maisie, can you watch Ivy and Juliette while I run and grab Ricky from soccer?"
"Mom," she argues.
"I'll be right back." I say. She stomps her foot.

Jack arrived home from his meeting early. Well, earlier than expected. The kids are already fed, and homework done, Ju-

91

liette has had a bath and the kitchen is clean. He comes in the house, drops his keys and his wallet on the counter. He takes his shoes off, grabs a beer from the fridge and retires to the couch. He turns on the television to a news station.

"How was your day?" I ask, sitting on the couch next to him.

"Tiring," was Jack's reply.

"Jack, a few girls are going to the mountains for a girls' weekend." Jack is already lost in the news.

"Jack." I sigh. I want to talk to him about my coffee meeting. About Michael. "Jack, there's something I want to tell you." My phone buzzes and I pull it out of my pocket.

New Facebook message from Michael, "Anni, meet me at the Inland Tavern tonight." I quickly move through the kitchen and out to the porch. I should have known that this would not be over so easily.

"Michael, this is not a good idea," I reply.

"Anni, please."

I look into the living room where Jack is now snoring on the couch. The TV is now airing some show about serial killers. The kids have been asleep in their beds since 8:00, except Maisie who usually falls asleep watching TV. I look at the messages again. No, Anni, this is not ok. I can't believe I am giving this thought. My keys are hanging on a key ring Maisie made in wood shop, and my purse Jack bought me for my birthday is sitting on the counter. I bite my nails, watching Jack sleep. Maybe just a few minutes. I open the side door and quietly close it behind me. No sense in waking up Jack.

I pulled into the tavern parking lot, trying to talk myself out of this terrible decision. The parking lot seems full and I wonder if I will run into anyone I know. What would I say? Is this even OK to do? I make a deal with myself to tell Jack about this when I get home, just in case. "Oh, honey, I didn't want to wake you after a long day", I'll say.

The crowd here is much younger than me. These twenty-something's clench their beer bottles, leaning in to have conversations, laughing and swaying to the beat of the music. Bruno

Mars, it's which is too loud for my taste. Guys have their arms around their girls, sneaking a kiss, or hugging their buds. The girls are flipping their hair and heading to the bathroom in pairs. I stretch my neck to find Michael and he gives me a wave. My pulse races. He's gotten a head start on quenching his thirst judging by the amount of empty beer bottles on the bar in front of him. I wonder if he is drunk, then again, he probably has a high tolerance. He smiles and I feel my heart flutter. When I am within arm's reach, he leans out and puts his arm around my waist and pulls me in. I stiffen at his touch, unsure of his motives. I put up a guard around my guard. Michael is tricky, he'll make you question everything.

"I knew you'd come," he says with a smirk. "Can I get you a drink?"

"No, thank you, Michael." I proceed with caution, but in his presence, I find it difficult to resist.

"Just one," he insists as he calls the bartender. "What do you drink?"

"Just water," I say to the bartender.

"And a glass of white wine," Michael adds, "You seem like the wine type," he adds. I give him an disapproving glance, raising my eyebrows in protest.

"Come on Anni, don't be a stiff," he says and smiles. The bartender returns with another beer for Michael and a glass of wine for me. Michael holds his bottle up and we cheer to something, I'm not sure what yet. I lift the glass to my lips and take a sip while Michael stares at me. Michael was cautious at the coffee shop, I guess feeling me out how I would react to him. But now, now this is Michael. How am I going to keep myself from being pulled in?

"See? I knew you were a wine drinker," he grins.

"Oh, how did you know that?" I ask sarcastically.

"Minivan, kids, skinny jeans."

I look down at my skinny jeans, dark blue denim and thin maroon sweater.

"Oh, really?" I struggle between wanting to let myself enjoy this and to be skeptical of his motives. I had never resisted him. What is different now?

"I'm not wrong," he says glancing at the lipstick marks on my glass. He watches me take another sip.

"Drink up, my girl," He says, holding up his glass to mine.

"I'm not your girl," I say immediately.

"Really?" he asks playfully.

"So, Michael. Why on earth would we be here together at a bar right now?" I ask to cut the awkwardness.

"Anni, I'm offering to buy you a drink. That is all. Don't over think everything." Over-thinking everything was my talent. And I haven't forgotten that Michael was always my weakness.

I become aware Michael still has his arm around my waist and I take a step back to give myself some distance. I take a seat at the bar next to him, remembering I have snuck out of the house while my husband snores on the couch after a long day at work. I get an uneasy feeling. It's not just sneaking out with a man. It's sneaking out with Michael. Far more dangerous.

Michael stares at me, "What?" I ask.

"So, what else is new, Anni?" he asks. I laugh at his trivial questions. He brushes a piece of hair behind my ear and my skin tingles at his touch. I look around to see if I recognize anyone in the bar, suddenly feeling guilty of being here. I want to run. But I want to stay. I want to enjoy his touch, his arm around me. Even if just for a minute. But, I chose Jack. Because Michael didn't choose me.

"Everything," I say.

Michael grabs the stool I sit on and drags it so my knees are resting between his legs. I silently protest, but nothing comes out.

"I'm staying in town for a few days. Hanging with Doug and Scott. Brandon is home."

"Oh," I said. I cringe at the names Doug, Scott and Brandon. I'm jealous they have had Michael all these years.

Michael is leading me on, I can tell. Anni, you need to leave. I try not to think about where this conversation is going. No, I already know. What if someone sees me here at the tavern with this man? Is this a normal, innocent thing? People talk in a small town, they love a good juicy story. Anni, don't let your guard down, I remind myself.

"Michael, I shouldn't be here with you alone." Even though I want to.

"Anni, I missed you." He leans in and kisses my cheek. I'm instantly back in the 90s. Don't take the bait, Anni.

"That's the beer talking." I missed you too, Michael.

I try to say goodnight to Michael. It's time for me to go back to my family. I should be home coaxing my husband up to bed so we can take advantage of the time we have alone while the kids sleep. Not here with Michael, my former soulmate, who shows up a lifetime later. I admit, it was my fault. I struck first with the Facebook request.

"Michael, I'm sorry. I need to go. I feel... I feel like I shouldn't be here with you." I get up and grab my wallet and phone and head to the door.

"Anni, I'm sorry. Don't go. I want to chat, reminisce. That's all. Remember when we went for a ride in the Jeep with the top off and it poured? We had to drive back home soaking wet." I smile at the memory. "And how you gave the best back scratches ever?" He grabs my hand and looks at my fingernails. He glimpses my diamond ring, the one Jack gave me when he asked me to marry him.

"Damn, Anni, look at that thing. I see you have done well." Reuniting with Michael feels too comfortable, which is why I need to leave immediately. People don't change, Anni. I remind myself how smooth he is. Michael will find the one loose string in your sweater and unravel it. One loose string that hasn't yet been cut off because you don't want the sweater to come undone, so you tuck it in neatly and hope it doesn't come loose again.

"Michael, it was so nice catching up with you again. But this is not going anywhere. I am married, I am a mom, I have a life. I don't know what your situation is, but," I pause, "we will not be friends".

"Shit, Anni. Why do you always have to act so fucking perfect? Live a little." Ah, he's found the string in my sweater. Realizing I had gotten comfortable again, I get up off the stool again and head for the door. Michael follows me to my car and grabbed my hand. "Don't." I say.

"I'm sorry I said that." He leans in and kisses my cheek. God, I hate him so much right now. And when I say hate, I mean want. "Michael, this ends right here. Good night." As I drive home, I second guess myself. Maybe I was overreacting.

I sneak back in the house like a teenager breaking curfew and find Jack had moved from the couch. I take my shoes off at the door hoping not to wake anyone and head to the kitchen to grab a glass of water from the fridge. Out of the corner of my eye I see shadows in the window, and I open the door to the deck to find my 16-year-old daughter lip-locked with a boy. I close the door quietly hoping she didn't hear me or see me, but sort of hoping they did.

I head to the bathroom and wash my face and brush my teeth, change my clothes.

"Where were you?" Maisie asks, returning to her room. I jump in surprise.

"Out," I snap. Maisie raises her eyebrows, and I'm sure she can smell the alcohol on me. "We needed milk.," I add.

"Where were you?" I ask Maisie.

"Downstairs getting a drink," she says. Well, then I guess we are both lying. I don't press Maisie because I don't want her pressing me, or yelling and waking Jack. I let it go, and walk to my bedroom. Maisie rolls her eyes and walks back to her room. I climb into bed and thought Jack was asleep. I move close to him so I can feel his warmth.

"Anni, where'd you go?"

"I'm sorry Jack, I didn't mean to wake you. I needed to run out to the convenient store for milk for breakfast tomorrow". That was the first lie I have ever told to my husband. I haven't thought of sneaking or lying at any other time in my marriage. But then again, I've never faced Michael. Once my soulmate. Once?

"OK," he said rolling to my side and wrapping his warm arms around me.

With Jack purring in my ear as he drifted back to sleep, I removed my phone from the nightstand, and I opened Facebook. The screen illuminated the room and I type "Michael Carter" into the search bar. *Anni*, I said silently to myself, *you are so stupid. You can't handle Michael. You should have never tried.* I scrolled down to the bottom of his profile and touched the screen. "Unfriend." *Are you sure you want to Unfriend Michael Carter? I am sure.*

Chapter 13: Summer 1995

Michael

The plastic straps of the lounge chair stuck to my sweaty skin while I sat on the pool deck waiting for Anni to finish her work for the day. I looked up to the second-floor balcony where she vacuumed, admiring her legs in those short shorts. July has been so hot and humid that the island is busier than usual.

A while later Anni came down the stairs carrying supplies, toilet paper, spray bottles, rags.

"Hey," she said, breathless and perspiring.

"How was cleaning?"

"Fun." She rolled her eyes, "let me change and I'll be right out." A few minutes later she is back in a black one-piece bathing suit with a pink sarong tied around her waist and a giant beach bag flung over her shoulder.

"What do you need that bag for?"

"Stuff."

We walked the usual path through the dunes and down towards the ocean. Since the tide is going out, we settled at the water's edge. There was a heavenly ocean breeze coming off the water cooling us from the oppressively hot day. The beach wasn't as crowded as usual. The difference between the breeze off the ocean and a breeze off the bay was flies. Green-headed flies that bite came in on a westerly wind.

Being on the beach with Anni was easy. We had a routine. As soon as we got settled, she got out her book. She always read at the beach. I got my radio out and flipped through the stations until I could get a good reception.

Anni sat in her beach chair, the straps fraying at the edges and I sat on my towel. Anni is probably reading a romance novel. That's probably where she gets relationship ideas. Anni dug her toes in the sand, curling them up and then pushing, making a small hole. Her toenails were painted hot pink to match her fingernails. It added to her already sexy look. Her skin was tanned from the sun and she wore her hair in a high ponytail on her head.

I thought about how much I wanted Anni, but the guys have been questioning me. Scott asked what's up with Anni. I tried to convince him it was just beach and pool stuff, but I knew he didn't believe me. Scott knew that Anni was at my house on nights we went out. And he knew that I stopped by the motel to see her on my way home from parties or the beach.

"You're distracted, man," Doug said. "You're leading her on."
"Man, you kick her out of your house so you can go fuck other chicks, I've seen it," Scott said, bluntly, "that's messed up Mike."
Scott was right, I was messed up. How could I do that to her?
"You need to cut it off, Mike, she thinks you love her," Doug said.

"No, she doesn't," I lied. She knew I love her because I told her often. I thought about what the guys said. I was leading her on. She questioned me about drinking and smoking, and she made me feel guilty. It was annoying, but I tolerated it because I loved spending time with her on the beach, on the roller-coasters, or by the pool. I loved kissing her soft lips. And admiring her amazing body. Sometimes I wanted more of her. All of her. Anni was simple, but our relationship was complicated. She wanted a commitment, and I didn't. At least for right now. I knew she would be there for me when I was ready. Or I hoped so.
"Maybe she's a good time," Scott elbowed Doug.
"Just shut the fuck up," I said, protectively. No one got to talk about Anni like that. Doug looked at Scott. "I should talk to

her," I said.

I looked at Anni, beautiful, sweet, fiercely loyal. We complimented each other, my wild side, her innocence. An unlikely match.

"Why do you keep looking at me like that?" she asked.

"Anni, you know I love you, right?"

Anni looked at me over her book, tipping her sunglasses down.

"Weird," she said returning to her book.

"I just feel…. I need some space." She moved her beach chair further away, and I tipped my head back.

"Anni, I'm serious," I said.

"Space for what, Michael?"

"I don't know," I shrugged my shoulder. This conversation wasn't going to the way I planned.

"We're just… different, that's all."

"No, we're not." She stood up protested, folding her book shut and throwing it on her chair.

"Look, I'm not saying we can't be friends, you… I need distance." I instantly wished I could take that back.

"Distance." She softly repeated, standing with her hands hanging by her side.

"Anni, that's not… that was a bad choice of words."

"Michael, that's all we are. Friends. You think I don't know what you're doing out cruising at night?" Her hands moved to her hips. She looked so hot in that pose. Her pink sarong hanging off her hips, her sunglasses too big for her tiny face. Focus, Michael. Anni voice became louder and caught the attention of the people around us.

"I think that's why I need space."

"So you can go get laid more? So you can kiss me and tell me you love me and then sweat all over some strange girl under the boardwalk? Random girls get to have sex with you, but I get nothing?" she yelled. People were staring at us but Anni didn't seem to care.

"Yes, that is why we need space. I'm hurting you. Wait, you want to have sex with me?" I asked, suddenly hearing her words. Has she thought about that? She ignored me.

"I hang around waiting and waiting, knowing where you are, but I'm not good enough." Tears trickled down her face.

"Stop it, Anni," I begged.

OK," she said.

"OK, what?"

"Just, ok."

I suddenly wanted her to argue with me. Maybe I didn't want space. Shit! What did I want?

Anni turned her back to me and I immediately felt regret. I didn't mean to hurt her, I'm actually trying to protect her. I grabbed her hand, the one I put the tin ring on years ago. The hand that beat my high score in pinball, the hand that scratched my back with just enough pressure to feel good and hurt at the same time.

"Anni, you're my girl."

"Right, leave me alone Michael," she said, shaking my hand off hers.

"Anni," I grabbed her shoulders, "We will get married someday, remember? It's just, right now I need time." I knew I was confusing her because I don't know what I want anymore. My heart sunk knowing I was hurting her. After the words came out, I realized that isn't what I want.

"Just stop," she said. She took a deep breath, her face wet with tears and her cheeks flushed. I knew I was messing with her head. I was a selfish asshole. I already knew that. I wanted to have Anni and my fucked-up life with the guys, but that wasn't fair to her. I didn't want to upset her anymore.

"Anni, I don't want to lead you on," I tried to justify myself.

"Too late Michael," she said.

I watched Anni pack up her beach chair and fling her bag over her shoulder. I should have begged her to stay, but I had already hurt her enough. I watched her walk up the beach and down the path until I could no longer see her. The day didn't turn out the way I planned. I didn't even have this plan. I don't know why I did this to her. I've made a bigger mess.

∞∞∞

"I need you," I cried to Sarah. I knew my voice was shaking, but I was trying to keep myself together.

"Anni, what's wrong?" she asked.

"Michael," was the only word I could get out.

"Oh, Anni, not the arcade guy?" she said, "I'll be right over."

I looked in the mirror in my bedroom.

"Anni, why are you like this?" I asked myself. "So…. goody two shoes." My mom always said, "goody two shoes" when she referred to someone who thinks they are so perfect. Isn't that what Sarah said, "stop being so perfect, Anni". Look at where it had gotten me, dumped by my boyfriend, dumped by my non-boyfriend, laughed at by my friends. I had nothing in common with anyone. I sat on the edge of my bed with my head in my hands, and I felt the hot tears roll down my face.

"Anni, I brought you a milkshake," Sarah said. I recognized the cup from Dustin's and I knew then that Sarah got the magnitude of my depression. She wiped the tears from my face with the back of her hand.

"What happened?"

"Michael said he needed space."

"What the hell does that mean?" she asked.

"I don't know," I took a sip of the milkshake. Vanilla. She really knew I was upset. "I thought Michael, and I were friends. Just friends."

"Anni, you will never be good enough for him, let that jerkoff go." I was angry she was speaking about him like that. "And you are about as perfect as they come, Anni. If he doesn't love you like this, he's not going to."

"That's my problem, too perfect. Why can't I be like you? I mean, no offense." I asked through the tears.

"Oh, Anni, you don't want to be like me," she laughed. "People think I'm the high school lush, the girl who gets around. Trust me, you don't want to be like me." I felt a sense of hurt in Sarah's admission. I never thought of her like that. Sarah was always the center of the party, so much fun, easy to make friends, get the boys' attention.

Sarah hugged me tightly. "You are perfect, Anni, never change for anyone. Do you honestly think Michael would be any different if you were like me?"

"You're right," I said, holding her tight.

"Well, except you probably would have had drunken sex with him by now," she said, trying to make me laugh.

"I would have probably liked that." I wiped the tears from my face, grateful to have her as my friend, grateful that she rushed over and brought me a vanilla milkshake.

August days were stifling and many of the college students have left, so I had to help clean rooms on my day off from my other job at the shop.

"Anni, grab fresh towels," Natalya said in her thick Russian accent. The sweat was beading on my forehead and my upper lip, and I wiped it away with a dirty towel as I head down to the laundry room to grab some clean ones. After several hours of sweating and making beds and scrubbing bathrooms, I threw on my one-piece black bathing suit and sat in the pool. The water was warm come the end of August after a summer of blazing hot sunny days. I sat on the edge of the pool, near the 4 ft sign and dip my feet in, then slid off the side. I crouched down until my entire body is underwater and dip my head back, wetting my hair. Cupping my hands, I splashed water on my face and got out of the pool. My beach towel was spread over the hot straps of the lounge chair and I settled in with my book. The children in the pool splashed and played and I tried to drown the sounds of their laughter. Overhead, seagulls soared around, hoping to catch an unattended snack. The sun kept dipping behind the clouds and the sky alternated from bright to dim.

I reread page 136 several times before I put my book down. The thoughts in my head and the surrounding noises were too distracting. It had been a few weeks since the beach with Michael, and it took all my willpower to stay away. Twenty-three days to be exact. Every time I tried to concentrate on my book my thoughts intruded. It felt like a breakup. Like my break up with Ben. The empty feeling, the extra time, the nights wishing Michael would call from the payphone outside my window. They never came. I put my chair in a fully reclined position and laid on my stomach, hoping to even out my tan. Maybe I'll drift to sleep.

I am startled awake by a warm hand on my back. I turn my head without getting up, and Michael was sitting on the lounge next to me.

"How long have you been there?" I asked.

"Not long."

"What do you want?" I snapped.

"I'm leaving this afternoon to go back home. Our lease is up for the summer."

"Oh," I said, sitting up on my lounge. I wrapped my damp towel around my body, feeling exposed in my bathing suit. If Michael left today, we wouldn't have a chance to make things right.

"I know this summer didn't go as planned, but we're just different, that's all Anni."

"Michael, stop. You're making it worse." He got up and sat next to me on the lounge. He wrapped his arms around me and kissed my forehead and then my lips. As he stood up, I tried to hold back the tears that were burning in my eyes.

"Keep in touch, Anni," he said as he walked away. I laid back on the lounge and buried my face in my towel hiding the hot tears, my lips still tingling where his lips were.

∞∞∞

The city looked busy from the 19th floor of the hotel. Taxis and busses filled the streets, and buildings rose up from the ground to the sky. From the window I watched the airplanes take off and land at the airport, and I tried to imagine what adventures the passengers are returning from. Kroy University is about 20 miles from here, the one I hope to attend next year.

"What time is he picking you up? My mom asked.
"Five o'clock."
"Where are you going?"
"I don't know, out to dinner." I said.
"Please don't stay out too late, Anni," she told me.

I put my coat on over my red sweater and bootleg jeans and headed down to the hotel lobby. Michael's yellow Jeep pulled around to the revolving doors, and he jumped out. I held my breath as I took in the sight. He eyed me up and down and pulled me into his body, melting me with his cocky smile. He was in a pair of light blue jeans and a long sleeve collared shirt, and he looked even more attractive in this than in shorts and t-shirts.

"Anni, look at you," he said as we both sat in the Jeep.
"It's me," I said as I stared at his perfect face.
"I missed you so much."
"Really?"
"Really." He looked over at me before pulling out into traffic.
"Are you hungry?" he asked.
"Starving."
"Good, because we are going on a date." He grabbed my hand and squeezed it. His hand was warm and soft, and memories flood back of the summer when he told me he wanted to be left alone. I stared out the window wondering if he would apologize or if it

wasn't a big deal to him. He seemed excited about meeting me in the city when I called him on the phone yesterday.

"Hey," I said when he answered the phone. I tried to picture his house, his room, the street he lives on, but I have never been there.

"Anni?" he said, surprised, "How are you?"

"I'm fine, I'm just calling because I want to look at a college in the city, and I know it's short notice, but I thought, maybe, you'd be free or something. I'll be there tomorrow," I rambled.

"Oh, wow, yeah Anni, that sounds great! What time will you be free?"

"Well, maybe after 4. My mom and I are staying at the Airport Holiday Inn."

"Great, I'll be there around 5:30 OK? I'm so glad you called."

"See you then, Michael." I hung up the phone, excited and nervous.

Michael and I sat at a tiny table in a quaint little Italian cafe. I wouldn't have thought from the outside this gem of a place existed. It smelled of fresh bread, basil and garlic and other spices I couldn't recognize. Waiters with white aprons and Italian accents scurried from table to table. Michael reached across and took my hands.

"I missed you," he said again.

"I missed you too." Distance. Space. That is what he wanted. He broke my heart. Can we move on from that? Are we moving on from that?

The soft Italian music played while we talked.

"How was Kroy University?"

"Good, I think I want to go there."

He stared at me for a few seconds and I had to divert my eyes to the floor to escape his gaze. I looked back to Michael. "What?" I asked.

"Such a smart, college girl," he said. "You amaze me. So perfect."

"Perfect, that's me," I laughed sarcastically.

"How's the party life at Kroy?"

"I didn't ask."

"Good." He always wanted me to be a good girl until I was too good.

"Anni, I know I hurt you, and I'm sorry. I just, I know we want this friendship to go in different directions."

"Do we?" I asked. Michael's lips turn down.

"Why do you say that?" he asked.

"I don't know," I said. I looked down, stirring my drink with the straw. "You kissed me."

"Yes, I did."

"Why?"

"Because I'm attracted to you," he said, "I've never denied that. You're beautiful, and you want me, too."

I missed his sarcasm. "Oh, I do?"

"You kissed me back." Touché.

"Anni, I hate hurting you."

"Then let's get married now." Michael's eyes fixated on my face, and he kissed my hand.

"A married college girl."

"I won't go to college. I'll stay home and clean motel rooms and have babies."

"Now that sounds like a plan."

"So, what now?" I asked.

"What do you want?"

"You know what I want," I said, "Isn't that why we are having this conversation?"

"Anni, I don't want to lose you, I need you in my life. You are my soulmate." I felt my eyes burn and water because I felt that way too. But it's true, our interpretation of our relationship is different. I could commit to Michael now for the rest of my life. There was no one else I felt this way with. I doubted anyone could ever live up to him.

"Let's just see how the summer goes," he said.

"So, are we back together? I mean, as friends or whatever?"

"Yeah," he said smiling at me, his eyes burning through my soul. "As friends or whatever." We sat quietly and ate dinner, enjoying the atmosphere, dark, with a candle flickering between us while opera plays in the background.

Michael paid the bill, and we headed back outside. It was cold out, and I zipped up my jacket and put my hands in my pockets. We walked through the city, and I admired the tall buildings and lights and I took notice of people walking. These things amused this small island girl.

Michael put his hand out and I and laced my fingers with his. His hand was warm and familiar. Hand in hand we walk for a few blocks. I saw his yellow Jeep, and I wished it was parked farther away. It would be a few more months until I saw Michael again, and the thought hurt. Michael didn't write letters like he used to, and I had to pay my mom for long-distance phone calls.

Michael opened the door of the Jeep and I got in, sitting sideways in my seat so my legs hung out the door. He leaned in and stood between my knees and took my face in his hands. His lips pressed against mine, and I instinctively put my arms around his neck. He slid me to the edge of the seat, pulling me in closer to him. His kiss was soft and slow and it was driving me insane. My heart pounded, and my head swirled into the clouds. His hands grabbed the back of my hair and pulled down gently tilting my face up towards his. He kissed me again, opening his mouth so our tongues danced as if they had been choreographed. He released me, taking my hands in his, and let go. I put my head into his chest and he kisses the top of my head. I felt his heart beating quickly, and I matched my breath with his.

"Why do you do that?" he whispered in my ear.

"Our relationship is a big head game."

Chapter 14: Summer 1996

Anni

The June air was warm and dry and the sun was low in the sky as the class congregated outside the gymnasium in their blue and white robes. I hung my yellow National Honor Society Cord around my neck and secured my cap to my head.

"Anni, we did it!" Sarah whispered, squeezing my hand as we lined up, two by two. Fifty-seven students of the 1996 graduating class of Beacon Prep proceeded from the gym to the field alternating boy/girl.

Pomp and Circumstance blared out of the speakers on the football field as the graduating class processional approaches. Proud parents, grandparents, friends, and family filled the bleachers.

"Welcome," said Jennifer Gordon, Student Council President, and Valedictorian. She talked about high school memories and starting a new chapter in our lives. I looked around at the students I've spent the last lifetime with Amy, Megan, Cindy... would I see them again after graduation?

I couldn't help but feel nostalgic about leaving Beacon Prep. The breeze blew through the microphone while they announce each name.

"Please hold your applause until the end," the principal said, even though hoots and hollers could be heard after each name.

I ascended the stairs to the stage as Principal Reese announces my name, "Antonia Marino." I grasped my diploma with one hand and shook his hand with the other, just as we had practiced all week.

"Classmates, please join me in turning your tassel," Jennifer said. "I now present to you the class of 1996." Our family and friends cheered from the bleachers as white and blue caps floated through the sky. Sarah and I found each other, and we hugged so tight.

"Let's make this summer epic," she said. Our friends gathered around embracing and saying goodbyes. Some we would never see again, some would settle here in Beacon, joining the culture of seasonal employment or labor work. Some were heading to college. Sarah and I would start separate schools in August, apart for the first time. My eyes leaked with emotion.

I remembered the day I received my college acceptance. I called Sarah right away.

"Sarah, I got accepted to Kroy University." It was my first choice. High standards, high SAT score requirement, letters of recommendations. I had everything in order. I knew I would get in. Sarah screamed into the phone.

"I am so excited for you, Anni!"

"I'm going to Bordon State," she said.

"That's exciting." Sarah was a good mind-reader.

She knew I was disappointed that we wouldn't be together next year. She had not applied to Kroy even though I had begged her to. She knew her grades and SAT scores wouldn't be good enough, but it would have been great to go to the same university.

"It will be fine, Anni," she said. "We'll see each other on holidays and summers."

"I know."

∞∞∞

Sarah and I laid on the beach the day after graduation, reminiscing about our senior year and planning the coming summer. "I'm working 2 jobs," she said. I had always worked two jobs, the motel, always, but my second job changed each summer. One summer at Dustin's Ice Cream and Mini Golf, another summer at the novelty shop, another summer waitressing at Lobster Landing. That summer I was checking beach tags.
"Did you get your roommate assignment yet?" Sarah asked.
"Yes, did you?"
"Yeah, I talked to her once, she seemed strange."
"I'm sure it's hard to tell over the phone, Sarah."
"My roommate's name is Stephanie. But I haven't talked to her. I'm so nervous."
I turned on my stomach to even out my tan and used my arms as a pillow to rest my head. The beach was crowded, the sound of children playing and the waves crashing was such a familiar summer sound.

Michael

Driving over the bridge to Beacon with the top off, the salty air engaged my senses. I can feel it on my skin, taste it, smell the ocean. It had been a long, cold and lonely winter. The sun warmed my face, and I cranked up the bass in my car. My Jeep was packed with clothes and beach chairs and towels. The Turtle Crossing sign was a sure way to know you've arrived in Beacon. Where else could you find a Turtle Crossing sign?
As I crossed the big bridge, I could see the smaller bridges, particularly the one leading over 44th Street. I pictured the time Anni, and I climbed the bridge and jumped into the bay. We had our rafts and floated as boats and jet skis and kayaks

moved around us, creating ripples in the water. Anni loved adventure as long as it wouldn't get her in trouble. That's what surprised me about bridge jumping.

"Michael, follow me," she said. I grabbed onto my raft and paddled after her to the dock and climbed out of the water. She walked to the highest point of the bridge, jumped over the fence and landed on the pipe that runs underneath. I did the same, sitting on the rusty pipe next to her. She grabbed my hand and glanced at me.

"Scared?" she asked, teasing.

"Nope," I answered. Anni stood up and balanced herself on the pipe, and I followed her lead.

"On the count of three," she said. Anni screamed all the way to the water. I took her hand as we surfaced from beneath the salty bay as we tread water. I looked back up towards the bridge to see a "No Jumping" sign and thought, my "Anni, the rule follower."

I pulled into the grassy lot of our beach house, and I looked around at the familiar sights, the beach to the east, motels, and shops to the west. Beacon was only a mile wide. You could walk from the ocean to the bay and most activities revolve around the water.

The first thing I did when I get to the island was drive to Anni's motel. Before I could get out of my Jeep, Anni ran towards me.

"Michael!" she screamed. She hugged me tight, and I kissed her head.

"Look at you!" I held her away from me to get a better look. Her cute floral swimsuit cover-up clung to her body, and I noticed she had a curl to her hair.

"Come on," she took my hand and led me to the pool. It was pretty crowded for June. It was hot and humid and the salt air was thick. The sun was covered by the clouds, and it looked like it might rain. Anni dipped her toe in the pool and delicately walked down the stairs until she was standing on her toes, the water up to her waist.

I followed her and moved to feel the chilly water on my bare skin. We dunked under at the same time, shivering at the cold water covering our skin.

Anni and I found a corner ledge to stand among all the other people in the pool looking to cool off. I pulled her close under the water so our bodies touch and my hands rest on the bare skin of her back. She felt so nice against me, so familiar. I had to push down the thoughts I was having about her wet body. She put her wet arms around my neck and I shivered.

"So, how have you been?" I asked.

"Good, I guess."

"Any new boyfriends?"

Her face smirks. "No, you? Girlfriends?"

"No."

"Well, let's keep it like that!" She said. I pulled her closer.

"I missed you," I said.

"I missed you too."

Chapter 15: Summer 1997

Anni

I don't feel like going out tonight I told Sarah when she asked if I wanted to go to a party. I was hoping I would hear from Michael, and he would ask if I wanted to take a ride to the jetty. On some nights we drove down there and sat on the wet rocks. I would lay back into his warm body, feeling the rhythm of his breathing, or the vibration of his voice. Sometimes he kissed me.

"You're not waiting around for that guy, are you?" she asked. Michael isn't that guy, but I didn't share my feelings. Especially after sharing my feelings last summer with Sarah when Michael said he needed space. She has way too many opinions and she wouldn't understand our relationship.

She knows we kissed, and she knows I am still a virgin, so there is that. "So, you've been hooking up for three years, you haven't had sex with him, you're not his girlfriend, but he goes out every night and gets drunk and laid?" she would say. "And he calls you afterwards? Anni, you're pathetic." Sarah would lecture me. The brief glimpse she got into our friendship last summer when Michael said he needed space was enough.

"Come on Anni, maybe you'll meet someone."

"I don't want to meet someone." Besides, she said the Beacon High guys would be there, and Michael hung out with some of them. "I'm going away to college in a few weeks anyway."

"Oh my God, Anni, not a fucking boyfriend. Loosen up a bit."

I thought about it for a few minutes. If I didn't go, I'd probably be home by myself reading a book. It was fun going out with Sarah, I enjoyed watching her work her way around a party like it's her job. I always had a good laugh.

"OK, I'll go."

"Yes! Anni, you'll have fun, I promise. Look, I have to go help my mom. Pick me up tonight." She said before hanging up the phone. I pushed the button to hang up the phone and placed it back in the charger.

Sarah and I pulled up to a small cottage type house, an island original. The party was already in full swing with people spilling outside. We could hear the music pumping as we walked up to the porch.

"It looks crowded," I said, chewing on a fingernail.

"It's all right, Anni, you'll be fine," she squeezed my hand. As soon as we walked in, the smell of cigarettes and beer hit my senses. I coughed in response to the smoky air. Sarah stretched her neck, looking for someone.

"Who are you looking for," I said, loudly over the music.

"No one in particular." She gave me a wink. I knew she was lying. Sarah headed to the back porch, knowing that is where the kegs usually are. Of course, she knows these things, and in the middle of the back deck was a keg, set in a tub of ice. She tilted her cup and pulled the tap. An expert. didn't offer me one, she knew I wouldn't drink it, anyway.

We moved down off the back porch and found a seat at one of several patio tables. The backyard had a pool, which had a few people in it, but the patio surrounding the pool was crowded. It was difficult to tell if there was anyone here I knew. I looked at Sarah and she had spotted someone, waving them towards us.

"Anni, this is David, he works at the bookstore with me." David was tall and good looking, bronze suntanned skin and dark blond hair. He looked like he spent a lot of time at the gym. I'm not surprised Sarah came here to meet him. David and his friend sat down at the table with us.

"Nice to meet you, Anni," David said. "This is my friend Ryan." Ryan held his hand up.

"Do you work at the bookstore too?" I asked. I don't know what else to say, I'm not good at this. Ryan wasn't great looking like David, but he had a cute dimple in his chin that catches my attention. I wondered what I was supposed to do with Ryan, and I got nervous. I realized Sarah is probably trying to set me up.

"No, I'm just in town for the week."

"Oh, ok."

"Anni, Ryan is going to Kroy," Sarah said.

"Oh, wow, that's great. You must be smart."

"You need a beer, Anni?" Ryan asked.

"No, I don't... It's my turn to drive."

"Ok, cool." He answered. From the corner of my eye, I noticed Sarah and David stand up, so I stood.

"Anni, I'll be right back, going to refill." Yeah, I'm sure that was where they were going. Ryan and I sat back down. He moved his chair closer to mine and attempted to make more idle conversation.

"So, you live here?"

"Yeah, north side of Beacon. My parents own a motel."

"That must be cool."

"Yeah, I guess." I'm always a little uncomfortable because people make weird assumptions when they find out your parents own something. I tried to change the subject. "So, what are you going to study?"

Many out-of-town visitors thought it must be so amazing to live in Beacon all year, but really it wasn't all that great. The schools were small, in the off-season the businesses were closed, houses were empty. It was pretty desolate. But, by the end of the summer, we were ready for the change of pace. A slower, more relaxed time of the year. Come May, the residents were welcoming back the tourists and the livelihood that came with it. The job opportunities and a steady paycheck.

"Engineering," he said. "What about you?"

"Psychology," I said. It doesn't sound as impressive as engineer-

ing. "I want to be a clinical psychologist," I explained further.
"Are you sure I can't get you a beer?" I laughed, taking the hint I needed some loosening up.

"I'm sorry, I'm just.... I don't really drink. I mean, Sarah drags me to these parties and I.. I'm sorry if I am boring." I usually say at least once at every party Sarah has dragged me to.
"No, it's not that at all," he said. "Do you want to get out of here?"
"Um…" I could only manage a stutter. I felt foolish that I wasn't expecting he would try to hook up with me. He stood up and grabbed my hand and I felt a wave of panic come over me.
"Come on, we'll just go somewhere quiet," he said. "How about your car?"

"My car?" I answered, confused. The car seemed like an unusual place to want to escape to, but I led him there. He sat in the passenger seat and reclined the back as far as it could go. I leaned my seat back, too.
"This is actually nice," I said, happy to be away from the noise and the smoke and the pungent smell of vomit from people drinking too much.

"Sarah said you were really hot," he said. "She wasn't lying." Oh God, Sarah. I feel my cheeks flush and I turned my head away.
"Sarah is embarrassing," I replied.
"No, it's fine. Don't be embarrassed. It's a compliment."
"Thank you," My palms were sweaty, and I realized that he is going to make a move. Ryan leaned over the console and I felt him pull me close, kissing my lips. It took me by surprise, and I pulled away.
"What?" he asked.
"I'm sorry, I…I wasn't ready for that." He leaned in and kissed me again and I tried to enjoy it, but it was terrible. His tongue was in my mouth like a lizard and I couldn't wait until he came up for air. He attempted to put his hands on my breasts and I pushed him back.

"I'm sorry, Ryan, I am ready to go back inside," I said, sitting my seat upright. Anni, you're such a prude. I thought of Michael and his soft, tender kisses that melted me. And his arms around me, holding me close to him, and his smell and how I had to stand on my toes. Will anyone ever be able to come close?

"OK," he put his seat back up and opened the car door. I opened my door, and we walked back inside. Ryan put his hand on my back and guided me through the house back out to the patio to find Sarah and David.

"Sarah, you left me," I whispered in her ear.

"Anni, did you hook up with Ryan?" she said.

"Briefly."

"Oh, God, Anni." While Sarah was talking I saw Doug, Michael's friend, emerge from the pool house with a girl. My knees buckled, and I struggled to keep myself upright, knowing that if Doug was here, that probably meant Michael was here.

"You ok, Anni?" she said, "you look like you're about to be sick."

"Sorry, I thought I saw someone," I answered.

"That guy? Why would he be here?"

"I saw his friend."

"Oh, shit," Sarah said, adding to my nerves. "Go hang with Ryan," she suggested.

"No, it's fine." I said. "I like Ryan, but he kisses like a lizard." Sarah laughed.

"Oh my God, Anni, you are hilarious. I will go get another refill on my beer."

"OK, I'll wait here." Sarah disappeared into the crowd towards the deck with her red cup. I glanced over at the pool house where I saw Doug. There he was. Michael with a tall blond girl. My heart stopped, and I felt like I would vomit. I froze. Someone must have bumped into because I think I had forgotten to breathe.

I frantically scanned the party for Sarah, as she should have been back by now. My senses were on alert, and I heard someone say my name. It was Ryan. I turned around to find him walking towards me. "Have you seen David?" He got a look at my pale face, my eyes wild and my heart pounding.

"You ok?"

"Fine," I snapped.

"Look, I'm sorry about before. I... I thought you might want to."
"It's fine," I didn't want to talk about that now. He was distracting me from the fact that Michael just went into the pool house to get laid by some blond, probably a stranger. I pushed my way through the crowd of people and out through the door to my car. I thought I heard the faint voice of Ryan calling after me, but I didn't stop. After getting in, I sat with my head against the window and sobbed. I knew Michael did this, picking up girls. I had never witnessed it for myself. I wished I never gave in to Sarah. My body shook as hot tears rolled down my face. Sarah and Ryan interrupted my breakdown knocking on my car window.
"Get out of the car, Anni," Sarah demanded. "You are not having a fucking meltdown over this guy."
"Go away," I said. Instead, she went around the car and got inside.
"What is wrong with you?"
"I saw him go into the pool house with a chick."
"That Michael dude?" she said.
"Yeah," I let out a sob that trembled my body.
"Oh shit," she said.
"Everything ok?" Ryan asked, leaning into the car next to Sarah.
"Yeah, her ex. Saw him going into the pool house with a chick."
"Ouch," Ryan said. "Come on out, Anni. I'll be your arm candy."
Ryan attempted to lighten the air. I smiled and wiped my wet face. Why were there so many boys that were nice and wanted me, and I wanted the only one I couldn't have?
"OK, Ryan, make this guy jealous," Sarah suggested. It made me think, *I wonder how Michael would respond if he saw me kissing someone.* I watched Ryan walk around the car and he held out his hand for me. Reluctantly, I got up. He wiped my face with his shirt and ran his thumb under my eyes, cleaning my smeared eyeliner. We returned to the party and made our way through the crowd.
I warmed up to Ryan, perhaps I misjudged him. He was funny and sweet and he wiped my face with his shirt after I pushed him away in my car and cried over another guy.

I spotted Michael again from across the yard, talking with Doug and Scott. Ryan noticed my wide eyes and pulled me in, his lips touching mine. It wasn't lizard-like this time, but just enough to drive Michael wild, I hoped, as I noticed him looking in my direction. We made eye contact. Michael stared at me, blankly, for what seems like forever.

"I'll be right back," I said to Ryan. I crossed the yard, squaring my shoulders, trying to be confident, but I was dying inside. I saw Michael look away from me as I got closer.

"Hi,Michael," I said, flatly.

"Hi, Anni," Michael said, looking down at my eyes. I was sure he'd been drinking, but not sure how much he had. I wasn't sure what else to say, so I turned and walked away. He would show up tonight at the motel, that I was sure of.

"You OK?" Ryan said when I returned.

"Yeah, I guess."

Ryan, trying to distract me, asked me about college. It was the last thing on my mind, but I tried to focus. Did he ask if I was excited?

"Um... yeah, you?" I pulled myself together.

"Yeah, my second year. Maybe I can show you around some-time."

"That would be great." But, I knew I wouldn't call him. I definitely did not want to start off college with someone I met at a summer party. I looked around the yard for Sarah and spotted her by the deck. I had to get out of there. Sarah begged me to stay.

"Sarah, I can take you home if Anni wants to leave," David offered.

"Do you mind, Anni?"

"No, it's fine. Ryan, it was nice meeting you. Thanks for being so kind and understanding during my meltdown."

"Hope to see you around campus, Anni."

I made my way through the house and out the front door to my car. Driving through the empty streets of Beacon, I sobbed. The traffic lights and neon signs blurred through my tears. I pulled into the parking lot of the motel, wiped my face and headed inside. There was the possibility that Michael would call me from the payphone on his way home. A strong possibility. I only wished I had the courage to not answer the phone. But I sat and waited.

Michael

Doug called and said there's a party tonight on the south side. There will be girls there from the city, one for each of us. I made a plan to pick him up.

I jumped in the shower, thinking about what the night would bring us. I put on a pair of denim shorts and a t-shirt and laced up my sneakers. This is the cologne Anni loves, I thought as I sprayed it into the air, stepping into the mist. The old wooden dresser drawer that held my socks also held my stash of condoms. I threw a few in my wallet and headed down to the Jeep. Scott jumped in with his usual cooler of beer and we head to a house party. I'm not sure whose house this was, but it was a small cottage type house set on the south side of the island.

"Hey Mike. Hey Scott," Doug said, already at the party, and handed us each a beer. He was smoking a cigarette and motioned to a tall girl with brown hair. "College girls," he said, putting his arm around her when she came over. College girls meant nothing but Scott and Doug were in high school. They were still impressed. "This is Natalie." He blew smoke out of his mouth, turning his head away from her, and then handed her the cigarette.

I looked across the room for Natalie's friends the reason we were here. Two more girls approached, a petite girl with short brown hair and a blond.

"These are my friends, Nicole and Michelle," she said.

Scott took Michelle's hand and kissed it. She acted flattered, so he made conversation. That left me with Nicole. She was a blonde with a knockout body.

"Do you need a drink?" I noticed she didn't have one.

"Yeah, thanks," she said. I went off to find the beer and returned with a cup in my hand.

"So, city girl or the island?" I handed her the beer.

"I live in Vermont, but I go to college in the city. Michelle is my roommate, this is her parent's beach house."

"Cool," Although I was not interested in a conversation. The party is getting crowded quickly, and we made our way to the back deck.

After a few beers, I felt more comfortable making a move on Nicole. I took her hand and walked her around the side of the house and leaned her up against the outside shower. She puts her hands around my neck as I kissed her, and I grabbed her ass pulling her into me. With little privacy, we moved back towards the crowd and spotted Doug and Natalie. Michelle and Natalie danced to the bass booming from the inside of the house, raising their cups in the air.

"Just came from the pool house," Doug smiled and elbowed me. I laughed, taking a sip of my beer from the red plastic cup. I gave him a high five.

Nicole made her way back towards me, and I put my hands around her tiny hips, "Do you want some privacy?" I asked. She reached up and kissed me, and I took that as a "yes." I led her to the pool house. Intoxicated, she seemed eager to get on with it.

There was a futon couch against the wall, and I guided her over to it and sat down. Nicole took my beer and placed it on the table and climbed up in my lap. We became tangled up in one another and I pushed her dress up. I removed her panties, rolled on the condom. I moved her off my lap and climbed on top of her. I could tell Nicole was experienced, she has done this many times before. She wasn't clumsy or awkward as she moved her body, rocking her hips. We emerged from the pool house with satisfaction on my face. I saw Doug, and he shot me a "hell yeah" look.

Nicole and I walked back to the deck. The crowd had thickened, and the music was loud. There was a stench of beer and cigarettes, suntan lotion and hair spray. People were making out everywhere, in the pool, the outside shower, the pool house. The air was hazy and red cups littered the grass. Across the backyard, I spotted a familiar face. What the fuck? No. She would never come to a party like this. Not my girl. I turned my body to face Nicole and led her in the opposite direction.

"What's wrong, Mike?" Scott asked, emerging from the pool house.

"Anni's here," I said.

"Oh shit, I tried to warn you about hooking up with her. 'Oh, Michael, why won't you be my boyfriend'," he mocked her.

"Shut the fuck up." I looked at Nicole, taking a shot with Natalie and swaying to the music. Doug walked to the edge of the pool where I stood with Scott.

"Anni's here," he said to Doug, filling him in.

"Fuck, who's she with?"

"Probably her friend Sarah. She's the only one who could get her to a party like this."

"That her?" Scott nodded in the direction of the patio. I turned to look. I saw Anni lip-locked with some dude, and I saw red. What the fuck was she doing, and why did I feel this rage?

"Well, looks like you have nothing to worry about, Mike," Doug said, patting my back.

Anni looked up and saw me. Her big brown eyes were locked on mine, and I couldn't blink. She crossed the patio, painfully slow making her way over. Fuck!

"Hi, Michael." Anni had no inflection in her voice, though I was trying to read her tone.

"Hi, Anni." What the fuck else was I supposed to say?

After a few silent moments, she walked away. My stomach turned, and I struggled with my feeling of rage seeing her kiss someone else. The confusion that she was even at this party in the first place and worried she had seen me with some girl, whose name I couldn't even recall at this moment. I wanted to fucking run after her and tell her she had no right to be mad, that I'm sorry for what she saw. I wanted to yell at her for kissing random guy, and I wanted to fucking drag her in the pool house and tear that dress off her goddamn perfect fucking body.

"Let it go, man," Doug said. Nicole came over and took my hand and I followed her back outside to the pool house, looking over my shoulder. I must find Anni, but not yet.

Anni

From the payphone outside my bedroom, Michael called at 1:30, as predicted. I wished I had the self-control not to answer. I didn't want to see him or talk to him. But I did.

"Anni, come outside," he said. I told him no and beg him to go home, but I eventually gave in, like I always did because I craved Michael's attention like a drug addict.

"I didn't expect you to be there," was the first thing Michael said. He lowered his chin, and his gaze was fixed on me.

"It's fine Michael, just leave." My eyes watered and I wiped away a tear. Illuminated by the lights from the lampposts, his face softened.

"I can't just leave. You're upset." My heart ached, and I wanted to escape to my room where I could cry tears into my pillow.

"Anni, you're not my girlfriend," Michael turned defensive. I curled up on a chair and pulled my knees into my chest while I endured this emotional torture. You aren't my girlfriend. You aren't my girlfriend.

"Why?" I asked. "Why am I not your girlfriend? You tell me you love me, I'm your girl. But I'm not your girlfriend." I blubbered like a runaway train. Michael hated feelings. I knew by spilling it all out, I risked losing him. He wouldn't come around anymore. Just like last time. But how much longer could we go on like this?

"Anni, don't."

I have had enough trauma for one night. I turned around to walk back inside.

"Wait, I'm sorry, Anni. I'm a fucking asshole, that's why." It didn't make me feel any better because it was so familiar.

Michael hugged me, and I cried into his shirt, my shoulders shaking. My feelings confused me. I wanted to push him away, but I couldn't bring myself to do that. He kissed the top of my head nestled under his chin.

Chapter 16: Summer 1997

Anni

The motel was full this time of the year and the 'No Vacancy' sign flashed in the office's window. The summer air was sticky, and the beaches were crowded with people celebrating the last hurrah of the summer. Soon children would return to school and the weather would cool and the island would become still once again. This week was the last week I would be here in Beacon before I left to begin my first year of college.

The motel was short staffed, and I had to help clean rooms. I used to enjoy helping so I could get tips to play games at the arcade. But now all my extra money went into gas and car maintenance. I sighed to myself, adult responsibility is not as fun as I thought. After I finished cleaning, Michael met me by the phone booth outside my bedroom window.

"Hey," I said as I approached him. He took my beach chair and flipped it over his shoulder.

"It's so hot!"

"Yeah, I can't wait to get down to the water."

"I heard it's warm this week," I said.

"Anything is better than this heat," Michael answered.

We made our way to the sidewalk towards the beach and walked under the boardwalk to pick up the wooden path between the dunes. The summer breeze was warm and blew the dune grass back and forth. The beach was long and the tide was out, so it felt like a hike getting to the water. I set my chair up on the sand and pulled my cover up over my head to expose my new purple bikini. Michael stared at me from behind his sunglasses, then tipping them down so I saw his eyes.

"What?" It was not the first time he'd seen me in a bikini. "Pick up your jaw, Michael." I kicked a clamshell awkwardly before walking to the water's edge. My body briefly shivered from the ocean which was not as warm as I had expected. But I was so sweaty from cleaning all day. I walked in slowly until I was deep enough for the waves to break over me. I leaned back and let the water soak my long brown hair. One more dip under a wave and I smoothed it back. I looked back at Michael who was still staring at me. He was acting strange. It was confusing. It made me uncomfortable, but I enjoyed his attention.

Feeling refreshed, I walked back to the beach chair, careful not to step on broken seashells. Once I had to have lifeguards wrap a gushing wound on my foot after a run- in with a broken shell. I picked up my towel and wiped my face, then laid it on the chair. I sat and noticed everything around me. There were boats on the horizon and a banner plane flying overhead advertising Ladies Night at the Pier House Tavern. The beach was buzzing with volleyball games and joggers, kids throwing Frisbees and loud music. Moms sat on the beach while their little ones became covered in sand, hoping to read a few lines in their People magazine. Young couples took turns rubbing sunscreen on each other's back.

"How is your packing coming?" Michael asked.
"I got my roommate assignment and I've bought a few things."
"Are you nervous?"
"Yes!" I said. "I'm nervous about meeting people and finding my classes. What if I don't like my roommate! What if I get lost?"
"You'll be fine. I'll come to visit you. You're right outside the city. Twenty-minute ride."
"Promise?" I asked. He smiled. Michael and I barely talked after school started, except for a few phones calls. But when the

summers came, we picked up right where we left off. He would come to see me at college. Fresh college girls, keg parties, no parents.

I stretched out on my beach chair taking in the warm sun. My body, now cool from the ocean, absorbed the sun's rays as it tans my skin. The ocean breeze gave me goosebumps, and I rubbed my arms. Beads of seawater covered my skin and my wet bikini clung uncomfortably to my body. I closed my eyes, taking in the sounds of the ocean, children playing and lifeguard whistles. Michael, his beach chair set up next to mine, scoped out the girls as they walk by, as his hand rested on my knee. I looked at him and smiled, noticing that glossy look on his face again.

"You are being super weird today."

"Super weird?" His lips turned up.

I love to read at the beach and I searched my bag for my book. Moments later Michael spoke. He always seemed to interrupt me when I'm reading.

"You have no idea what I am thinking right now."

I chuckled, keeping my focus on the pages of my worn paper-back book, "You're right".

"It's that bikini," he said. "It's fucking with me."

"What?" I lifted my head up. "What is that supposed to mean?"

"I need to go cool off." He abruptly headed to the water. That was awkward.

I walked back toward the water to catch up with Michael. On my way past the lifeguards, I noticed Tyler from my Pre-Calc class. He was standing on the edge of the lifeguard stand with a pair of binoculars up to his eyes, a whistle around his neck and his nose white with sunscreen. His chest was bare and red board shorts hung on his hips. As I got closer I saw Amber, his lifeguard partner. She went to the same school, but I don't think we had any classes together. Amber's parents owned a bagel shop on Beacon. I stopped to talk to Tyler.

"Tyler, hey," I said as he leaned on the lifeguard stand.

"Anni!" he jumped down and hugged me. "How is your summer

going?"

"Good, busy and getting ready to leave for college. How about you?" Tyler's skin was so tan from being outside all summer. His long blond surfer hair was messy from the salty breeze.

"Me too, I'm pretty excited about going away. What are you up to tonight? We're having a send-off party for the lifeguards heading to college. You should come." Lifeguard parties were known to be meat markets for guys. They invited all the girls who talked to them on the beach and got sloppy drunk. There was loud music and drinking games and promiscuous behavior.

"Tyler, you know me better. Lifeguard parties aren't my scene."

Tyler laughs back and flips his hair, "It's not one of those. Just a send-off. I promise."

"OK, maybe I'll stop by."

"Awesome! I gotta get back on the stand." Tyler signaled up the lifeguard stand where Amber was sitting. He gave me a hug. "See you tonight!"

I headed into the water to find Michael.

"Who was that?" He must have seen me talking to Tyler and sounded somewhat annoyed. Could he be jealous? No. Michael wasn't the jealous type.

"Tyler, from school. Invited me to a lifeguard party."

"You're not going to a fucking lifeguard party, right?" Michael's mouth fell open.

"I am."

"Anni, you know what lifeguard parties are like. Not your thing. You're going to get hurt."

I laughed at the hypocrisy, and Michael's cool wet hands grabbed my arms and tossed me in the cold ocean water. I screamed and splashed him back. Michael pulled me against him in his arms and glanced over at Tyler.

"Jealous?"

"Protective." He said with a smile.

"Right!"

"But, you're not going." He said, definitively.

"Come with me, you can protect me."

"No." He grabbed me around my bare waist and pulled me towards him.

I walked back and sat in my beach chair, aware Michael was jealous of Tyler. I smiled.

∞∞∞

Later in the evening, Sarah and I headed out on our bicycles to the address Tyler gave me. We weaved in and out of parents with children in strollers standing in line for ice cream, while the bar scene picks up, with bouncers stationed outside checking IDs. We pulled up to yet another million-dollar bay front home and threw our bike in the front yard. I wondered what these people did. Locals didn't own these homes. They were seasonal owners who came down from their high-paying jobs on the weekends. Tyler was right. This party seemed full of mostly locals, and lifeguards, and their friends. It was crowded, but not too bad. I hated crowded parties. How was I going to survive in college?

"It's our last week, Anni!" Sarah squealed as she squeezed my arm. "Do you want a drink?"

"Water." Sarah rolled her eyes and skipped away returning with water, a beer and some of our friends.

"Anni!" Kate yelled over the music. Kate was tall with short black hair. She was in my biology class this past year, and we became friends dissecting frogs. She danced over, beer in hand and gave me a giant, sloppy hug. "Where have you been all summer?!" she asked.

"Work mostly. The beach."

Several other fellow high school graduates gathered around, and we reminisced about teachers we loved, classes we hated and what college would be like.

"I have an 8 am class... blah," Sarah moaned.

"I hope I can figure out how to do my laundry!" Kate whined.

"Who wants shots?" I heard from a voice. Kate's brother, a junior at the state university, was holding a tray of Jello shots.

"Come on guys, grab a shot," Sarah yelled.

"I'm good," I said holding up my hands.

"Let loose Anni, it's our last week!" Kate said. I rolled my eyes and looked for a way out. I passed through the foyer and to the front lawn where Sarah's ex-boyfriend, Dan, was lip-locked with the girl who sat in front of me in English.

I found a spot to sip my water and escape the loud music. Anni, you are such an old lady. As people went in and out of the house, several greeted me. I twisted the cap off the water bottle on and off, fidgeting my hands. Tyler came out and sat next to me.

"Thought you'd be out here alone."

"Sorry, I'm not the party type. I don't know how I will survive college." Tyler laughs.

"I'm glad you came tonight."

"You are?" I instantly felt stupid saying that.

"Yeah, saw you on the beach a few times this summer. I hoped you would come and say hi."

"Oh, I'm sorry, I rarely notice the lifeguards." I felt stupid saying that, too.

"So," He said awkwardly, tapping his hands on his lap.

"So."

"Yeah, can I kiss you?" His question was unexpected. Who asks before they kiss?

"Um, yeah," I said. Making out with boys, what's next Anni? Drinking? Tyler leaned in and kissed my lips, sticking his tongue in my mouth. It was weird but OK. He tasted like beer, which solidified my decision not to drink it.

"Sorry," he said. "I've been drinking some. But I really wanted to do that." I smiled at him, and he took my hand and stood up. I stood up too, and he hugged me tightly. "Let's hang out sometime when we are home from college."

"I'd love that," I answered. And I think I really meant it. Suddenly Sarah burst through the front door and hurled in the bushes. Gross. But I moved to her and held her long hair back. She made several more heaving motions and then stood up. Her mascara was running down her face and she looked wrecked, not to mention the vomit on her clothes. Please, never let me get like this in college, I prayed.

"Oh God!" She moaned. "Anni, where were you! They made me do shots! I needed you to stop it!" I don't mind being Mom to Sarah. It's fun watching her drink, but not when she gets sick.

"Let's go home, Sarah," I said as I led her to our bicycles.

"You're a good friend, Anni," Tyler said. He kissed my cheek and pulled me in for a tight hug. I wondered why we didn't hang out more.

"Oh my God, Anni, you made out with Tyler!" she yelled, struggling to keep a balance on her bicycle. Tyler watched from the house and shook his head.

"Well, I wouldn't call it making out." Or would I?

Michael

I paced the floor waiting for Scott to call or stop by so we can go out, but he didn't come by tonight. Maybe Anni would want to come to hang out and watch a movie. I suddenly re-membered she was going to a lifeguard party, and I felt a twinge of jealousy wondering if she would hook up. No, I felt white hot jealousy. She probably won't though. Anni didn't do that. Maybe just that one time. I loved and hated that about her. If she did, I could have moved in on her, friends with benefits. Some days I wanted to cut it off with her, our friendship. It got too much for me to handle. We spent a lot of time together as friends and it was torture.

That bikini though. Purple. Strings. That body. She was fuck-ing oblivious I was struggling to control myself. I searched the beach for a distraction. Yellow bikini, blue bikini, but the only one I could think of was the one I wanted to get off her body. And then Anni talking to the lifeguard with the curly blond mop top. Shit. His hands all over her bare skin, hugging her.

"You're not going to a fucking lifeguard party, right?" I asked when she told me this dude invited her. It surprised me at the feelings I had, lust for Anni, jealousy, desperation to keep her from a party known to prey on girls. I had enough of my thoughts. I grabbed her arms and playfully push her into the ocean, and she laughed and splashed back in retaliation. I pulled her close our bodies being swayed by the current of the waves, trying to keep our footing as we sank into the sand. Our bodies touched beneath the water and her breasts pushed against my chest. I looked at the blond mop top and gave him a nod.

I had already apologized for the other night when I found her at the same party. I knew that must have been difficult for her. I wasn't sorry, though. I was sorry she got upset, but it should not have been a surprise to her. She knew me. Anni mentioned the tin ring which I don't regret giving her, but it's her go-to secret weapon. She'd held on to it for so long, a reminder of our friendship. It wasn't a lie though, I would marry her someday.

Aware Anni was out, I found it difficult to concentrate on anything else. I turned on the TV and flipped mindlessly through the channels. There was nothing that could keep my focus off of her. I closed my eyes and tried to drift off to sleep. My mom was asleep already, or at least in bed reading a book. My mind kept wandering to that purple fucking bikini. The way it clung to her wet body. Oh, my fucking God. The strings tied around the back of her neck. I willed myself to picture the 13-year-old girl playing pinball but, it didn't work. I grabbed the keys to my Jeep and headed out the door.

I drove down 26th Street, hoping not to find Anni's car in front of the house known for these parties. I didn't see it. Perhaps she rode her bicycle. I drove around the block again, and I saw Anni. There she was sitting on the porch, but she wasn't alone. Mop Top was with her and he was holding her hands in his lap. I wanted to stop and jump out, demanding she gets her ass home. Fuck. I kept driving and prayed she didn't notice my Jeep stalk past the house. Fuck again. I didn't want her to think I was stalking her. Even though I was. I knew he would kiss her. And she would kiss him back.

I headed toward the south end of the island. Aimlessly, I found myself at the inlet and parked. Eleven o'clock. I wondered how long she would stay. I heard my friends reproaching me.

"Mike, you're stalking her," would be Doug.
Scott would tell me I'm leading her on. But, I wasn't. I was open and honest with her. She knew where I stood. Although, I'm not sure where I stood. I was sitting alone at the inlet, after driving around looking for her. Damn Scott for not calling. I needed a distraction. Some cheap beer in a random hotel room on the beach. A party in a boarding house filled with foreign girls.

That reminded me of the time Doug and Brandon and I crashed a party at the Seaside Manor, foreign girls everywhere. Doug couldn't even pronounce the name of the naked girl he was with in the dirty, dusty room, devoid of any signs of having been cleaned since they arrived. The girls would work all summer, sometimes several jobs. Ride operators, ice cream servers, standing outside with candy samples. They would do anything for an American guy. I mean anything.

I checked the clock in the Jeep, 11:15. The air was cool and damp, and a full moon hung high in the sky. I remembered the last full moon when Anni and I walked down to the ocean. The beach was lit up by the large, bright moon rising above the water. We were barefoot and Anni wore her cut-off jeans and a blue Beacon Prep sweatshirt. I held her hand as we walked, enjoying the change of pace from a night out with Scott and Doug. It was quiet and peaceful. I put the blanket I was carrying under my arm down on the sand, and Anni and I sat, listening to the ocean's thunderous roar. We watched the stars twinkle in the sky as the moon climbs higher and higher into the night.

"I love this," Anni said, her face lit up by the light of the moon.

"What?" I asked, pulling her into me.

"Just sitting here, listening to the ocean, being away from all the people." She looked back towards town. The lights, and cars and the roller coasters, the faint sound of people talking and laughing and screaming not too far from the peace of the beach. Off to the left, two teenagers were making out on the lifeguard stand, which earlier that day sat two lifeguards, scanning the ocean for swimmers in distress. "I think I will miss this when I go away to school."

"What about me? Will you miss me too?" She punched my arm lightly.

"But I'll be closer to you," she said.

"But not here, on the beach, at night, alone." She climbed over me and sat between my knees and leaned back into my chest. I wrapped my arms around her and breathed in the smell of her hair, vanilla. There was definitely something about being on the beach at night you couldn't get in the city.

"I'll miss this too," I said. She leaned her head back to look at me and I kissed her forehead. More and more this summer I wished I could give myself to her completely. I wanted to make her happy. Give up Doug and Scott and drinking and smoking and girls. We sat quietly for a while, feeling the warmth of our bodies against each other.

I leaned back and pulled her on top of me and she giggled, rolling over on her stomach.

"What are you thinking about?" she asked.

"Kissing you," I said. She tilted her head and gazes at me. We laid on the blanket facing each other, and I moved close to her face, touching her lips softly with mine. She wrapped her arms around me and curled up into my body.

"Kiss me again," she said, her big brown eyes looking up at me. I put my hand on the back of her head and pulled her closer, kissing her once more, parting my lips and grabbing her face with both of my hands. She smiled, pulling away and laid back on the blanket on her side, propped up by her elbow. I stared at her, taking a deep breath, trying to avoid doing something more than I'd regret later.

"God, Anni," I said.

"What?" How can she be so gorgeous and so fucking clueless to my feelings?

I pulled her in towards me wondering if she can feel my body respond to her.

This was a moment, a memory I relived often. I wondered where we might be now if things had gone further that night.

It's 12:00 midnight. Anni has got to be home by now and I pull out of the spot to drive to the motel. I am reminded of the vision of Anni on the porch with Mop Top. Did he kiss her first? Did she kiss him back? The image of her lips on his made me burn up. This wasn't the first time I've called from the pay phone outside her window in the middle of the night. Usually, I'm on my way home from a night of drinking and mindless hookups. Why am I so fucking nervous?

I called Anni's room, but she didn't answer or look out the window. What if she was still at the party? I sat in my jeep and put my head back into the headrest and look up at the stars. I will wait.

She passed by on her bicycle around 1 am and didn't notice me until she locked it up. It was hard to miss my yellow Jeep.

"Michael, what are you doing?"

"I wanted to see you."

"Are you drunk or something?"

"No." I put my arms out to hold her. She pulled away, confusing me. "I promise you, I haven't left the house all night except to come here and wait for you."

"How long have you been waiting?"

"A while," I said. She didn't mention seeing me stalk past her earlier.

Michael, its 1 am, go home."

"I can't," I whispered, pulling her into me once again.

"Why not?" She was so fucking clueless.

"Because I want you," I pulled her closer into me and our lips meet. Her eyes closed for a moment, giving in.

"What's that mean?" she said, confused.

By the end of this night, our relationship would be different. My intentions were unclear, but I couldn't get that bikini and that body out of my mind. I had grabbed a condom out of my glove compartment and put it in my pocket, ready if she let me. I briefly thought about the consequences, of Anni's expectations for afterward, but all I could think of right now was getting her clothes off. I could deal with the consequences later. I was confident she would let me, but I wasn't sure I wanted her to.

I took her hand and led her up to the deck where we have had many conversations about life, about friendships, about us. It was dark except for the familiar neon sign of the ice cream parlor, and I sat her down on a lounge chair. I sat next to her, grabbing her face in my hands, pressing my lips against hers. She trembled, but put her arms around my neck, pushing her body into me.

I felt her breasts against my shirt and my breathing became shallow. I pulled her on top of me, pushing her dress up so she could straddle my lap, and I ran my hands up her perfect, smooth legs. Her skin prickled at my touch. I pulled her down towards my face and kissed her, harder and with more urgency. She was responding with her body and her actions. I knew she was feeling it, too. I positioned her on me so she could feel the hardness through her panties I was going to soon have off her. She smelled like lavender, and I breathed in a deep breath, committing it to memory.

"You OK?" I asked her.

"Yeah," she breathed hard, looking around to see if anyone saw us there.

I kissed her neck, and she tipped her head back, exposing her skin. The emotions running through my head were new. The salty air of the ocean and the darkness reminded me of the night on the jetty, holding each other, feeling grateful to have her back in my life. I wanted to kiss her that night, but I was so nervous I couldn't bring myself to do it.

"Anni," I said trying to figure out what she was thinking. I noticed her eyes wet, and I knew she was overcome with emotion. I laid her down on the lounge and ran my hand up her leg, pushing up her dress, wondering how much I could get away with out here on the deck.

I reached my hand further up her dress, cupping her breasts in my hand over the lace of her bra. She gasped. I pushed my body against her so she could feel how much I want her. I didn't know how much longer I could wait. I had never taken my time with anyone, and Anni was clearly driving me out of my comfort zone. How did she get through my guard? I stared down at her face, her expression unreadable. My heart pounded in my throat.

"If you're going to stop me, then do it now," I said, barely able to catch my breath. I was desperate to know if she wanted me, too. She stared in my eyes without saying a word. I would be crushed if she stopped me.

"Anni," I said again, willing her to say something. My hands, under her dress, traced a line down her spine. Her body was shaking and I felt her heart pounding against my chest.

Anni

"If you're going to stop me, then do it now," he said, out of breath. I didn't know what to say. I wanted him to stay, and I wanted to continue feeling his body on mine, kissing my lips and my neck, pushing and pulling. But was there a point where I would want to stop? *I didn't want to stop.* Michael stared in my eyes with a look of want and desperation, his chest rapidly rising and falling. I didn't know what I wanted.

"Anni" he begged. He continued kissing me, running his lips down my neck. My heart pounded in my chest. Why was he here tonight? What does this mean? Was he really home before he came here? Are we going to.... *Anni, stop thinking.*

"Anni," his voice pleaded. My eyes burned as a hot tear escaped and ran down my cheek. Michael laid me down on the lounge and ran his hand up my leg. It prickled under his touch, and I shivered. He pushed my dress up, and his hand crept, touching the bare skin of my back as he ran his fingers along my spine. My head pounded as my heart raced faster. He pushed his body weight onto me, reaching his hand further up my dress, cupping my breast over my bra. I worried we will be seen, although I know for sure there have been others that have had similar experiences on this deck and they didn't get caught. Including Sarah.

"Let's go inside," he said. I considered the logistics of trying to sneak him past my parents in the middle of the night, but it wouldn't be the first time.

"If we wait any longer, I am going to take this fucking dress off of you right here on this deck," he said as his chest rises and falls rapidly. My head spun hearing Michael talk about taking my dress off, and I fell apart. I didn't know if I could go through with it. The emotional side effects would be too much for me to handle. I wished Michael had been drinking. Knowing he was here sober, on his own free makes me weak. I am sure he had considered the consequences.

I stand up and smoothed out my dress before walking down the stairs from the deck to the front door down towards my bedroom. Michael locked my door, and I felt a lump rise in my throat. Calm down, Anni. It's now or never. Michael pulled me close to him, his hands on my waist and rested his head on my shoulder. Tears swelled in my eyes again, and I tried to force them back. *Don't be so emotional, Anni.* But it was Michael, my best friend. Things had been so difficult for us the past two summers. Michael had hurt me so many times, telling me he needed space, seeing him at a party, drinking and drunk dials. But he loved me. I was his girl, always. He told me.

I felt so warm and calm in his embrace, though my heart beat fast. He dropped his arms to my hands and then let go, looking around my room. He stood in front of my shelves looking at pictures and books. Michael opened my senior yearbook was on my dresser and read "K.I.T. Anni, From Steve." I couldn't take my eyes off of him working his way around my bedroom.

Was he thinking about something? Oh, God. Maybe having second thoughts? He found a basket of triangle-folded notes and flipped one over in his hand, "Steve?" he asked.
"No," I chuckle, "From Sarah." Michael opens the jewelry box on my dresser and found the ring. He put it in his pocket. Michael pushes play on my cassette player and 80s ballads play from the speakers. He lowered the volume, no doubt he hated that music. I laughed at the thought of making out with Michael to rap music.

Michael wrapped his arms around me and pulled me close. He kissed my lips gently, and I responded to him, allowing myself to give in. He put his hands in his pocket and pulled out the ring and put it on my finger. It was too tight considering he gave it to me 5 years ago when I was just 13 years old. He pulled the ring to stretch it and slips it back on. I giggled.

"I want you so fucking bad, Anni," he said, "This" he gestures to my body. "This is killing me." His words made me completely lose touch with my surroundings.

Michael's warm body swayed with mine, as I breathed in his scent. The cologne reminded me only of Michael. Just as I calmed myself and feel comfortable, he slipped his hand underneath my dress and pulled me closer. Michael looked at me, and my knees went weak as he undid the clasp on my bra. I held my breath and my body trembled once again. His hand cupped my bare breast, and I instinctively grabbed his arm, unsure if I should stop him or let him go. My body tensed and we made eye contact.

"Do you want me to stop?" he whispered. My skin was alive everywhere he touches me, and it surprised me at how my body responds to him.

"I'm scared," I admitted. Terrified actually. But I wanted to continue.

"Anni, I want to do this with you," he said. My heart fluttered and my head got dizzy and I knew there is no turning back. He was all mine tonight.

"Are you sure?" I asked. He was sure, Anni, he had his hands up your dress.

"I love you," he said. I smiled, and I knew now I had never been more ready for this. He pulled my dress over my head, and I stood before him naked except for my underwear. He pulled me close to him as he sat on the edge of my bed and I stood between his knees. He ran his hands across my hips and up my sides, leaving electric sparks everywhere he touched. My body shook. Michael took off his shirt, and taking my hands, placed them on his bare chest. His skin was warm and I could feel the muscles of his chest, which makes me want to touch him more. He pulled me into the bed and we melded our bodies, my bare breasts against his chest, my hips against his. He pulled off my underwear, and I felt my head spin. Our bodies entangled with one another as he wrapped his legs around mine, kissing my lips and running his hands down my body. I begged myself to let go, but my body was so tense.

Michael handed me a condom. It's a gold foil packet, shaped like an arcade token. My hand trembled, and I handed it back to him to put on. I held my breath. Michael looked in my eyes, and his body shook. He was nervous too.

"Anni," he breathed.

"Oh my God, Michael," I said, grabbing his bare shoulders. My head spun, and I felt light-headed.

He pushed me gently back on my pink pillow and bent my knees as he climbed on top of me.

"You ready?" he asked. He kissed my lips as he pushed into me. I wanted to scream as I felt my body full of Michael. The pain and stinging and the way he grabbed my hips sent me into a sensation spiral. I struggled to keep up, tilting my hips

141

towards him, trying to find a rhythm. Tears rolled down my cheeks, emotion and agony. I breathed through the pain which has faded, and I moved my body to meet his. I dug my fingernails into his arm as he pushed harder.

"Anni," he said, gripping my arms. Sweating and panting.

"Michael, oh my God... Michael," I answered him.

"You OK?" I nod.

Michael moved with more desperation in his thrusts. Then, he stilled for a moment, finding his release and collapsed on top of me, his breathing labored.

"Oh, my fucking God, Anni." he panted. I froze in disbelieve we had crossed this line. What did it mean? He traced my body with his fingertips and ran his hands through my messy hair. This moment was years in the making, pinball, roller coasters, literally and figuratively, the kiss... two years of kissing, of begging. Michael, please, let me be your only one.

"Say something," he whispered. Michael's face was soft and glowing in the faint light of the lamppost outside. I thought I saw wetness in his eyes.

"I feel..." I couldn't think of what to say.

"It was a first for me too," he said, kissing my forehead, "With someone I love." My heart melted. Was that what it meant to wait for the right one? The one I would marry, anyway.

"I thought it was time," he said. I tilt my head, confused.

"Time?"

"Well, I've been trying to keep my hands off you since you grew boobs," he laughed. I poked him with my elbow, but I was grateful that he lightened the mood.

"Why do you fight it, then?" I asked. He could have me if he wanted, why try?

"Shh," he said. He placed his finger on my lips. "Don't." He ran his fingers down my face, leaving a trail of warm sparks. Michael always tried to keep me from talking about my feelings. "Don't," he always said to avoid uncomfortable conversations. That was how we got to this point, he shushed my feelings so he didn't have to think about it.

"It's called a commitment," I said, softly. I know that word wasn't in Michael's vocabulary. I wondered if he would ever be capable of committing to one person. My heart sunk.

"Be patient Anni." An ominous, unsettling feeling came over me. I had been patient, I would continue being patient because I knew he loved me and we would be together someday, and he would commit only to me. But everything changed then. I laid here naked in Michael's arms. How was I going to move on from this knowing he wasn't mine?

"It will be ok, Anni," he said, reading my thoughts.

"Michael…." I began.

"Anni, stop talking, I don't want to ruin this moment," he whispered, pulling me close and kissing my lips. Another redirecting strategy. He knew what I would say.

We sat quietly while I was over-thinking all my thoughts and emotions. One day on the beach I had overheard Michael's friends discussing a "conquest". A get the girl contest. I didn't know the exact rules of the contest but I recalled the gist of it being one point for each girl. I felt instantly mortified, ashamed, and humiliated. I had just let Michael make love to me.

"Can I ask you a question?" I said, sitting up on my bed.

"What?"

"How many points is a virgin?" I stared into his eyes trying to get a reading before he spoke. He didn't respond right away. "I heard you the other day talking to Scott about points. A contest. A virgin must be worth a lot of points, right?"

"Why are you saying that?" he asked, "You aren't some point, Anni."

"A lot?" I ignored his response.

"Stop, Anni, that is not what this is and you know it. Don't ruin this." His voice hurt and defensive. I thought in my heart I knew it was not a game to him, but I was feeling overwhelmed. My head swirled with thought after thought.

"Did you use me?" I asked, as tears flood from my eyes.

"Why would I do that, Anni? I could have had you a long time ago if you were a game." I tilted my head to look at Michael, trying to understand his wording. He was probably right. I never had it in me to stop him.

"I'm here because I love you," he said. He ran his fingers through my hair. I turned my face into his chest and cry. My body shook.

"I'm sorry, Anni, I can't give you what you want right now. Maybe someday." And with those words, I feel like he had taken a part of my soul. "You ok?" He knew what I needed. He knew how I was. He also knew how I felt. So, I said the only thing I could say.

"I love you too."

Chapter 17 : Past

Michael

Two words: party hopping," Doug says. "I'm in."
Anni and I sat at Pizza Palace on the boardwalk across
from the amusement pier. Families with strollers and
bags and over-sized plush prizes surround us as we sat at the
counter on stools. The sky looked ominous as a storm suddenly
rolled in from the west over the bay. The Pizza Palace quickly
got crowded as people tried to take shelter. A crash of thunder
jolted us upright in our seats.

"Scared me!" Anni yelled clutching her chest. A few more rum-
bles of thunder followed the crash as the storm moved through.

"Hey Anni," the guy making pizzas said to her.

"Hey, how's your summer, Tommy," she responded turning her
attention away from the storm. Who is Tommy, I wondered
while she makes idle chit chat about whatever?

"This is my…." She hesitated, "Michael."

"What's up," he nodded. Anni and I each ordered a slice of
pizza and soda.

"This is my Michael?" I teased.

"Shut up, Michael, what the heck are you?" Another boom of
thunder made Anni jump.

"Do you want to hang out tonight?" she asked. She took a bite
of her pizza. Anni was wearing a red sun dress which hiked up
around her legs as she sat on the stool. I couldn't help but stare.

"We can go to the movies, or play golf and get ice cream or go to the beach." The look in her eyes made it hard to turn her down.

"I can't, I have plans," I said, looking forward to party hopping tonight with Doug and Scott and Brandon. Scoring free alcohol from people who thought we were supposed to be at their party, anyway. It was always a good time. Anni looked down at her fingernails, disappointed. I knew this was the last week we had for the summer.

"Why don't you come with me," I hesitated before I asked. She stared at my face trying to decide if I was kidding.
"Are you feeling OK?" she touched my forehead with the back of her hand. "Have you been struck by lightning?"
"I'm feeling fine. You said you wanted to come out with me, and I'm asking you if you want to. That's all."
"Well, what are you going to do?"
"Party hop." I smirked. I waited for her reaction. "Michael, that's not a good idea" I heard her say in her head. She took a deep breath, contemplating her decision.
"Who is going?" she asked.
"Me," I answered. "Does anyone else matter?" I tried to read Anni's thoughts. "There will be drinking, and smoking, and making out, and sex, and maybe we might even get arrested."
"Oh my God, Michael," she said, covering her eyes. "I'll go!"
"Seriously?"
"Yeah, unless you don't want me to," she added.
"No, I want you to."
"Well, I want to, too!" she leaned over and hugged me.

Just as we stepped outside of Pizza Palace onto the boardwalk, there was a tremendous boom of thunder. Anni practically jumped in my arms. The rain we thought had ended came pouring down in buckets and we huddle under a store's overhang, which wasn't providing us much protection.

The lightning bolts created an impressive display over the ocean as the storm moved out. Once the rain slowed, we made a run for it. I grabbed Anni's hand, and we ran down the wet boardwalk, she screaming and I laughing. Anni ran and slid across the wet wood and I followed her. Her drenched red dress clung to every inch of her seductive body while her wet hair dripped in her face.

We arrived back to my house to pick up the Jeep. I ran in to change my wet clothes, and I helped her in to the front seat and buckle her seat belt. She always laughed at me for buckling her, but I liked to reach across her, inhaling her smell, some kind of coconut today. It started when she was 14 and could barely get into the jeep on her own. But now it gave me a change to touch her body. I took Anni back to the motel so she could put dry clothes on, even though I was really into that wet dress adhering to her body. But she put on an equally amazing yellow dress, thin straps, flowing skirt. Her hair was still wet and frizzy, and she smoothed it back into a ponytail. I grabbed her hand and squeezed it before pulling out of the parking lot. I drove towards the bay and parked in front of Scott's house. Anni and I got out, and I took her hand as we approach the door. Scott opened it, looking surprised.

"Mike," he said, putting out his hand. He glanced at Anni and back at me with a wide-eyed stare.

"Hi," Anni said.

"What's up?" Scott answered, hugging her and giving me another death stare. I shrugged. Anni walked back to the Jeep ahead of us.

"What the fuck are you doing, Mike?" Scott asked.

"She wanted to come," I said. I brushed off his question like it wasn't a big deal.

"She will ruin our night."

"It's only one night, Scott, it will be fine." I got back in the Jeep and Anni sat next to me. I held her hand as I drove to pick up Doug and Brandon. They hopped in the back seat and I smirked, looking back at all three of them squished together. Doug sitting in the middle flanked by Brandon and Scott.

"I hope you know what you're fucking doing," Doug whispered from the back seat.

I parked the Jeep on 30th Street in the middle of the southern section of the island that has many motels within walking distance. I took Anni's hand as we walked towards the Surfside Inn, trailing behind the guys. We had partied here before. I knew it for renting to under-aged teens. We spotted a room with the door propped open and a keg just inside. Doug headed up first. "Yo," he said. "You guys from the city?"

"Yeah, who are you?" a girl in a tight black dress asked.

"I'm Doug, I live here in Beacon, this is my friend's place," he said, motioning towards the motel, lying.

"You live here all year?" she asked, impressed. That was always Doug's modus operandi, a sense of pretentiousness for living in this so-called paradise all the time.

"Mind if my friends and I join you?" he asked. Doug motioned for us to come up to the room. "What's your name?" he asked her.

"Kerri. And this is Jennifer." She pointed to her friend standing with her. We headed inside the room where it was stuffy and hazy with cigarette smoke. I looked at Anni who has a death grip on my hand.

"You OK?"

"Sure," she said smiling. Kerri handed us each a can of cheap beer. Anni handed her beer over and I open it and gave it back to her.

"No, thanks," she said. I shrugged and took a sip. The music was loud throughout the room and I wondered if the adjacent rooms would complain to the manager. I put my hands on Anni's hips and moved to the beat of the song, trying to loosen her up while taking a sip of my beer. Doug shoot me a look from across the room as he moved in on some girl sitting on the couch.

"So, what's it like living here all year?" I heard her ask Doug. I knew he had her now, it's like a season pass to city girls.

"What do you think, Anni?" Scott said.

"Scott, I've been to parties before, just not with you." She snapped.

"Oh, shit, OK," he laughed. "Where's your beer?"

"I don't have one," she answered. I pulled her close to let her know I would not let him harass her. Scott left and made his way around the room talking to girls, trying to impress them with his stories of the island. They were captivated. It felt unusual to have Anni with me rather than trying to pick up chicks.

"You guys ready to roll?" Doug asked. He motioned towards the door. The trick was to leave before people complained or threw up and causing a scene which makes it more likely the police will show up. We walked a few more blocks, passing motels that were quiet. Some nights we would hop from pool to pool, but not tonight.

Doug put his arm around Anni as we walked, talking to her about something I couldn't hear. I knew she was uncomfortable with his beer breath on her face as he leaned in to her ear. But she was being a good sport so far. She laughed, and he pulled her tighter.

"How about this place?" Brandon asks as we approach the Islander Motel. It was brightly lit with strings of white lights draped throughout fake palm trees. There was a group of teens hanging on the deck, overflowing from a motel room with cups in their hands.

"Let's try it," I said. We sent Brandon in to test the crowd. He motioned us up a few minutes later, already palming a beer.

"This is Matt," he said, patting Matt on the back.

"Hey Matt, you mind if we hang?" I asked.

"No, man, come on in. Do you want a shot?" He poured a few shots into cups and handed one to each of us. Anni held her cup, sniffing it and twisting her face. I took it out of her hand and threw it back, encountering the aftertaste of cinnamon burning in my throat.

I watched as Doug took Anni's hand, as my head swirls. He led her inside the motel room where there was another crowd of teens. He looked back at me.

"She has to go to the bathroom," he explained. Some time

passed, and they had not emerged from the crowded motel room yet, so I looked for them. Doug, with a beer in his hand, and Anni were standing in a corner talking. His hand was leaning on the wall over her shoulder, his mouth close to her ear. She laughed with him.

"Mike," he said. He pushed off the wall. "Ready to go?"

"Let's get out of here," I said. We got Scott and Brandon and headed down the stairs, thanking the crowd for the free beer and shots. I kept my eyes peeled on Doug and Anni.

Doug put his arm on her back and led her down towards the sidewalk.

"What the fuck are you doing, Doug?" I grabbed his arm and pulled him aside. Anni looked on.

"What?" he asked. He tilted his head.

"Keep your fucking dirtbag hands off her," I said, "You're going to hurt her."

"Mike, I think she's capable of handling herself. You don't need to go fucking parental."

"Fine,"

"Fine?" Doug asked. He stepped up. "Tell me she's your girl and I'll leave her alone, Mike. Say it," he looked at Anni who was staring at us.

"Do whatever the fuck you want, Doug," I said in his face, knowing he is right. But I also know Anni, and Doug isn't her type.

"Stop, Michael," she said, pushing me away from Doug. Doug grabbed her hand and walks ahead of us. She willingly went with him making me question what the fuck is going on. He whispered in her ear and she threw her head back, smiling. I saw red. Brandon and Scott grabbed beers from their pockets they lifted from the first party and we walked down towards the beach.

I lagged behind everyone. I couldn't move in on Anni because she would think I was jealous or possessive or whatever word she used. Ahead I saw Doug hug her. She seemed like she was enjoying his attention. My heart pounded, and I felt drawn towards intervening in this intentional display of trying to make me feel things. I took the last swig of my beer and threw the can onto the sand, hurrying to catch up.

"Anni," I said, careful not to slur my words. I didn't want her to think I was drunk, though my thoughts were fuzzy and distant. I took her hand as she held Doug's in the other. Doug smirked at me and shook his head and I wanted to punch his fucking face. He dropped her hand.

"Mike, if anyone's messing with her, it's you," he said walking away. I knew he was right.

"Doug," she said watching him walk away. He turned back to her and pointed his finger in her face, "He won't fucking say it, Anni, remember that." Doug walked back towards her and kissed her lips. Without thinking, I stepped to him and pushed him down. Scott and Brandon stepped between us.

"Seriously, Mike?" Scott yelled. I let them walk ahead of us towards the beach, while Anni stayed behind.

"Anni," I said, turning back to her. Her eyes stared a hole in my head, as my brain was foggy and spinning.

"Michael, what was that?" she said, her hands were on her hips.

"Sorry about Doug," I looked for a reaction. Anni shook her head.

"Why? We were just having fun, Michael."

"Fun."

"Yeah, fun." Anni pushed me. "Michael, you're jealous!"

"Maybe," I admitted, pulling her close into me. I put my head down into her shoulders, smelling the lavender scent of her hair. I didn't kiss her because I know she would not want me to after drinking and smoking. It felt unusual to be here with her and the guys, like two worlds collide. I would normally look for girls. The guys probably weren't getting any girls tonight because we brought Anni. I didn't care. I enjoyed being in her company, but I knew I wouldn't invite her out with me again. She did things to me. Made me have feelings.

"Do you want me to take you home?" I asked.

"Nope," she said confidently. We caught up to the guys as we made our way down towards the water. Scott dropped his clothes on the sand and streaked past us to the ocean disappearing into the dark.

"Oh my God," Anni gasped, covering her mouth with her hands.

"He always does this," Brandon said.

"Do you?" she asked me, stretching her neck to look at me.

"Sometimes," I winked. "I'll do it if you do."

"Not naked," she protested.

"Dress off." I compromised. She looked around at the blackness of the night, the guys standing behind me. Doug and Brandon and I held our breath. Anni pulled her dress over her head and throws it to the ground and locked eyes with me.

She put her hands over her mouth. The guys looked at me, but I couldn't take my eyes off her gorgeous body. She ran towards the water wearing only her panties and bra, screaming as she hits the cold ocean. I looked at Doug's mouth hanging open and I was done. I threw my clothes on the sand and ran after her. Grabbing her in the dark of the night, the moonlight shining above. She dipped beneath a wave to smooth out her hair while my hands found their way around her bare waist. I undid the clasp of her bra and took it off, throwing it in the ocean and plunging under the water with her. Her heart pounded against mine, and her breathing was fast. I was so eager for her, but I tried to control it while the alcohol broke down my inhibitions.

"Anni, you are amazing," I ran my hands over her wet body. I leaned my face in to her and kissed her lips forcefully with so much frustration I had been holding in all night. I cupped her wet, naked breasts in my hand. I looked back towards the sand, as the guys looked on, clumsily turning away as I made eye contact. Yeah, they were staring at us.

Doug, Brandon and Scott turned their backs and walked up towards the boardwalk. I took her hand leading her out of the water. She looked around, holding her arms over her bare chest. The Beacon lifeguard boat was parked on the sand and I guided her towards it, stopping at my shorts to grab a condom. Anni's eyes widened as she realized what I'm planning to do. It was only a few days ago in her bedroom she gave herself to me. I climbed into the boat with her, naked and wet, and we sat on the bench. I leaned over to kiss her face, moving closer so our bodies were touching. I ran my fingernails down her back as her body responded to mine, her skin prickled and shivered at my touch.

"I want you," I breathed into her hair, my brain still fuzzy and spinning from the beer and shots. Anni didn't seem to care about that right now as she moved her body in response to mine. I slipped off her panties and threw them to the ground. I dragged my fingers along her legs, making my way up her body. I cupped my hands between her legs and she grabbed my arm. I felt her, her body ready for me and I pulled her on my lap, lowering her body onto mine. I pushed and pulled her hips moving her in rhythm with me. I kissed her neck and her breasts and I pulled her close as she moved to meet me.

She threw her head back. "Michael," she said, grabbing my arms. I came apart at the sound of her saying all my name, my body was shaking. She leaned down and her lips met mine. I pulled her down wrapping my arms around her bare skin.

"I love you," I slurred. She climbed off me and pulled her panties back on, suddenly worried someone is around. It was possible the guys were still watching, and I didn't care. I dug a shallow hole and threw the condom in, kicking the sand back over it. Hopefully, the tide would carry it out before some kid dug it up making a sand castle.

Anni pulls her dress over her head. Her bra floated somewhere out in the ocean. I pulled her against me again, kissing her face, her lips, her neck. I could get used to this. I took Anni's hand, and we headed off the beach.

Doug, Scott, and Brandon have moved on and I do not see them anywhere, so Anni and I walked back a few blocks to the Jeep.

"Michael, let me drive," she said, knowing I was pretty drunk. I handed her the keys. No one else had ever driven the Jeep before. What did she do to me?

I headed over to Doug and Brandon's house the next day to make peace with Doug after last night.

"Doug, are we cool?" I asked, sitting on the deck watching jet skis race up and down the channel.

"I'm cool, but what about you?"

"What's that mean?" I asked.

"You can't do this to her. How long has it been, 5 years? I know you're fucking her, Mike. You said you weren't. I saw you in the ocean, there's no way you're not."

"I don't see how that is any of your damn business," I yelled, feeling my face flush.

"People have girlfriends Mike, if you want her, then go get her. But don't fuck around with her."

"I don't know," I said, blowing out a breath I have been holding. "I'm not ready."

"Why, Mike, because you want to go out with a bunch of high school kids, getting drunk and laid every other day? Jesus fucking Christ, you are 21 years old Mike, hanging out with us, 18. Well, Brandon's 20. Grow the fuck up."

"I'm going to let her go," I had been thinking about it, she deserved more. Next week she would leave for college and I needed to cut my ties now. I felt my eyes fill, but I tried to keep cool.

"You're a fool."

"Doug, what do I have to give her? Like you said, the 21-year-old child."

"No, I said grow the fuck up."

"Even if I did, even if I committed to her, I'd ruin her. I'm not meant for that."

"Then I guess you lose, Mike." He said, patting me on the back.

Chapter 18: College

Anni

Ryan, the first person I saw when I arrived to check in at Kroy University.

"Hey, you," he said as several students approached my car to carry my things to my new home. Ryan was holding a clipboard, and he checked off my name.

"Room 104," he instructed the others and they move through the lobby with my belongings.

"How was the rest of your summer, Anni?" he asked. My face flushed thinking about the encounter we had, seeing Michael with a blond, crying in my car, Ryan's lizard-like tongue.

"Good, I guess." I tried not to appear overly friendly, but not rude.

"Cool, my dorm is right over there, room 213. Stop by sometime."

"Yeah, sure, OK," I said knowing I won't. I grabbed a few bags of my stuff and head up to room 104.

I stood in the middle of my freshly painted blue cinder block walls, two loft bed frames, 2 desks and 2 closets. It would need a lot of fixing up to be comfortable for the next few months. Stephanie's things were tucked neatly to one side of the room in large plastic totes, though she was not in the room.

"You must be Anni," a loud voice from the doorway called.

"You must be Stephanie!" She ran in and hugged me, swaying

back and forth as she did. Stephanie was overly friendly. She was adorable, with a short brown haircut and bangs, wearing a denim skirt and navy blue t-shirt. I instantly liked her. She reminded me of Sarah, so outgoing and excited, which could also mean trouble. I recalled all the times I held Sarah's hair as she puked in the bushes. I wondered if it would be the same with Stephanie.

We unpacked our books and clothes, placing them in drawers. Stephanie brought a small refrigerator, and I brought the TV. We arranged our room, hung our posters and added touches from home to brighten up the dankness of the dark dormitory room.

"The Cranberries, I love them," she said, eyeing my poster as I fixed it above my bed.

Stephanie hung a string of lights across the window that added the perfect touch and I put pictures of my friends up on the wall.

I showed Stephanie a picture of Sarah. "She's my drunk friend I take care of."

"We will be such good friends."

"Who's this?" She picked up a 1/2 strip of photos from an arcade photo booth. "He's cute."

"That is Michael. He's my..." my voice trailed off as I searched for a word. "Let's put that in the drawer for now." I took the photo out of her hand and looked at it. Two pictures from a strip of 4, ripped in half top to bottom. Michael has the top two and I have the bottom two. Goofy faces and the last one, Michael kissing my lips. That was unexpected, I remembered. Six summers, three of them kissing, touching, making love, and yet I didn't have a title to give him. Then he disappeared. No returned phone calls or goodbyes. Just gone. I tried for days before I left to call him. I cried myself to sleep the last night when I realized I would not see him before I left. I guess I knew then it was over. Stephanie gave me a puzzled look but shrugged her shoulders. I put it in the drawer. I'm thankful she asked no more questions.

"Well, OK." Stephanie said. "Are you hungry? Let's go get some food!"

"Yes, starving!" We headed to the basement of the student center to the cafeteria. It reminded me of my high school cafeteria with its trays and cafeteria workers dishing chicken nuggets and meatloaf. The smell of grease and fried foods and something burning filled the room.

I handed the cashier my student ID, and she deducted a meal from my meal plan. Stephanie and I found a table in the corner.

"So, Anni, what are we going to do the first night of our college career?"

"Well, I was thinking I would map out my classes and maybe get started on reading."

"Oh God, Anni." Stephanie cried dramatically.

"Bowling? Movies?" I suggested, shrugging. Stephanie rolled her eyes.

"Don't worry, I can help you. My brother left us some party starters in the mini fridge." Wow, I was right about Stephanie being so much like Sarah.

"I don't drink." Stephanie smiled as if I was her new project. It was a typical response. Sarah had given up trying to make me conform to her party life.

"So, like, are your parents alcoholics or something?" she said, confused by my declaration.

"No, I just… don't see the point," I answered.

"Well, OK." She said, "But will you still come out with us."

"Us?"

"Yeah, some friends I met at summer orientation. They live downstairs."

"I will go, but we have classes early tomorrow so we can't stay late." Ugh, I was already bearing my only friend here.

"Anni, you are not wearing that to the party are you?" Stephanie asked as she cracked open a beer from the mini-fridge. I turned to look at myself in the mirror. Jeans, t-shirt, red flannel and hiking boots. "No?"

"No! Not unless you're planning to spend your college years

single and celibate. Try this." What's wrong with single and celibate? Stephanie pulled out a tight black shirt with a plunging V neck. "Do you have jeans that fit better?" I pulled out a pair of tight jeans and she gave me black boots with a heel. Stephanie put makeup on my face and fixed my hair.

I inhaled at the sight of myself. "How Do I Look?" I asked, glancing in the mirror.

"Smokin'!" she blurted out. "Let's go get em!"

I followed Anni out the door and we headed down the hall to another dorm room. The thing I was learning first at college was that partying is a process. You don't just "go to" a party. You "end up" at a party.

Stephanie introduced me to some of her new friends. She leaned in and whispers 'Upper Classmen". She winked.

"This is Anni, she's my roommate," Stephanie said.

"Hi Anni, I'm Dave, I live downstairs. And this is Kristin and Leslie and Michael."

Why did there have to be a Michael? I instantly knew I would keep my distance from him. Dave opened the mini-fridge in Leslie and Kristen's room and pulled out a bottle of liquor. "Who wants shots!?" he asked, swaying the bottle in the air above his head. I thought this was a dry campus.

Dave poured shots in some plastic cups and passed them out.

"No, thank you," I said. Dave shrugged his shoulder and moved on and I was grateful he didn't make a scene.

"She doesn't drink," I heard Stephanie say and my face flushed. "We'll work on her."

When everyone was primed, we headed to the frat party. It was right off campus. The house was pretty much what you'd expect from a house full of guys. An expansive run-down house occupied by a Greek fraternity with bed sheets hang from the balcony. As we got closer, I realized the writing on the sheets were welcoming back the brothers of whatever Greek letters they were.

People were everywhere, crowded in corners, on couches and around the keg. We passed red cups in exchange for a few bucks. The damp air and smells of cigarettes and pot hit me. I was shoulder to shoulder with people and I didn't know a single one except the ones I came with. I grabbed Stephanie's hand, desperate not to lose her, and I followed her into another room where I can breathe. "You OK?" she asked me.

"I'm fine." But I was lying. I wanted to go back to the dorm, curl up in my bed and read a good book. I hated crowds, but I square my shoulders. I didn't want to be a bore.

"Stephanie, who is that?" I motioned toward a guy talking to Dave.

"That's Will. He is Dave's roommate, a sophomore." I felt instantly attracted to Will. He reminded me of the guys who vacation in Beacon. Stephanie suddenly perked up, "You like him?" Her eyes got wide and excited. I thought back to my breakup with Ben, my kiss with Tyler, and losing my virginity to Michael and I thought, why not? What have you got to lose Anni?

"Introduce me." I said. "Wait! No!" Stephanie handed me a red cup. "Here", she said. I looked at the cup, took a sniff of the beer and put it to my mouth for a tiny sip. I looked at Stephanie and she nodded an approval. I tried not to think of the taste and quickly drank the remaining beer, twisting my face in protest of the taste. "Liquid courage," Stephanie proclaimed, and she clapped her hands. "YES! Anni! You're a rock star." She handed me another beer. I chug that one too, surprised at how easily I caved to this new freedom. My parents weren't here to be disappointed in me, or lecture me and I didn't have to drive anywhere.

"That wasn't bad!" I said, surprised. Stephanie looked so excited that she didn't have to waste her energy on corrupting me. She took my hand and dragged me through a crowd. The floor was sticky, and I worried about getting cigarette burns on my clothes as I brush by people standing close together. My head feels a little woozy and I can feel my body loosen up.

"Anni, this is Will. Will, this is Anni". Stephanie said. Will smiled at me and my heart does some kind of flutter thing. I was feeling the buzz from the first two beers I've ever consumed, aware it went straight to my brain.

"Nice to meet you, Anni." Will said as he shook my hand. "Do you need a beer refill?"

"Uh, no... no, thank you!" I felt out of place and my head was spinning.

"Is this your first year here?" Will asked.

"Yeah, this is kind of my first beer too, so excuse me if I seem... stupid." Will chuckled. He quickly turned his back to another guy walking past who pat him on the shoulder.

"Hey, Bro! How's it been?" They do a half hug, half back pat.

I stood there for a minute feeling awkward, but Will has moved on. I turned to head back to Stephanie who has left me to fend for myself and stumble into people I don't know. I made my way through a crowd of football players.

"Where's Will?" Stephanie asked.

"That didn't go well."

"Nonsense," Stephanie said, "I saw him eying you up."

I shrugged my shoulders. Anni handed me another beer, and I took small sips, deciding I hate the taste. "It's an acquired taste," Sarah used to say, "You get used to it."

"Hey, Miss I-don't-drink!" Dave teased. He stood shoulder to shoulder with Sarah and me.

"You should have seen her!" Stephanie chimed, "trying to get Will's attention."

"Stephanie!" I protested.

"Will, huh?" Dave teased. "All the girls like Will." My heart deflated, he is probably taken or worse, he's like Michael. The room spun as Dave was talking and I realized this is what being drunk feels like. I kind of liked it. Dave put his arm around me in a friendly gesture and we chatted about majors and classes. As he talked, I found it difficult to concentrate, his words were getting farther and farther away.

"Will!" Dave grabbed his shirt as he squeezed through the crowd. "Have you met Anni?"

"Yeah, hey!" he smiled. "Can I get you another beer?" Will was so smooth, making his way around the crowd, clearly popular with everyone. His words flowed out of his mouth like butter.

I wave my arms in front of me, "No, no, no!" I slurred.

"Oh my God, she's so drunk," I heard Stephanie say.

"So, where are you from, Anni?" Will asked.

"I'm from Beacon," I try to concentrate on each word. Will's face become blurry.

"Oh, cool, I've been to Beacon. Senior Week! Class of 95! Good times," he said. Locals really hated Senior Week. Invasion of high school graduates, unsupervised, drinking, destroying properties, fights.

"Will! Shots!" I heard a tall blond girl call from the make-shift bar. Will headed towards the blond, embracing her. I hid my disappointment. I wondered if that was his girlfriend.

"Anni, shots?" Will yelled back.

"Oh, God no!" Will points at me, "talk later?" he asked. I shrugged. The room spun and my stomach didn't feel that great. Sarah always told me it was worth it. I was not so sure.

"The room is..." I couldn't think of the word, so I motion my finger around in a rotation, trying to hold myself steady.

"Yeah, that happens," Dave laughed. I looked at him and his face looked fuzzy. I squinted to stop the double vision.

"Here, drink water," Stephanie said. She handed me a bottle. I wished I could make the spinning stop.

"Anni," I heard someone say. I couldn't make out the voice but it sounded so far away. I looked at Will's face in front of me, smiling, but his voice is so distant. "You OK, Anni?" he asked. I couldn't think, my brain felt disconnected, everything was spinning and my senses were deceiving me.

"She's going to be sick," I heard someone say. The next thing I remembered was leaning over a bush outside pouring out the contents of my stomach with every violent thrust of my body. I felt a hand on my back, holding my hair in a ponytail. I wiped my face with the sleeve of my shirt and rolled over into the grass. I panicked seeing Will kneeling next to me.

"Better?" I nodded and closed my eyes. "Come on, I'll walk

you back to the dorm." Will lifted me up off the ground with his hands under my armpits. I made a deal with God; I will never do this again if he took away the spinning.

It was dark and quiet on the way back to campus. It was a cool night, and I felt cold and clammy. I stopped on the way to vomit once again into a trashcan while Will, my new crush, rubbed my back. I assumed my chances with him were dead on arrival after this display of inexperience. A random bench appeared on the path and I decided I need to lie down. I had to stop this spinning. Will sat next to me.

"Is it always like this?" I mumbled.

"No," he smirked. "You just went a little crazy. You have to start slow." I laughed with him and at myself.

"I'm so embarrassed," I slurred.

"Happens to all of us," he said, rubbing my hair. I felt myself falling asleep on the bench. In the distance I heard people walking toward us. I stayed still hoping they didn't stop and notice me.

"Sit up, campus security," he said.

"I can't get arrested, my mother will kill me," I said desperately.

"Don't worry, you're not getting arrested." The security guards walked past us and I sit upright, careful not to draw any attention to myself in this state.

"See, you're good," he said. "Let's go." Will stood up and held his hand out to pull me to a standing position, which was much more difficult than I anticipated. I stumbled into him and he put his hands around my arms, leading me down toward the entrance of the dorm.

"Give me your key," he said as we arrive at the door to my room.

"Stephanie has it," I felt defeated, as I slid down the wall and sat on the floor in the hall. Will sat next to me and I leaned into him and passed out.

"Oh my God, Anni," Stephanie said. She unlocked the door. I'm not sure how much time has passed since I have been sitting here. She helped me to my feet and into our room and I banged my knee on the frame as I climbed into bed.

"Feel better," Will said as he turned to leave the room. "Thank you," I slurred in my sleep. The room rotated as I drifted off, and I prayed tomorrow had mercy on me.

Chapter 19: College

Anni

I took in the vast campus spread before me on my way to class. The new buildings mixed in with the old. The library to the right where I would spend many nights researching and studying for exams. The gymnasium was to my left which I imagined loud basketball games and the squeaking of sneakers and thunderous cheering of the crowds.

My backpack pulled down on my shoulders with books and binders and notebooks ready to be studied and critiqued. My stomach felt twisted as I walked towards the science building in anticipation of what will be required of me this semester. Tests, research papers, projects, late night study sessions. The magnitude of the knowledge that surrounded me made my brain thirsty for learning.

Beacon Prep was a small school where you knew everyone. A small one-story school building with teachers who were on a first name basis with your parents. That's just the community it was. I felt so far away from home here, so out of my element. Amazing buildings, a campus that stretched beyond my vision, thousands of students walking around, none of whom were familiar. I wondered if I'd run into Ryan again. He saved me the night I ran into Michael.

My heart sank. Michael. I've only thought about him a few times, distracted by the newness of the college and new friends and a fresh pool of great-looking guys.

"Hey," I heard from across the walkway on my way to class. I turned around, and I saw Will running to catch up with me. My first thought was to hide behind a tree. I cringe with embarrassment.

"Hey!" he said again, slightly out of breath. "Anni." He held out his hand. "We met the other night at the party." My chest tightened as I realized I don't quite have all the details about what happened that night. Was I so out of it Will thought I wouldn't remember him at all? Would I remember him if I hadn't already noticed him when I was sober? Oh my God, did Will and I.....?

"I'm Will, Dave's roommate." There was an awkward silence where I thought I was supposed to say something.
"I'm sorry about that," I apologized. "I just…" he interrupted me with a wave of his hand.
"Where are you heading?"
"Science building," I said.
"Cool. Cool. How about lunch? Meet me in the cafeteria in South?"

"Uh, sure. Sounds good." I was grateful he doesn't bring up the whole vomiting incident the day before classes started. That was embarrassing enough.

I entered the science building and looked around at the expansive lobby. The building was obviously new and state-of-the art. I found my classroom, A6, and took a seat at a long black lab table. I did not know a single person in class. The shelves around the classroom were lined with microscopes, goggles, skeleton models. The professor handed us a 24 page syllabus. I flipped through it and bit my lip.

"Tonight you will read Chapter 1-4." She said. I browsed through the textbook and see Chapters 1-4 is 117 pages long. Some pages included pictures and graphs, but I swallowed hard. In high school it would take us a month to finish 4 chapters, maybe longer.

The sky was gray and the air warm as I walked to the cafeteria in South after my Chem Lab. I looked around, but I didn't see Will anywhere. I sat on the bench outside the cafeteria hoping that he showed soon.

"Anni," he said, "you made it. How was Chem?"

"Electron configurations in atomic energy levels, anyone?" I said.

"Ugh, no thank you!"

"What class did you have?" I asked.

"Statistics, Standard deviation? Normal Bell distribution?"

"Ew."

We make our way through the cafeteria line, and I took a turkey sandwich and a bag of chips and a soda. The cashier swiped my card, and we settled at a table by the window overlooking the park across the street.

"Well, you look much better than when I left you the other night." I felt my face become hot.

"It was the first time I had a drink," I explained. "I am so embarrassed."

"Don't be. I could tell you stories upon stories."

"I was always the designated sober friend. My friend Sarah likes to party. I guess I am kind of a drag." Will smiled and my heartbeat quickened. I remembered Will making his way around the crowd so smooth and lively, as if it were his own party. He seemed liked by everyone. I wondered why he was here with me, or why he left the party to take me back to my dorm.

"I'm sorry you had to leave the party."

"It was my choice," he shrugged. "I've been in your position before, and I wanted to be sure you made it back safely."

"That was kind," I said, thankfully.

"So, what's it like living in Beacon all year?" *I dreaded this question, and I got asked it a lot.*

"In the winter its kind of boring, quiet, just a few people, blinking traffic lights." The blinking traffic lights was definitely a bonus, though. Locals looked forward to driving through the island without stopping every block for a red light.

"Hey, Will," a small blond girl said, sitting at the table next to us. He nodded to her. I got slightly jealous.

"I think it would be neat to have the island all to yourself," he said, not giving her much interaction. I liked that.

"Yeah." But inside I was rolling my eyes. Such a typical conversation. Oh my God, you're from Beacon. That's all I ever heard after people asked where I was from.

"I can't believe you grew up in Beacon and never partied!"

"Well, I've been to parties, I just..." my voice trailed. Why does everyone make me feel so guilty for not getting drunk. "I just choose to be sober."

"That's cool," he said, smiling.

"After last week though, I don't know if I will ever drink again."

"Well, you just went a little crazy," he said, smiling. "Stick with me, I'll show you how."

"OK."

"So, any boyfriend back in Beacon missing you, Anni?" he asked. Smooth. I looked down at my fingernails and pushed a cuticle back.

"No, no one is missing me anywhere," I said. Will smiled. "How about you?"

"No," he looked around the room like he was searching for someone. "I'm kind of coming off a bad breakup." His voice cracked, and he cleared his throat. I bit my lip and imagined myself as a rebound girl, one to make him feel better about getting his heart broken. I guess I was kind of on a rebound myself ever since Michael disappeared, but by social definition, it wasn't really a break up.

Will checked his watch and stood. We threw our trash out and placed the trays on top of the trash can. I took one last sip of my soda and tossed it in the bin. I felt grateful he has a class because I wasn't sure where this would go after lunch. We walked out of the building and it drizzled.

"I'll talk to you later, Anni. Thanks for having lunch with me."

"Thanks for inviting me." I watched him hold his backpack over his head and run across campus.

"Anni, I think I'm falling for you," Will said as we walk to school one morning. I stopped and look at his face, his bright green eyes and short, dark blond hair, just a highlight of red. I had to look up as he was taller than me, thin and somewhat lanky.

"Really?" I felt caught off guard.

"Don't you feel it too?" he asked. He stepped closer.

"Yes," I said, locking eyes with him.

Until now, Will had not acted like he was interested in me, other than a friend. I had wondered why he didn't kiss me or take advantage of the times he walked me home from parties after I drank too much beer. There had only been lunch dates and walking to class and hanging out. I thought we were destined to be friends. Maybe it was because of his break-up. He seemed so cool and popular around campus I felt silly thinking he would be interested in me.

I had been heartbroken over Ben several years back, and Michael, well, where was Michael? He disappeared and left me torn apart with a giant gaping hole in my heart. I wanted someone to really love me. I wanted a guy to ask me to be his girlfriend and tell me he loved me and take me on dates. I wanted him to introduce me to his parents and his friends and call me every night to say "I love you".

But what about Michael? Is he coming back for me? What if I give myself to Will and Michael changes his mind? He said he wanted to marry me and I knew he would come back one day. I thought about that night in my room and how much love I felt. When he left, I knew he was mine forever. I needed to just be patient and wait. But I did have feelings for Will. Can you love someone and have a relationship with someone else? And, how can I fall in love with Will when Michael owns my heart?

I smiled at Will to let him know I was feeling it too. I put my hand out for him to hold and we walked to class. We walked down the hill towards the science building and before turning to leave, Will took my face in his hands and kissed my lips. My body tingled. "I can't wait to see you later." He said. He smiled before he turned and walked to his class.

I stood with my feet frozen to the ground as I watched him

disappear into the building. My hands touched my lips. The warmth of his hands on my face lingered. I practically skipped to class, still tingling.

I walked into my dorm room and found Stephanie studying on her bed. I dropped my backpack to the floor and slumped into my desk chair.

"Ugh, Calculus!" she groaned.

"Ugh, Chemistry!" I groaned back.

"So, Will kissed me." She jumped up to her knees in her loft bed, nearly hitting her head on the ceiling.

"I knew it!" she yelled.

"Knew what?"

"I knew he liked you, Anni."

"How did you know?" I asked. I tossed a pillow at her.

"Let's see, he walks you home from parties, he asks you to lunch, he walks you to your classes, you hang out in his room."

"But I figured he liked me as a friend, why wouldn't he make a move?"

"Some guys are descent." She said. I thought Michael was descent. I waited and waited for him, clinging to all attention I could get. "So, how was it?" She asked, sitting on the edge of her bed. I took a moment to bring myself back to the present. Thoughts of Michael kept interrupting my life.

"Nice."

"Nice?"

"Well, it was just a kiss, in the middle of campus.".

"That's not a kiss, that's a declaration," she said.

"A declaration?"

"Yes, Anni, he likes you! He kissed you in front of people." She explained. I shrugged. It reminded me of Ben kissing me many years ago at the Homecoming bonfire. Getting caught by a teacher, seeing my classmates walk by. I guess it was a declaration. Will didn't care who saw us kiss.

"But, he seems so.. popular." I said.

"Anni, you underestimate yourself." Stephanie jumped off her bed and put her hands on my shoulders pushing me towards the mirror. "Look at you." I looked at me. "You are gorgeous, you are hot, you are super smart. You're a respectable, beautiful, likable girl." She hugged me.

"Stop being so hard on yourself," she added. I loved her and I loved that she was so much like Sarah.

"Thank you." Her words humbled me.

"I am going home this weekend," she winked. My heart skipped a beat. I knew that was a hint for Will and I to be alone for the weekend in our dorm. But, I haven't given that any thought. Being intimate and alone with Will. How could I ever be with someone intimately after Michael? Would I always compare each kiss, each touch? Would anyone ever be able to live up to him? I don't know if I was ready to sleep with Will when I couldn't get Michael out of my heart or my head.

"Oh, no, I can't." I looked down at the floor.

"Yes, you can." She opened her desk drawer and showed me where she keeps her condoms. "Just in case."

"I don't know," I nervously chewed my fingernail.

"Well, you will know when the time is right," she added.

"I aced my Chemistry test," I said walking home from class Thursday afternoon. Will stops and gave me a high five.

"You are amazing, you know that?"

"Well, I studied hard."

"We should celebrate, tonight." He pulled me close. I wasn't sure what he meant, but I felt my heart pound.

"The football house is having a party," he said, "Should we go?"

"Sure, that sounds fun."

The air was cold and crisp as November rolled in, and I zipped up my coat as we left my dorm. Will held my hand as we left campus up the road towards the football house. It is an old building with a shaky wooden porch that wraps around the house. The football team lived at this house. We walked up the stairs and opened the large front doors where we were met with a cloud of cigarette smoke and a doorman collecting money.

"Will!" he said, hopping off his stool and shaking his hand.

"This is Anni," he said, "This is Greg, We went to high school together."

"Will was our quarterback."

"You don't play anymore?" I asked.

"Nah," he shakes his head, "too much commitment and I probably wouldn't be that good at this level, anyway." Greg handed him two cups, and we made our way through the house to the back. Will filled my cup with beer and I took a small sip, still have not "acquired" to the taste of it. He laughed as my face contorted to the bitterness. A crowd formed around us as people pile into the house. Will turned to say hi to guys, girls hugged him and he engaged in conversations.

"This is my girlfriend, Anni," he would say every once in a while. I'm not sure when we took on these official titles. I think it was just assumed. It surprised me the first time he said it.

"You introduced me as your girlfriend?" I said.

"Is that ok?" he said, "I thought we were, I mean, when I told you..." he stuttered. It is rare I can make someone else nervous, it is usually me who stutters. I leaned over and kissed him.

"Yes, I'll be your girlfriend."

"Oh, thank God," he said smiling and pulling me close.

"Anni, try this," he said, handing me a shot glass.

"Um, no," I protested.

"Come on, you just drink it all at once and let it go down your throat," he explained. I took the small glass from his hand and smelled it.

It burned my nose with it's aroma of cinnamon. The scent reminded me of whatever shots Michael was doing the night of motel hopping. The taste of cinnamon on his tongue. I tried to push down the thoughts of Michael and be present with Will. "It's not bad, I promise."

I tried to put the whole shot in my mouth at once but I only took half. I held it there unable to swallow.

"Swallow it," someone said, looking over Will's shoulder. My mouth was on fire and my eyes watered.

"Swallow it," I heard again. I swallowed it. Will pulled me in towards him.

"Oh my God, Anni, that was awesome!" he said. He hands me the rest of the shot. I had a crowd now. Always entertaining when the rookie did something new.

I tipped the glass to my mouth and took in the rest as my nose burned and my eyes teared. I swallowed it down hard, my face wrinkled in response to the taste. Stephanie would be so proud. Sarah wouldn't even believe me if I told her. I took a sip of the bitter beer to wash down the cinnamon.

"Did you like it?" he asked, putting his arm around my shoulder.

No, not at all. Let's never do that again!" Will smiled and pulled me towards him kissing my forehead.

"I need water." Will and I make our way to the kitchen and he grabs a bottle of water from the refrigerator. I chug half of it, hoping to stave off getting too intoxicated.

"You OK? Any spinning?"

"No. I feel good, just a little buzz." Will and I headed down to the basement which is hot and crowded.

The lights were dim except for some kind of red and green and blue moving lights. There were a few kegs scattered throughout the room, and a few old couches. Couples were making out in the corners and there was a makeshift dance floor where students moved to the loud bass coming from the speakers. The floor was sticky and there was a haze in the air. Will and I made our way over to a group of people.

"Will!" A guy patted his back. There were a few girls who recognized him and I lace my hand in his to claim him.

"This is Anni." He doesn't introduce me as his girlfriend this time, and I wondered if it was because of the girls. Maybe one is his last girlfriend.

"Hey, Anni," said a short dark-haired guy, "I'm John." He put his arm around me. "Where are you from?"

"Beacon," I expected an interrogation. But John doesn't seem to have any connection to Beacon, so he doesn't press on. John was very touchy-feely, and I gave Will a wide-eyed stare. He took notice. He grabbed John's arm and pulled it from around my neck.

"She your girl?" he asked.

"Yeah," Will said confidently, then pecking his lips to mine. He took my hand and we make our way through the crowd.

"Hey," I heard as someone touches my shoulders, " Aren't you in my math class?" I turn to see a girl with shoulder length light blond hair. "Antonia, right?"

"Hi, yeah, Anni," I said.

"Megan," she held her hand out.

"Don't you think Professor Martin is horrible?" she said. My head is slightly fuzzy and Megan sounded like she is far away. I squinted to see her better.

"She is OK, I guess."

"Really? Maybe you can help me sometime."

"Yeah, sure," I said, as I turn towards Will. He pulled my hand, and I followed him.

We passed through the dance floor and I moved my body to the beat of the music. I couldn't make out the song but I felt the rhythm. Will noticed me grooving and stopped and pulled me towards him. He moved with me holding me against him. The room swayed, and I lost my balance. Will caught me and put his hands on my waist, pulling my pelvis closer to his. My arms wrapped around his shoulders and he kissed me. His hands moved up my back as he opened his mouth, our bodies still moving to the music. He moved his kisses down my neck.

"Want to get out of here?" he asked.

"Yeah," my breathing hitched, and I felt my knees go weak. Was this lust? I had never felt that before. Did alcohol do that?

Will and I walked out the front door of the football house into the cold air. It felt so good on my skin after being in the hot basement. I pulled my coat on and we walked down the road back towards campus. I stumbled on a crack in the sidewalk and Will grabbed my arm.

"Anni, we are off campus, don't get us arrested."

The cold air was sobering, and the spinning stopped. I felt just enough buzz.

"Where's Stephanie?" he said.

"Went home for the weekend."

"What? When were you going to mention that," he said, laughing and grabbing me around the waist. He kissed my lips, and we continued walking back.

I fumble to get my key in the door of my room, as Will stood behind me kissing my neck. His touch sent sparks straight to my belly. We were both feeling the effects of shots and beer and smelling of cigarettes and marijuana. Will plopped down on my bed next to me. My head was woozy, but I didn't think I drank that much. Maybe it was the shots. At least there was no spinning. With Stephanie gone, I had no one to sit in the bathroom with me. I put on a CD to break the silence as the Red Hot Chili Peppers played softly in the background. Stephanie's string of lights provided just enough light for me to get back to my bed without tripping.

I climbed up into my bed and Will's face had a look of longing, touching my face and brushing through my hair with his fingers. He tipped my head back, kissed my lips, and I reminded myself to breathe.

Will's the small lights illuminated face, and he looked incredibly hot wearing a thin sweater and a pair of dark jeans with a belt.

"Is this a teddy bear?" he said, pulling my stuffed bear out from under him.

I grabbed it out of his hands, "That's Mr. Teddy." I threw Mr. Teddy down the end of the bed.

His kisses grew more urgent, and he pulled my body into his. I felt his erection against me. I met his urgency and his breathing became louder. He kissed my neck, and his hands touched my skin under my shirt, proceeding with extreme caution as he gazed into my eyes to read my thoughts.

"Do you want me?" he asked, breathing heavily.

"Yes," I whispered, as my chest rises and falls rapidly. He pulled my shirt over my head and ran his fingers along the outline of my bra, making his way to the back and unclasping it with one movement of his fingers. A thought of Michael pops in my head and I try to push it down. I wasn't ready that night, even though it was amazing. But this is different, expected, raw desire, lust.

I pulled his shirt over his head, amazed by my courage to take initiative. I ran my hands down his bare chest, his skin warm and sensitive to my touch. Reaching down, I grabbed his erection through his jeans, and he took a sharp breath. I fumbled with his belt buckle and then pulled the button open and slide them off. My nerves were tingling, and I shook with anticipation.

"Oh my fucking God, Anni," he said, breathless. He slipped off my jeans and underwear and we laid naked, his hands caressing my bare breasts. He slid them down my body and I held my breath as he reached between my legs. I gasped in surprise. "Yeah, Anni," he breathed in my ear.

My body was alive with sensation and excitement and I put my hand over his urging him to continue. "Don't stop," I begged, moving my hips in response. A low groan escaped from my throat.

"Come on, Anni," he whispered, his breath hot on my skin. I felt an unfamiliar warm sensation building and finally my body trembled as I came undone. We locked his eyes, and I'm sure he realized it was the first time I'd experienced that.

He grabbed a condom he had put under my pillow. I thought of the gold foil condoms Michael had, and I tried to push down those thoughts.

Will slowly pushed into me. I tipped my body up to meet him and met his movements, as I grabbed around his chest. He glistened with sweat. Our bodies moved together, and I grab a fistful of pink comforter. Will leaned down to kiss me, his breath shallow and quick as he moved faster.

"Anni," he say, panting for air, and then collapses on top of me, satisfied. "Fuck." He kissed my neck as he trembles. His limp body weighed down on me and I wrapped my arms and legs around him, trying to slow my breath.

"You are so... fucking beautiful, you know that?" he asked, rolling on his side. He puts my hand up against his chest and I felt his heart pounding.

"That was amazing," I said. "I didn't know my body could respond like that." I took deeps breaths to slow my pounding heart as I lay my head on his chest.

"Anni, you weren't a virgin, were you?" he said, his eyes wide with concern.

"No, but, just... I don't know." I looked up at the ceiling and I couldn't help but remember the pain of my first time. The fear of what was happening. I couldn't concentrate on what my body wanted. I didn't even know that is what I wanted. I was grateful he asked no more questions. I felt guilty for thinking about Michael right now but, then again, if this had been my first time, could I have enjoyed it this much? I could at least thank Michael for that.

Will pulled me close and kissed my lips, wrapping his naked body around mine.

"You're so perfect, Anni," I smiled, but thought about "Perfect Anni". "You don't have to be so fucking perfect," I heard Michael's voice say in my head. I looked at Will and felt a pang of guilt knowing I wouldn't give him all of me. When Michael comes back, I'll break Will's heart.

Chapter 20: Present

Anni

"Anni, it's only for 4 days," Jack assures me, as I sit on the bottom step of the staircase. Truthfully, I don't mind his business trips all that much. It does not differ from when Jack is home. We chat mostly by text messages and phone calls. I still need to get the kids dressed and ready for school, and run them to their practices and games, and cook dinner and straighten up before Jack gets home late every evening. Jack kisses my cheek and then he carries his bag to the airport shuttle.

"You'll be fine, Anni."

"I know," I watch the car pull away. Someday I can join Jack on his trips. I can lie on the beach and relax while he spends all day at dull medical conferences and then join him and his colleagues for dinner and drinks. But, that is not a possibility now.

I think about all the conferences I missed out on in the past 15 years. After graduate school I had a promising career in psychology. Perhaps I would present new research on the neurobiological process involved in addictive personality types or behavioral theories on anxiety and depression. Maybe I would discuss my new publication in the Psychology Today Journal. I mourned the death of my career years ago when Maisie was born. I loved her so much that I couldn't have someone else raise her or miss all her milestones.

In a few hours the children will arrive home from school and ask when their Dad is coming home and I will have to remind them Dad is away at a conference. It will disappoint Ricky, Jack will miss his soccer game once again. Maisie and Ivy will not care so much and I must help Ivy with her math homework. They will all climb in my bed at night and claim a spot, and I will move to the couch at some point, after a struggle to maintain my space. I secretly adore all of my children falling asleep in the bed together. I look at all their sleeping faces and my heart melts with love. It is a peaceful moment in this chaotic life.

The airport shuttle pulls away and I close the door. I walk back to the kitchen, grab a trash bag and begin my way around the kitchen. I throw away food wrappers, and water bottles and old school work. I put away cereal boxes and wipe down the countertops. As I sit down on the couch and flick on the TV, my phone buzzes with a FaceBook message.

"Anni, meet me at Pizza Palace," Michael writes.

"No," I immediately reply. Unfriending Michael apparently doesn't block him from sending me messages. *I guess I could technically block him for good. Technically.*

"Anni, it's just pizza." Why does he always seem to make question my thoughts. I know it's only pizza, but it's Pizza Palace. Michael knows what he is doing.

"OK," I say with instant regret. *Still his puppet, Anni.*

"I knew it" he texts back, adding a wink emoji. I throw my phone down on the couch, angry he knows he can still control me. I'm angry at myself allowing it.

The drive into Beacon always makes me restless. I travel the boulevard, cutting through the wetlands. The marsh and all of its water trails are where we rode jet skis, or cast our crab traps, or docked our kayaks. I approach the bridge over the bay leading into town. Some days the drawbridge would go up, stopping traffic to allow for tall boats to pass underneath. Always, when you were in a hurry. The drive in is different now. The landscape of the island has changed from small shops and motels to over-sized restaurants, and homes, and condos.

I roll the windows down in my minivan and smell the salt air. The island is desolate on a weekday in late September, but the weather remains warm and humid. I pull into a parking spot outside of Pizza Palace and check my car for quarters for the parking meter, before realizing it is after Labor Day and you no longer have to pay.

Pizza Palace is overlooks the beach, and the sound of waves crashing is carried on the wind and sounds thunderous and peaceful. The last time I spent a peaceful moment on the beach may have been about 20 years ago when I could take a book and my beach chair to the water's edge just close enough that the breaking waves reached my feet before returning to the sea.

I could finish a whole novel in one day when I went to the beach alone. If I had my beach chair in the car, I would have loved to go down to the beach after lunch. Trips to beach now includes umbrellas, beach bags and coolers, sandy kids and beach toys. Though I haven't been to the beach in this town in 20 years. Gone are the days I can relax with a novel, close my eyes and listen to the pounding of the ocean.

My thoughts interrupted by the realization of what I am doing, visiting Michael while Jack is away. The betrayal, the sneaking and the lying is becoming too much for me. I wonder if there is a point where I will say no. I let that sink in for a minute, because I hope that point is coming. Michael is ma-nipulative, I know. Feelings of guilt swirl in the pit of my stom-ach. I think of the messages I found on Jack's phone years ago from a female colleague that made me suspicious. Jack swore it was nothing, and I believed him because I trusted him. Now and then I think about those messages and wonder what else I don't know about Jack. But this has to end with Michael sometime. Maybe today.

I look at Pizza Palace, happy it is still here after all this time.

Many businesses did not make it through the new millennium on Beacon. I feel nostalgic being back here and I feel a lump form in my throat thinking of the last time I was here, the last night I saw Michael before going away to college. The beach, the lifeguard boat, the taste of beer on Michael's lips.

"Anni, hi," Michael says. He takes my hand and kisses my cheek. I follow him to a table outside, facing the ocean. There is a cool, ocean mist that touches my skin. We take a seat at a table and the waitress brings over some menus and Michael and I sit in silence for what seems like an hour. Intrusive thoughts of Jack keep entering my head, and I imagine how it would feel to know Jack is having lunch with someone he once cared so deeply.

"Do you still like mushrooms on your pizza?" he says. Michael hates mushrooms, and he always said "Anni, mushrooms on pizza is not right."

"Yes, I do still like mushrooms on my pizza." I admit.

"I'm glad you're here," Michael says. I smile, unsure of how to respond. We still have not spoken of the events that lead to the end of our relationship or even any memories of the past. I wonder whether I imagined all the drama that surrounded our friendship and maybe Michael doesn't remember it the way I do.

It's been 20 years. Are my memories all false, distorted in my mind by the passing of time? But, I fear that I can't ignore it much longer, and I feel a strong urge to rehash the past with Michael. Maybe if I get closure, I can move on. I want to lay it all on the table.

"Isn't this amazing, Anni? You and me, back here in Beacon at Pizza Palace? All that is missing is your purple bikini," Michael's eyes narrow. "You don't still have it do you?" My breathing is shallow and I have an empty feeling in the pit of my stomach. Michael isn't holding anything back. He knows all of my triggers.

"What's wrong?" he says.

"Nothing, Michael, just taking this in, that's all," I answer.

"So, you unfriended me on Facebook the other night."

"Yeah."

"Why would you do that, I thought we had a good time," he says.

"You don't have any boundaries Michael, you never have."

"And yet, here you are, Anni," he smirks, "on your own free will."

"I didn't want the temptation."

"To do what?" he asks, not breaking eye contact with me.

The waitress brings over a bottle of beer for Michael and an ice water for me. I am grateful she interrupted us. Michael and I make small talk about life in the present. I'm finding it difficult to concentrate as all these memories come flooding back. My brain feels foggy and I felt slightly faint.

I grasp at an image of 20-year-old Michael drunk at my doorstep. Anni, I missed you. I feel sick hearing him telling me I am too clingy. Anni, I need some space.

I flashback to Michael in my bedroom that night. Anni, I love you.

I need to leave Pizza Palace.

"Are you OK?" Michael asks.

"Yes, I'll be right back." I get up and place my napkin on the table. I walk to the ladie's room and let the tears flow. Get it together, Anni. I look at myself in the mirror. What are you doing here? I am aware of the pull Michael has on me just as he did two decades ago. This is all your fault, Anni.

Jack would not approve of this lunch date. Would he? I play the scenario in my head as I say "Jack, I had lunch with an old friend today." And Jack would say "Nice." And that would be the end of the conversation. He wouldn't wonder who it was, or where we went.

If it were me, I would analyze every detail of Jack's lunch date. I would want to know what they talked about, what was she wearing, where they went. I would be suspicious of text messages, and phone calls, and meetings. I would check her social media page. Did anyone see them together and speculate he was cheating, or did they think he was having a business luncheon? I would wonder why Jack didn't love me anymore and Jack would try to convince me it was just lunch. Snap out of it, Anni.

I decide to go back and confront Michael. To lay it out and see if we can put the pieces of my memory back together. I want to know if Michael has the same memories and what his perspective is. Psychologists say flashbulb memories occur in a highly charged emotional event. These phenomena sear an image into your brain allowing you to recall it with extraordinary detail. Think of where you were on 9/11. That is a flashbulb memory. I am certain my memory is still accurate.

"Anni, is everything OK?" Michael asks.

"Yes," I lie. I am such a coward.

"You seem nervous."

"I am…. nervous." I admit.

"Why? It's just me," Michael says. But I hardly know this person sitting in front of me. And when I look at him, all I can see is a 21-year-old in a 40 something year old, very attractive man. All I can hear is Michael telling me he loves me and he will marry me. And touching me, laying naked with me, telling me he's getting married. My thoughts become too much and I blurt out.

"Michael, what do you remember?"

"What do you mean? About what?" He cocks his head to the side.

"About us, I mean, things that happened."

"A lot," he says.

"Specifically?" I prompt.

"Specifically, how much I adored you. How you were always different."

I stare at his face while he is speaking and try to put together what he is saying. "Different how?"

"You never cared about what others thought. You had your convictions and stuck with that. You didn't let anyone change you."

"You changed me."

"How?"

I looked down at my lap. I want to say I trusted no one for a really long time. That my 2-year relationship with Will ended because I couldn't get over him. I wanted to tell him I still think about him so often that I feel emotionally unfaithful to my husband. Some nights I have such vivid dreams of this exact moment, or my brain replays memories.

What if the memories are altered each time I dream? What if the dreams and reality are tangled in a new story that never happened? I'm afraid to tell Michael this because I fear his memories are different and I don't want to feel like a fool for carrying this pain around for a quarter of a century. Michael, you were my soulmate. I told myself for years if you walked back into my life, I would leave everything for you. And even on my wedding day, I thought, if you came back I could still leave. I stood on the alter looking at Jack thinking this should be you. And with each child I had it got more and more difficult to imagine myself walking away. I waited years upon years and you never came back and now I have a husband, four children, a dog and a home, you waltz back in.

Well, ok, I contacted you. I have never felt I belonged anywhere else and when you came back for me, I would let you lead me home. And here you are. But I can't say to him, because that isn't why he is here.

"Do you want to take a walk?" he suggests.
"OK," Michael took my hand and I stand up. He doesn't let go as we head down the sidewalk towards the beach. I slip my sandals off and place them by a light pole and we walk along the ocean, both of us trying to figure out what comes next.

This past week I tried to be strong and I couldn't. Just like I always have, I let him in and he controls my thoughts and behaviors and makes me feel things I don't want to feel. I try to find the courage to say what I am feeling.

Let's start off easy, I think. "Michael, do you remember when we met?" I ask.
"Yes, you were playing pinball, I remember. What was that

game called?" He says.

"The Earthquake," I remind him.

"Oh yes, 'Warning, Earthquake!'" he says. We both laugh at the memory and he puts his arm around my shoulder and squeezes, forcing my body into his. I breathe in his smell.. "That was a great summer. I remember being so bored.

My mom gave me $20 and told me to find something to do because I was getting on her nerves. She was so grateful after we met because I would be out of the house a lot. We had so much fun, didn't we Anni?"

"We definitely did," I said. I think of our time laying by the pool talking about parents and Michael would tell me about his friends back home. I would tell him stupid things my brother did to annoy me or how much I disliked cleaning dirty motel rooms. This conversation seems to go ok.

"Until you became friends with Doug and Scott." I joked.

"What about them?" Michael asks.

"Well, they weren't exactly a good influence on you. They kind of took you away." I said, with a chuckle in my voice.

"Oh," was all Michael replied. "We were just different, Anni, that's all."

"Yeah," I resign. It felt like salt in a wound to hear him give up that easily.

Michael smiled at me to break the tension and we continue walking in silence, his arm resting on my shoulder. I allowed myself to enjoy this one moment. We were just different, Anni, that is all, I repeat over and over in my head.

"Do you remember showing up at my room in the middle of the night?" I ask, hesitantly. My stomach knots as I wait for an answer.

"Which time" he smiles that crooked smile, that guilty crooked smile.

"The time you took my virginity," I say.

Michael stops walking and turns. "Oh, that time," he smiles. "How can I forget that time? Yeah, I was crazy about you." My heart sinks thinking about the night he came to Kroy. Doesn't he get it? That destroyed me.

"I was crazy about you, too," I respond.

"Anni, I've remembered that night in your room and the night on the beach every day for the past 20 years. I've had dreams about it, holding you." His eyes soften and he looks at my face. Michael takes my hands in his, facing me so our eyes meet.

I open my mouth to talk but nothing comes out. We stare at each other for a while before continuing to walk, my hand still in his.

"Me too," I pause. "But it was for points, right?" I say, hesitantly, unsure of his reaction.

"Anni, you were not a point." He stops and faces me and puts his hands on my shoulders. "Yes, there were points. It was a stupid guy game. Boredom. But you were not a point. I hope you haven't spent all this time thinking that."

"Actually, I have. You never came back. You didn't answer my calls or answer my letters."

"I couldn't. I hurt you. You wanted more. I didn't want to be selfish anymore."

"You said you would marry me," I say, "I still have the ring."

"What?"

"You gave me a ring. A tin ring. You said someday you would marry me." My eyes burn. "And then you showed up at my dorm and crushed me."

"I'm sorry, Ann. I was stupid."

"Is she still your wife?"

"It's complicated," he says. He pulls me in close and holds me. I want to drain my emotions and let the tears flow, but I keep my composure.

When we walked back to Pizza Palace, I took the car keys out of my purse in anticipation of getting in the car. I wasn't sure how to leave things. I felt some closure, but I guess I can just get on with having seen Michael one last time. I needed to get back to my life with Jack and the kids.

"Can I take you somewhere, Anni," Michael asks.

"That depends where," I reply.

"Get in my car."

"I'll follow you," I say, knowing getting into his car is not a good idea.

"Anni, please, just get in." I sigh, giving in to Michael once more. His convertible is immaculate inside, much different from the french fries on the floor of my minivan, and it smells like Michael. He puts the top down and drives the main street of Beacon.

My brain swirls, overwhelmed by the rush of emotions that come over me. The wind blowing my hair, the warm air on my skin, the terrible music on the radio.

"I can't do this," I blurt, "take me back to my car, please."

"Anni, come on, it's just memories, it's nice," he says.

A dizzy feeling comes over me as my stomach turns. Michael parks down at the inlet where we used to climb the jetty and listen to the band far in the distance. I can still hear the awful rap music in the Jeep, the scent of his cologne, the warm feeling leaning against him watching the stars. The smell of the sea and the salt air on my face. I remember all those things like they were yesterday.

"Remember when I brought you here after you put the letter on my seat?" he asks. I look at him, a 40-something year old man, and my mind returns to the present. To Jack.

"Yes." I swallow hard.

"I wanted to kiss you that night," he admits. I look in his direction and he smiles. "But I was scared."

"You were scared?" I try to avoid engaging in this trip down memory lane, but he pulls me in. I can feel my blood pump through my temples.

"Yeah, you made me so nervous," he says, "I remember not wanting to do something that would make you leave."

"I remember trying to do things I didn't want to do to make you stay," I admit. Michael looks in my eyes and I try to compose myself.

"I want to kiss you now," he says, catching me off guard.

"I know."

I know Michael. Even after two decades, I know Michael. He is playing the only way he knows how, grabbing my emotions, promising me things he can't give. But he doesn't kiss me, even though I want him to. Even though I have waited 20 years for this.

"Take me back," I ask of him. He nods silently realizing this is too much. He puts his hand over mine and we drive back to my car at Pizza Palace.

"Anni, come up to the room with me," Michael blurts.
"Um, no Michael. That is a terrible idea." I at least have the courage to know that.
"Why?"
"Because I already feel guilty about being here while my husband is out of town. Or in town. And because I don't trust myself. Or you. And because you are married. And I'm not even sure what I am doing here." I say. Michael takes a step towards me and pulls me close to him.
"OK," he says.

I am surprised at how disappointed I feel that Michael doesn't press me any further. And then he adds, "You always do the right thing." He kisses my cheek, and he is gone. I feel resentment cut me, but I know this is not over yet. Michael cannot leave me standing in the middle of Beacon. A familiar pain fills me once more as if a wrinkle in my life brought my past and present together.

My phone buzzes and I pull it from my purse. "Landed," is the text message I get from Jack. The message jolts me back to reality. I never told Jack about the coffee meeting, or the tavern and it's unlikely I will mention this lunch meeting. I am uncomfortable with the deception that has crept into my marriage.

In 17 years I have never lied or withheld information from Jack. Though our relationship has been lacking romance and passion for some time now, I have always remained loyal. If Jack looked through my phone or social media or hired someone to track me, I would check out squeaky clean without so much as an ounce of suspicion. Until now.

I get into my van and plug my phone into the charger, resting my head back on the seat. Hot tears fill my eyes and I wipe them away. I pick up the phone and dial Jack's number.

"Anni," Jack answers.

"Jack, I'm sorry to bother you but would it be fine if I went to the mountains with some girlfriends next weekend. I meant to ask you sooner, I mean, I asked you sooner but I need to give the girls an answer."

"Sure, Anni. I'm sure we can make it work. I hate to run, Anni, but I have to catch the hotel shuttle. Please tell the kids I said hi."

"Thank you, Jack."

Chapter 21: College

Michael

"**I** should probably go home for Christmas" Doug said. Doug had been staying in my basement for a few weeks after a falling out with his mother. Doug was lazy and has no credible employment or any motivation to do anything. This presented a problem at home and the old lady kicked him out. Danielle had been on my case about getting rid of him and she encouraged him to move back home on the island.

"I can get you to the bus station on Wednesday," I suggested. Doug rolled his eyes. I knew he didn't have any money for a bus ticket anyway.

"Anni," I said.

"What?" Doug asked, confused.

"Anni goes to college nearby, I'm sure she is going home for the holidays."

"Yeah, Michael, the girl from the motel? Not a good idea."

"Well, then I'll give you bus money," I offered.

"Fine, call her."

I wasn't sure if Anni would talk to me anyway. Ever since I met Danielle, I had been avoiding all of Anni's phone calls and letters. Anni called my parents' house and my father told her I moved and gave no forwarding information.

The last time we were together was pretty amazing. I wasn't

planning on taking her virginity, but that bikini she wore to the beach was stuck in my head. Even now I could see her in it. That night I was just planning on kissing, seeing where it went, but she didn't stop me. When I put my hands up her dress, she seemed willing. I remembered how nervous she was and how her body tensed at first, but she trusted me. She was my soulmate. Even though I miss her, letting her go was the right thing to do.

Underneath a pile of socks in my drawer, I found the letters Anni sent to my parents address several months ago. In one of those letters she had given me her college number begging me to call.

Now I needed a favor.

I dialed her phone number. My palms were sweating and my heart pounded in anticipation of hearing her. Before I could hang up, an unfamiliar voice answers the phone. Anni's roommate. She asked me to hold while she gets Anni.

"Hello?" she said.

"Anni, hi." She didn't respond. "Anni?" I repeated wondering if she was still on the line. After for what seemed like eternity, she spoke.

"Michael? This can't be Michael." I felt the tension in her voice. She wasn't excited to hear from me. I felt foolish now calling her, breaking my silence and asking her for a favor.

Anni

The ringing of the phone distracted me from studying for my chemistry exam. Stephanie jumped from the top of her loft bed as I looked up and followed her with my eyes.

"Anni, the phone is for you," Stephanie handed me the phone and gave me a shrug.

"Hello?"

"Anni, hi." Hearing his voice made me lightheaded and I felt my breathing quicken. I didn't know how to respond. I opened my mouth but words did not come out. Stephanie looked at me, sensing something was wrong.

"Michael? This can't be Michael?" Stephanie cringed and mouthed "Sorry."

"Anni, are you going home this weekend? I have a friend who needs a ride." Michael lived about 20 minutes from the University. Funny, considering we had always been hours apart, and now we were so close but no contact. I scratched my head and I must have made a face, because Stephanie put her hands over her face to stifle a sound.

"I'm sorry, Michael. What?" I said. My face flushed and I tried to understand correctly what I was hearing.

"You disappeared and then months later call my dorm and…" Stephanie fist pumped my lecture.

"OK," he interrupted, "Let's start over. Anni, how are you? How's college?" I opened my mouth again to talk, but I have nothing.

"Anni, I'm sorry. I want to see you, I have to tell you something. And I miss you."

"I miss you too," I blurted. Stephanie waved her hands in the air in protest.

"So, are you going home? Doug really needs a ride." Oh, not Doug. I don't know how I would last hours in the car with him. But I really wanted to see Michael.

"Yes Michael, I am going home this weekend."

"Anni, Doug and I will be there Thursday evening. You sure you don't mind? I can't wait to see you."

"I'm not leaving until Friday."

"I know, we'll go out. See you then?"

"I, uh, I guess." I had lost control of myself. Michael was coming here.

I looked at the phone receiver in disbelief after Michael hung up. I felt my face flush and tears welled in my eyes. I slid down the wall to the floor and put my head between my knees and cried. Stephanie sat next to me and puts her arm around me.

"That was Michael." I said. Stephanie laughs and makes me laugh.

"I figured."

"I don't really want to see him."

"I understand."

"But I do. What if he has reconsidered? What if he really loves me and wants to tell me so?" I sat up straight. "He said he has something to tell me," I said.

I tried to imagine what Michael could possibly have to tell me after all this time. He's sorry? He's in love with me? He's sick? Oh no, please do not let him be sick.

"No, Anni. Let it go. Hasn't he already told you he loves you? When you love someone, you don't let them get away." I got annoyed with her. She doesn't know anything about us. Maybe Michael had realized he couldn't let me get away.

"What will I tell Will?" Stephanie helped me come up with a plan. Michael and his friend would tell the staff they are staying with David and Will. They would sign into their room for the night and come up to our room.

"But wait, Will will know."

"Anni, it will be fine. Will won't even know he is here. And either nothing will happen and you'll have nothing to tell Will, or Michael will tell you he loves you and you'll have to let Will go anyway."

"God, Stephanie, just blurt it all out." I laughed until I started to cry.

"No, Anni, don't." She wiped my tears.

"Well, you didn't lie, Michael. You came to visit me at college," I said sarcastically when he arrived. Michael kissed my cheek and gave me a faint hug like he was unsure how I was going to receive him. He held me out and looked at me and smiled and my heart melted like butter.

It was so surprising seeing Michael here in my dorm room. My emotions were all over the place. I felt apprehensive, but my heart wanted to throw itself at him. I was moving on, though I thought about Michael often, especially when I tried to study in the quiet library and memories would distract me.

"College girl," he pulled me in close and kissed my head.

"This is my roommate, Stephanie," I said. Michael gave her a little wave. Stephanie eyed him up suspiciously.

"Anni, you remember my friend Doug?" I did remember Doug, holding my hand, making Michael furious that night on the beach.

I remembered Doug trying to make Michael say I was his girl and he wouldn't say it. I always blamed Doug for taking Michael away from me. He and Scott and Doug, scoping the island for girls, drinking and smoking pot. Doug kissed me that night while Michael seethed with jealousy. The memory actually made me smile. Jealous Michael.

"Thanks for giving me a ride home tomorrow, Anni." I shrugged my shoulders, hoping he slept most of the way so I wouldn't have to talk to him.

Michael looked around my dorm room, at pictures of my friends. New pictures added of people I have met. He picked up a picture of me holding a red cup.

"Water?"

"Beer," I flatly reply. He glanced at Stephanie who gave him an innocent look.

"You don't drink beer." He nudged my arm.

"She does now," Stephanie chimed in.

"I'm jealous," he said. "I bet you're fun when you're drunk, Anni".

"Oh, she IS!" Stephanie said. I rolled my eyes. I thought of all the times she has held my hair back in the past few months. Michael pulled me in for a one-armed hug and kissed my hair.

"Who's this?" he pointed at a picture of me and Will.

"My boyfriend." Michael frowns.

"Where's my picture?" he asked.

"In the drawer," Stephanie answered. I glanced at her with an evil eye. You had to admire her tenacity for coming to my defense.

"What? Why?" he asked. I gave him a sideways look. He knew why.

Michael jumped up on my loft bed.

"So, you like music and beer?" Stephanie asked Doug.

"Yeah, what's the plan?" Doug asked, looking to maximize his time at Kroy.

"Parties, kegs," she answered.

"Let's go," Michael said.

This felt so awkward, partying with Michael at college. But we still needed to talk, I can't let myself be compromised with alcohol. We walked across campus to a house with a crowd gathering on the front porch. The doorman frantically collected money trying to rush everyone in as quickly as possible to avoid the police catching on.

"Are you 21," he asked us.

"Yeah," Stephanie lied.

"OK, go in." Without asking for proof, he hands us a cup.

Michael looked around the dark basement, which was wall to wall with college students. Techno music blared so loud the beat felt like it was in your throat. A strobe light hung in the corner next to a neon Budweiser sign.

Doug returned with filled beers and handed them out. I took a sip and my face curls from the bitterness. Michael started at me trying to hide his expression.

"Anni, drink up my girl!" he said, tipping my cup back. Doug peered around the room, looking out of his element. I supposed the Beacon local skit could work on some of these girls, though. When I first got here, people were intrigued to hear about what it was like to live there. Stephanie worked herself around the room socializing with classmates and friends and I caught a glimpse of her smoking a joint.

Doug spotted her from across the room and walked in her direction.

"Where's your boyfriend?" Michael asked.

"I don't know," I answered. I tried to avoid Will tonight and I was guessing he went out with Dave. I really hope he doesn't decide to come to this party. It would be awkward. We usually stick to parties where Will knows the guys who live there. This was Stephanie's crowd.

Michael grabbed me around the waist with one hand, his

beer in the other and pulled my body against his. We swayed to the pounding music and he whispered in my ear, "I missed you, Anni." We needed to talk about this, but my body was feeling loose from the beer.

I glanced across the room and saw Doug holding Stephanie around her waist, talking close to her face. I thought back to that night motel-hopping, Doug leaning in to me so I could smell the beer on his breath. I realized he had ulterior motives, and that night ended with Michael and me making love on the beach under the light of the moon. The second most amazing night of my life.

As I watched them from across the room, Doug leaned in and kissed Stephanie's neck. Predictable.

"Let's go, Anni," Michael said.

"Where?"

"Back to your room." I felt my heart beat faster at the thought of being alone with Michael. Will crept into my mind. *What would become of us?* We made our way through the crowded basement up the stairs and walked back across campus. Michael stopped in front of the library and turns to me.

"I'm sorry, Anni." I turned my head and look at the ground. I don't know what he's sorry for. Leaving me without any good-bye? Crushing me? Breaking my heart in a million pieces? He hugged me tight against him and I felt at home in his arms. He took my hand and we continued walking towards the dorm. My head was slightly woozy and I prayed I didn't run into Will on the way back to the room.

Once back in the dorm, I jumped up in the loft bed next to Michael, our feet dangling off the side. Our bodies were touching and I felt myself starting to relax.

"Look at you. A College girl. I always knew you would do amazing things."

"Yeah, it's fun, and a lot of work."

"If only I could have gotten you drunk before!" he laughed.

"Then what?"

"I don't know." he shrugged. "Maybe you would have loosened

up." My mouth turned down. We both knew it wouldn't have changed anything.

Michael laid down on the bed and pulled me down next to him. I stared at the ceiling, trying to control my breathing, and wondered what was going to happen tonight. I didn't worry about Will because I knew it could be over between us tonight if Michael was ready.

"Michael," I rolled over to face him. " I tried to call you." Michael kissed my forehead and ran his fingers over my jawline. My body relaxed and I felt myself succumbing to his spell once again. Could he be here to stay? Maybe he had realized it was time and my patience has paid off.

"I know," And his lips make their way to mine, touching softly.

"I wrote you letters," my voice cracked.

"I know." And he kissed me again, opening his mouth while pulling my body even closer to him. I met his kiss with equal passion, feeling the anger and insecurities of the past leaving me.

"Michael…." I whispered, pulling away, but he interrupted me.

"Anni, I'm getting married." He turned to face me to see my reaction? What? What did he just say? Don't cry, Anni. But I felt my face getting hot. I felt my eyes beginning to fill. My stomach contracted and I felt like I was going to vomit. I wanted to leave the room, run away somewhere.

My body was paralyzed and my brain was not able to send message to my muscles to move. I curled up in a ball on my bed. I wanted Michael to see the pain he has caused. Michael reached his arms around me and pulled me close into him wrapping his body around mine. I sobbed, as my body shakes out of control.

Michael was quiet. He kissed my head and stroked my hair. My mind wandered to that night in my room and the way Michael touched me and how my body responded to him.

"Anni, say something," he begged. I opened my mouth, but I couldn't speak.

My face was puffy, my eye makeup streaked down my cheeks. I tried to slow my breathing, but I felt like I was hyperventilating. I jumped down from the bed and Michael turned to face me.

"Is she pregnant? Does she know how many partners you've had? Does she know you got drunk and had sex with half the island? You told me you would marry me! You told me I was your girl. You told me that!" I was crying, I was hysterical, I was hurt.

"Anni, no, she isn't pregnant and yes, she knows about my past. I know it's a shock and it's crazy. But life is crazy. I'm sorry." Michael put his arms out to hold me and I shoved him away.

"You're 21 years old. Who gets married at 21!" I yelled. My muscles tighten and my heart pounded a steady rhythm in my head.

'Anni, stop," he pleaded.

"But we were soul mates. You believed that. You said it. I thought you would come back for me. I thought that is why you were here!"

"We were. We are. Anni, you don't understand." he said. I gave in to him as he wrapped his arms around me. His shirt became damp with my tears.

My hysteria was interrupted by a knock at the door. Shit. Please don't be Will. I couldn't ignore it. I was sure he heard me yelling. I wiped my face and looked at Michael. He sat down in the chair by my desk.

I opened the door and Will was there. He smiled and leaned into to kiss me.

"You ok, Anni?" Will must have been confused seeing my face flushed and swollen.

"Yeah, allergies," I sniffled. I gave him a hug and then I opened the door farther so he could see I wasn't alone.

"Oh," Will said, surprised. He checked out Michael and then glanced at me.

"Will, this is my friend Michael. I'm giving his friend a ride home tomorrow, back to the island so he drove him up here."

"Hey" Michael put his hand out to shake Will's. "Nice to meet you, Anni has told me a lot about you." I looked at Will to see if he was buying it. He seemed confused but relaxed a bit.

"Well, I wanted to see if you wanted to come downstairs and hang out, but I see you are busy. Call me later." He kissed my lips and ran his fingers through my hair. "You sure you're ok?" he said as he turned to leave.

I followed Will out into the hallway and closed the door. "Look, Will, this is awkward, but Michael is just, well, a friend. His friend needs a ride back to Beacon tomorrow."

"Anni, it's OK. I believe you. Just that, you look upset."

"No, no, Will. Michael just told me he is getting married and we were just, I was just happy." Lying to Will was so difficult because he deserved so much more. I felt terrible.

"Where's Stephanie?" he asked. That was an easy question to answer.

"With Michael's friend, Doug," I responded. Will laughed and shook his head knowing that is a completely believable story. "Figures."

"I'll be down in a little bit." I leaned in to kiss him. I knew I would probably not be down there later. Will disappeared down the hallway and I took a deep breath before I went back into my room.

"I'm so sorry, Anni," Michael said, seeing me closing the door on my boyfriend, lying to him about Michael being here, lying to him about having allergies.

I turned back to Michael, "You ruin everything! Everything!" I pushed him with both of my hands. I raised my voice and waved my hand at the door.

"He wants me. Only me. He wants to make a commitment to me. He has sex with me....often. And it's amazing. Like, makes my body do things I never knew existed," Michael winced, I knew that would cut him.

Michael was so possessive of me, no one can have you Anni, except me. "He wants to call me his girlfriend and go on dates and introduce me to his friends. And he won't show up and tell me he's engaged to someone else."

Michael stared at my hysterical monologue.

"You were sooo afraid of me getting hurt, so protective. Don't go to parties, Anni, don't go down the beach with boys, Anni" I mocked him, wildly moving my hands around. "But you're the one that hurt me!" I stared at him, not blinking, not taking my eyes off of him.

"I don't know what to say," Michael finally broke the silence. "I don't know either." Michael stood up and put his arms around me and I sobbed into his shirt. He was crying, too.
He softly kissed my lips, "I love you, Anni. I always have."
I wiped the tears from his cheek and collapsed on the floor, hugging my knees to my chest.

I knew this was the very end. There was nothing left and there was never going to be anything more. Michael having a is fiance was a kiss of death. We held each other all night knowing in the morning he would leave and we would never see each other again. And we were right. We never did.

"Anni," Doug said as we crossed the bridge into Beacon. I looked at him, my eyes still swollen from last night. "He loved you."

I said nothing. I stared at Doug, emotionless, blank.
"Anni, I tried to warn you. That night on the beach, I tried. Do you know he came to me the next day? I told him to grow up. He loved you so much. He just, well, I don't know Anni. I don't know why he does what he does. He doesn't love her like he loved you."

I turned my head to look out the window. Tears welled in my burning eyes. Doug put his hand on my shoulder. I knew Doug would see Michael again. He didn't have to try to make it on without him.

Michael

The sky was clear and traffic light as I drove back to the city. My mind, however, was distracted by the past 18 hours. I thought maybe Anni and I would have one last fling before I get married. But her emotions, so raw and painful, was something I didn't anticipate.

My chest felt heavy and I struggled to maintain my focus on the road as I merged onto the highway. The city on the horizon came into view as I let out a deep breath. Anni. I was going to miss her very much. I allowed myself a moment to feel sick to my stomach, but I knew it was the right thing to do.

When we arrived at the college, Doug and I checked in as Anni instructed. I presented ID to security and he gives us an overnight pass. "OK, go ahead up". I skipped past room 205 to Anni's room. She opens the door and took my breath away. Her young face, glowing and her hair in a ponytail, swinging around when she walked.

Just like when we first met. Her smile lit up the whole room. College looked good on her. The memory of that night in her room drew to the front of my consciousness and I tried to push it back down. Her naked body touching mine, the awkwardness of her first time, teaching her how to move. This was going to be so difficult for both of us.

Anni and I made simple conversation in front of her roommate, Stephanie and Doug, though I tried to gauge her attitude from the tone of her voice. Sarcastic? Playful? Resentful? I wasn't sure yet. After the night on the beach, making love to her in the lifeguard boat, I made a decision to put an end to my relationship with her.

It had evolved into something I wasn't ready for. Kissing Anni was one thing. I could go on forever kissing her, but having sex with her was too much. That night put me over the edge emotionally.

"Mike, I can't believe you just cut her off," Scott said. I remembered Anni's pleas on the answering machine, the hurt in her letters.

Dear Michael,

Please, I need to talk to you. I'm sorry for whatever I did, just please call me. I promise, I'll leave you alone forever if I can just talk to you once more.

Love, Anni

I felt the desperation in her voice, in her letters. I'm sure she hated me, and rightfully so. But Anni was an addiction and I had to quit cold turkey. I tried to cut her off in the past, but I couldn't stay away. She deserved someone better. Someone that could give her everything she wants. And that wasn't me. Right now she seemed guarded.

I worked my way around her room, looking at the pictures on her wall. She had changed. Drinking, a boyfriend. I felt jealous of the boyfriend, just as I had with the dickhead high school boyfriend. I checked him out once more in the picture. He's young. Younger than me, I am guessing. I wondered if he's a virgin. Though he looks like the type who gets girls. Has he fucked Anni yet? The thought sickened me.

"Where's my picture, Anni?" I asked her. Her roommate told me it's in the drawer. I guess I deserved that.

We arrived at a party, some frat house or something. It's a hole in the wall dive for sure. It reminded me of Beacon parties, drinking, smoking, girls, loud music. I looked around the damp basement at all the smart, sexy college chicks and thought of the possibilities. Doug grabbed us some beer and I watched as Anni takes a sip, her face grimaced from the taste. I marveled at this new version of her. I tipped her cup back. I wondered if the boyfriend was going to show up tonight.

Anni drank a few beers and she chilled out a bit from being so uptight when I got her. I wanted to have fun with her tonight, knowing that my time with her was running out. I swallow hard thinking about it. She was going to be hurt, confused, angry and it was my fault.

I grabbed Anni and held her against me, moving our hips together to the beat of the music. Stephanie flashed me an evil look and I could only presume what Anni had told her. I buried my face in Anni's hair and inhaled her smell. Coconut? But familiar, nonetheless.

I lost sight of Doug and I could only guess that he had moved in one some girl, most likely Stephanie because she was convenient tonight. Anni's body molded with mine as we moved and I wanted to get her out of here.

"Let's go, Anni," I whispered in her ear. "Back to your room." I knew it would be wrong for me to make love to her tonight, but I really fucking wanted her. I prayed I could control myself. The boyfriend pops into my thoughts and I realized I don't need to try, Anni wouldn't allow it anyway.

Fucking boyfriend.

We walked across campus, Anni in my arms. She looked at me several times and I smiled back.

"You drunk?" I asked.

"No," she said. Her eyes are slightly glassy and I imagined she at least has a buzz going. We arrived back at the dorm and I jumped in her bed. Anni sat next to me, nervously biting her lip. We made small talk and I braced for the interrogation. With Anni, there was always an interrogation.

"Michael," she began. I pull her closer to me, kissing her forehead, feeling her face with my fingers trying to memorize every part of it. I try not to focus on what she was saying. Something about phone calls and letters and I didn't want to have to defend myself. I pulled her face to mine, kissing her lips to get her to be quiet.

She was apprehensive at first, but responded, leaning into my body. I put my hand on the back of her head, pushing her towards me, my other hand wrapped around her waist, pulling her hips into mine. I couldn't take it anymore. She had to know before I cross the line.

"Anni," I interrupted her, "I'm getting married." Anni's face turned red and her eyes wet. Her body convulsed in what I imagined were silent sobs as she pulled her body in, clutching her knees to her chest. I didn't know how to respond. In this moment, I wanted to call it off. I wanted to tell Anni I made a mistake and I wanted only her forever. But I knew that was just my emotions clouding my thoughts. I pleaded with myself to stay strong.

"Say something," I begged. Anni sobbed and trembled, her make-up running down her face. I knew I had caused her this pain. Anni finally spoke and became hysterical and indecipherable. I couldn't understand what she was saying through the tears, but it didn't matter. I reached out and wrapped my arms around her and she buried her face in my shirt.

The boyfriend. Shit. Anni opened the door, wiping her eyes with the back of her hands. I reached out and offered to shake his hand. "Anni's told me a lot about you," I say, hoping not to destroy this relationship for her, even though it made me wild with jealousy. Anni sent him away.

She closed the door and continues her meltdown. All I heard was amazing sex with Will and my body tensed. I felt like the green-eyed-monster. Everything she said was true, I was overprotective, I hurt her, I told her I loved her, I led her on, giving her hope. She hung in there. Anni was loyal to the end. My eyes burned and I turned my back and clear my throat, trying to compose myself.

"I love you, Anni. I always have." I said, taking her face in my hands and pressing my lips to hers. For the last time.

Chapter 22: Present

Anni

J ack arrives home on Wednesday. "Daddy, Daddy!' Juliette cries. Jack picks her up, and he tousles Ricky's hair. He puts her down and gives me a kiss.

"How was your week, Anni?" he asks.

"Fine. I actually had lunch with an old friend".

"Oh, nice." he says. "I'm going to bring these bags up to our room."

Jack responded how I thought he would to my confession. Uninterested. Not curiosity, interest or even jealousy. Suddenly, after years of an uneventful marriage, I want passion and lust and attention. I want Jack to make me feel like a wife. I want him to come home and kiss me properly and tell me he missed me. I want him to find a babysitter so we can be alone. I want Jack to text me during the day and ask how it is going, or offer to cook dinner one night. But most of all, I want to feel wanted.

Last weekend at the bar, I felt wanted. This week at the beach, I felt wanted. I haven't been able to get Michael out of my head since the moment I saw his face on my laptop screen. Maybe leaving me 20 years ago was just as hard for Michael as it was for me. Maybe Michael was looking for closure too.

It took all of my strength not to follow him upstairs to his room. I wanted to. I wanted to feel the warmth of his body again. I wondered if it would feel as familiar as it once did. Nobody has made me feel wanted in so long that I wanted to throw all my convictions and my vows into the ocean. Was this normal? Do married couples feel like this sometimes? Maybe I just need to talk to Jack and tell him I want to feel wanted.

Jack wasn't always distracted. I remember our first date after meeting in Rosie's Tavern.

Sarah picked out my clothes as usual for my first date with Jack. "This dress".
"No" I said, that dress is too desperate. "Not a good first date dress." Sarah frowned. She held up a pair of black pants and a low cut silk blouse. Why do I have so many low cut tops, I wondered. "Fine." I took the clothes and went to the bathroom. I opened my make-up case and applied some foundation and blush. I blended some eye shadow and apply black mascara.
"You look H.O.T." she spelled out. "Someone is getting lucky tonight."
Jack rang the doorbell and Sarah scurried down the hall. She'd planned an entrance for me. "Stay in here, I'll get the door. You come down the hall and act all casual, like you didn't know he was there."
"You mean, like I haven't been pacing the floor for the last 10 minutes?"
"Exactly" she said. I played along for Sarah's sake.

"Jack, welcome to our apartment, come in." Sarah said.
"Hi Sarah."
She sat him down on the couch. "So, where are you going to-

night?" she interrogated.

"The diner," Jack said.

"I hope you are joking."

"I am."

"Let me go see if Anni is ready." I hid in my room until Sarah came to get me.

"You know this is ridiculous, Sarah." She hugged me. "Be safe." She slipped a condom in my hand and gave me a smile.

"Ha! You know I do not need this tonight." I said, tucking it in my back pocket. Sarah shrugged.

I walked down the hall to the living room where Jack was standing with his hands in his pockets. I caught myself staring at how handsome he was.

"Hi Anni," Jack said, planting a kiss on my cheek. His dark hair was stiff, and he smells so good.

"Have fun," Sarah said. Jack led me out the door to his car and we headed to a restaurant on the island.

"I hope you like seafood" he said.

'I love it."

He pulled into the restaurant and my nerves tingled. Everything on the island is a memory I wanted to forget. But, I convinced myself to move forward and enjoy the evening with this superb looking man. His perfect chiseled jaw, gelled back black hair and a shadow of whiskers on his face gives me goose bumps. It had been forever since I had a real date. I didn't think people dated like this anymore.

We parked and Jack came around the side to open my door. He put his hand on my back as we made our way to the restaurant and my body warmed to his touch.

"Reservations, Evans." He said to the hostess, and we followed her to the table.

"Is that your name? Jack Evans?" I asked.

"Yes," he answered, not returning the question.

"So, Anni, what do you do?"

"I am a psychologist." I said. His face seems impressed, "who

waitresses" I added with a sense of defeat. Jack chuckled.
"Actually, I got a job offer at a private company, so I am excited about that."
"Wow, that is great, Anni, congratulations." Jack smiled. He had perfect teeth and his eyes squinted slightly when he smiles.
"How about you, Jack?"
"I'm in medical school" he said.
"Wow, smart and good looking!"
"If you say so." I can tell I embarrassed him. I thought if I was in medical school I would be shy to tell people. There's a lot of pressure on being a successful doctor.
"What kind of medicine are you practicing?" I asked.
"Orthopedics," he answered. "So, do you like crabs?" I give him a puzzled look. "To eat, do you like to eat crabs? They have great crabs. All you can eat!"

I laughed, "Oh, yeah, I do." Growing up on the island, eating crabs and catching crabs was practically a requirement. I recalled catching crabs with my brother down on the dock. We would take them to my grandfather who would clean and cook them.
"Do you want a beer or do you prefer something fancy?"
"Beer is fine. Beer is really the only adult drink I know. You know, college parties and all."
"Do you want me to ask for a red cup?" Jack teased. "You are 21, right?"
"Yes, Jack! I am 24."
"Oh good! I don't want to be an accomplice for underage drinking."
'How about you, Jack?"
"Twenty seven."
"Oh, an older man." I joke, thinking the last time I fell for an older man it crushed me.

The waitress brought our beers, and we clinked them together.
"You look pretty," he said, smiling and glancing at my face.
"Thanks," I answered, slightly embarrassed.

It's been a while since I've been on the dating scene and the last encounter was college, last year before graduation. Will and I didn't last through Sophomore year.

"You are emotionally unavailable Anni," he said, "always distracted. Why can't you give up the game and let me in?" I was so hurt by Michael, I was protecting myself. Then one night Will didn't answer my calls, and I needed my Psych book from his room, so I ventured over and found him kissing a sorority girl. "I'm sorry, Anni," he said. I turned and left without a word. I was thinking I was unlovable.

"So, tell me about your new job," Jack said, breaking my thoughts.

"Well, it's a small office, but established clients. I'll be doing family therapy," I said, which will be odd considering I don't have my family, or little experience to bring to the office. But I nod and listen and say "and how do you feel about that?"

"That's great." He reaches his hand across the table to hold mine. Is this how adult dating is, or have I been unlucky in love. There must be something wrong with this beautiful, sexy, polite, doctor-to-be.

"So, what do you want to do now?" Jack asked after we left the restaurant.

"We could go to Rosie's" I joked, "Ladies' Night."

"I was thinking we could go back to my place."

"Oh, well, we could do that too." I cleared my throat. Jack surprised me being so forward, but I tried not to sound too prudish.

"Unless, you don't want to," he said in response to my reaction.

"No, I want to."

"Ok." He puts his hand over mine and put the car in drive.

Jack's apartment was clean and sparsely decorated. I found a stethoscope on the counter and I picked it up and looked at Jack to see his response. He walked over and took the stethoscope and put it in his ears, putting the chest piece over my heart. I admit, I was finding this incredibly sexy. Jack listened to my heartbeat for a few seconds and I was afraid he would notice that it was pounding out of my chest.

"Sounds good." He took off the ear pieces and put them in my ears so I can hear my own heartbeat. I placed the stethoscope back on to the counter and Jack led me into the living room.

I look around to get a clue about Jack. There were no pictures to give anything away.

"Do you live alone?" I asked.

"Yes," he said, watching me inspect his home, as a cat brushed my leg.

"That's Snuggles."

"Snuggles?"

"You don't like Snuggles?"

"No, I do. I love Snuggles." I tried to pick up Snuggles, and she hissed at me.

"Snuggles is overprotective." He flashed me a smile that made my knees weak.

"Does she hiss at all the girls you bring here?"

"I don't know, you're the first." I wondered if that was true.

Jack broke our conversation by pulling me close. His lips touched mine lightly. They were soft and warm. He was taller, and I stood on my toes to meet him. He smelled of beer and crabs and Old Bay, but a faint smell of cologne. His cologne smelled familiar but I couldn't tell what it was. He was a good kisser. We moved to the couch where he leaned over and put his arms around my waist. By now, any other guy would have had my clothes off, but Jack took his time. He sat up and took my hands.

"Do you like ice cream?" he asked, spontaneously.

"Um, yes!" I answered. He walked to the kitchen and grabbed two bowls of ice cream and returned.

"I like you." he said handing me a bowl of ice cream. I smiled. Jack sat next to me and took a spoonful of ice cream and then put our bowls on the coffee table. He put his hands around my neck to pull me closer and our lips touched. It felt nice. Probably the best kisses. Slow and soft, not rushed.

I pulled the condom out of my pocket and held it up. His eyes widened. "Aren't you prepared!"

"Sarah gave it to me." He took it from my hand and put it on the table behind him.

"I think we will save that for another time." I felt disappointment but grateful to have that expectation off the table.

I was so awkward at adult dating. I gave him a smile that maybe showed disappointment, because he took my hand and pulls me closer. "But, I would like to take you out again soon."

"I'd really like that," I said.

I get in bed and I pull the comforter up to my shoulders. Jack is laying on his side with the remote in his hand, flicking through tv channels. I curl up to him and rest my chin on his chest. "Jack, how was your trip?" I ask.

"Fine, uneventful" he says.

"What did you do?"

He puts down the remote control and faces me, "The usual. Workshops and lectures".

Out of my bedroom window I see the motion detection lights activate and I remember last week when Maisie snuck back in from the deck. I consider going down and interrupting whatever is going on, drinking, smoking, boys, but something stops me. I don't know what it is.

"I thought you would have called to talk or the kids". I continue.

"Well, I know you're capable of handling it all. You always do." He kisses my forehead and turns back to the TV.

"Well, sometimes I want to talk to you. Like, have a normal conversation where you appear interested in me and the kids."

"What's this about?" He asks annoyed.

"It's just that I feel like I need more attention from you. I need to feel wanted. You barely even want to be intimate anymore." I argue, feeling my eyes swell, tears threatening to spill. Jack isn't impressed by tears so I try to hold them in.

"That's ridiculous, Anni. We have a bunch of kids. We have a little time alone. I want you." he says, like it isn't obvious it has been a month since the last time we were alone and intimate.

"We need to make time, Jack. You can't just ignore me all the time."

"I don't ignore you, Anni. We are both busy." He leans in and pulls me close and kisses my lips but I don't feel it. All I can think of is Michael and his invitation to go back to his hotel room. I pull away from Jack.

"What?" he says, confused by my request to be more intimate and my hesitation to be intimate right now.

I get up out of bed and walk down the hardwood stairs into the kitchen. I rummage through the dark maple wood cabinets looking for something to stress eat. I pull out a poptart and pour a glass of milk and settle at the kitchen table. Tears form in my eyes. I wipe them with the back of my hand as I hear footsteps on the stairs. I want it to be Jack, coming down to take me in his arms, tell me he is sorry, he will be more attentive, and he loves me so much.

"Mom?" Maisie asks, "What are you doing?"

"Maisie, hi," I say, "Just having a snack."

"A poptart?" she asks, raising her eyebrows.

"Maisie, who are you sneaking outside with?" I ask.

"Mom," she whines.

"Maisie, I understand. Believe me, I understand more than you know," I say, thinking of sneaking out with Michael at 16 years old, kissing him by the jeep, making out on the deck in the middle of the night, his hands on my naked body, the beach.

"Aiden," she says, her face softening.

"Your boyfriend?"

"I think so," she looks down at the floor and I feel her pain in the pit of my stomach. "He hasn't like, officially said."

"Ask him," I advise. "Ask him if he's committed to you."

"Where's this coming from Mom? Why are you being weird?" she says. Maisie is intuitive. "Is this about Michael?"

I feel my stomach drop and a nauseous feeling creeps up in my throat.

"What?"

211

"Michael," she repeats, staring into my eyes.

"What do you know about Michael?"

"Well, I know you snuck out the other night to see him. Who is it, Mom?"

"I didn't sneak out, Maisie."

"You told Dad you went for milk," she says, "that's lying." My heart pounds.

"Maisie, how do you know this?"

"Facebook Mom, you left it open on your laptop. I had to do a research paper."

"He hurt you didn't he?" she says. My eyes burn. I look at Maisie and see myself, a teenager, sneaking out, unsure of my place in a relationship with a boy.

"Mom?" she says. I struggle to breathe and I feel the tears spill over. Maisie gets up and puts her arms around me, her eyes wet.

"I'm sorry, Mom." She says. "Boys suck."

"Maisie, Michael and I were best friends in Beacon. He was my first."

"You loved him?" she asks, wiping away her tears.

"Yes, but I wasn't enough," I say. "Maisie, you are perfect, and you are enough. Never settle for anyone that doesn't make you feel you aren't enough. Settle for someone that makes you feel loved and wanted all the time."

"Are you going to see Michael again?" she asks.

"It's not like that Maisie,"

"What are you going to do?"

"I need closure," I say, forgetting I am talking to my teenage daughter.

"I trust you," she says, as she sits on my lap and wraps her arms around me. "You're the best mom and the best wife." I wipe my eyes with the end of my shirt sleeve.

"Maisie, are you having sex?" I ask, since we are being open and honest.

"Mom!" she barks. I think we need to talk about safe sex and protection and all that, but not right now. Maisie squeezes me tight and stands up.

"Good night Mom, I love you," she says.

"I love you too, Mais." She turns and walks towards the stairs.

"Mom, Aiden said his dad knows you. His name is Tyler. He was a lifeguard."

I open my laptop and turn it on. I dare you, Anni. But first I have to send a text message to Lily.

"Hey, I will not make that girls' get away. I have to go out of town for family stuff. Thank you for inviting me though."

"Oh, that stinks, Anni! We will miss you. Have fun."

My fingers shake as they touch the keyboard. I search for hotels about an hour's drive down the coast from the island. I find a beachfront room and type in my name, address and phone number. Actually, I type in a fake name, address and phone number. And then I open Facebook and send a message.

Dear Michael,

I will be at the Carriage Motel in Dune City on Friday. I will be there alone.

Love, Anni

I do not wait for a response before I close my laptop. I don't want any conversation, or to discuss anything. I just want to show up and see what happens.

I go to my closet and pull out a few outfits. I decide on a short navy maxi skirt and a short sleeve off white blouse, not too dressy, but an outfit I feel good in. I pack a pair of sandals, a bathing suit, some sweatpants and t-shirts and I throw in my toiletries.

My heart has been in my throat all week since I planned this plan to leave my family for the weekend in search of something. I'm not sure yet, but I will let it play out. I am satisfied with the decision for now. There is no way Jack will ever find out because he won't check up on me. He thinks I will be in the mountains with the girls and he will not text or call.

"Moooom, I have soccer practice after school. Who is going to take me?" Ivy says. I look at Jack.

"Um, I am." He straightens up, raising his hand.

"Mom, he doesn't even know where the field is!" She begs.

"I can call Sophia's mom and see if she can take you," I answer.

"Kids, we will work this out. I'm a capable guy." he says. "What else?"

"I have clarinet practice after school." Maisie says.

"What about you son?" Jack asks Ricky. He shrugs his shoulders and looks at me to confirm his schedule.

"I want to get ice cream," Juliette pipes in.

"I've written out a schedule. You may have to miss things this weekend. It's really hard for one parent to do everything." I glance at Jack, hoping he gets the hint. "It's only for two days. I'll be back on Sunday." I say. "Now let's go, you will miss the school bus."

Jack waves to the kids as they get on the bus and closes the front door. He turns and pulls me in close to him. "So," he says, as our faces are almost touching. "I have some time before I have to leave". His eyes are lustful and his smile playful. We both look over at Juliette who is playing dolls, oblivious to her surroundings.

He plants a long, passionate kiss to my lips and grabs my ass. I jump and Juliette notices.

"Well, I guess I'll have to take a rain check on that," Jack says. He kisses me goodbye before he starts out the door. "Have a good time, Anni." He looks at Juliette and walks over and picks her up and swings her around.

"Anni, what about Juliette?" he asks, confused.

"She goes to daycare, Jack." I roll my eyes. "You have to pick her up."

"I'll pick you up early, Juliette. We'll go for ice cream!"

"Yay!" she laughs.

"Anni, text me the address of the daycare." Jack winks and walks out the door, closing it behind him. I shake my head.

As Jack closes the door, my stomach drops. Foreshadowing, I think. I pop my cold cup of coffee back in the microwave and continue to get Juliette ready for daycare.

"Juliette, come here and brush your teeth."

"No, I don't wanna."

"Brush your teeth, otherwise you'll get a cavity."

"Noooo." I can feel my patience wearing thin, my nerves already sitting in my throat.

I gather Juliette and her lunch and backpack. "It's show and share day!" She cries. I cringe. Not show and share day!

"OK, how about your stuffed elephant," I suggest.

"No" Juliette protests.

"How about your painting we did yesterday?"

"No"

"Juliette, we will be late." I say urgently.

"I want my stephascope" she says. "The one daddy got me".

"Juliette, I haven't seen that stethoscope in a really long time."

"I WANT THE STEPHASCOPE!!"

Frantically tearing apart the house for a toy stethoscope, we find it at the bottom on a bin of toys. I scoop her up and get in the car, buckle her in and move to the front seat. How does Jack not know where the daycare is, I think to myself? I pull out my phone in the parking lot and text him the address. I check my phone in a few minutes and no acknowledgement of the message I sent. I shrug my shoulders. He never answers me anyway.

I pull into my driveway and put the car in park. I let out a deep breath I have been holding all morning. The sinking feeling comes over me again. I stare at the house, an oversized home, beautifully landscaped, thanks to Jack's hard work and dedication.

I am grateful to him for the things he provides our family. We have enjoyed nice vacations, fancy appliances, all the latest electronics.

Why am I still not satisfied? I feel guilty and I consider canceling my plan. I shake my head to get my brain to change the subject. I walk inside and grab my overnight bag. I throw it in the car and get in the passenger's seat. *I need to leave before I change my mind.*

Michael

I stare at my phone, Facebook Messenger open. Disbelief. Dear Michael, I'll be at the Carriage Motel... alone. *What is she thinking?* This is not very Anni-like. I know what I am thinking. *Shit.* My mind races with memories and seeing her again. Anni was everything I expected 20 years later. Beautiful, smart, successful, and still affected by me. Revisiting Pizza Palace, the jetty, the beach, Anni could barely hold it together. How has she held onto this for two decades? I put my phone back in my pocket. *How the fuck am I going to make it until Friday? What will I tell Danielle?*

I met Danielle at a family wedding. Danielle was a friend of the groom. She was from an affluent family and in line to take over a successful family business. I glimpsed her from across the large reception room after having a few drinks and mingling with family.

"Don't you hate weddings," I said as I handed her a drink.

"Completely," she sighed, raising her drink to mine.

"I'm Michael," I put my hand out to her.

"Danielle."

"Hey, you want to go outside for a while, I need to get out of here." I asked.

"That sounds great," she agreed. We walked out to a courtyard and sat at a small table.

"So, how do you know the bride and groom?" I asked.

"I work with Peter," Danielle sipped her drink, swirling the stirrer in the ice in her glass. "It's actually a family business, insurance. How about you?"

"Cousin" I said, "To the bride."

"So, what do you do?"

"Actually, I'm a freeloader living off my parents, I drink a lot." I said. Danielle laughed, but I wasn't joking. She didn't press me any further.

Danielle was tall and had a sweet round face and long dark hair she wore in curls for the wedding. She was unlike the many girls I had experienced in the past. She wasn't a college girl, or a shore girl. She was mature, had a job and her own place. At the end of the night I asked for her number.

My parents were pushing me to get a job and get out of the house. After dating for a little while, I moved in to her place to get my parents off my back. I needed to grow up. My friends had real jobs. No one was picking me up to go have beer and sex. After a few months, I asked her to marry me. Marrying Danielle is safe. I will be well taken care of.

But, Anni. She was feisty, passionate, innocent and strong. Anni knew what she wanted and wasn't afraid to go after it. She worked hard, harder than anyone I knew. And she loved me unconditionally, even though I couldn't give her what she wanted. All of me. She is going to get all of me on Friday. Every last inch of me.

Anni

"Hey, Anni," Miranda greets as I enter the cafe. "Your usual?" she asks.

"Yes, thanks." I say. "To go please." I am grateful the cafe is empty at the moment because I need to share my plan with someone.

"Miranda, remember my client I met with?" I begin, nervous to tell her. Miranda will understand though.

"Yeah, the hot one." she says. "I know he isn't your client, Anni, but go on." She says. I should have known my lie wouldn't fool her.

"He is the one I told you about. The one from my past I looked up on Facebook."

"Oh... OH... shit!" she remembers. "Anni, you devil." Miranda isn't the settle down, monogamous type. She has casual relationships with both men and women, never really settling. Her lifestyle seems so exciting at times, especially those stressful times of juggling four children and a less-than-enthusiastic husband.

"What are you going to do?" she asks, resting her chin in her hands on the counter.

"The girls invited me to go to the mountains this weekend, and I told Jack I am going. Or rather, I asked Jack if I can go because if I go, it requires a lengthy list of childcare and directions." I say. Miranda stares at me with captivation, willing me to go on. She then has an epiphany and jumps up excitedly.

"Oooh, and you told Jack you are going, ditching the girls and heading down to see your man in secret." She whispers. "It's a brilliant plot twist, Anni!! I love it!" Miranda loves a good drama.

"Miranda, try to understand the magnitude of this. It could ruin my life. You are supposed to be talking me out of this."

"Well, that's a lot of pressure!" She pushes off the counter. "So, what are your expectations? Hot and steamy or...." She lets that linger.

"I have no idea. Look, here is the information of where I will be, just in case." I say. I don't want to talk about it anymore with Miranda. My life isn't a drama unfolding... or is it.

Miranda comes out from around the counter and gives me a big squeeze. "Anni, you're a smart, beautiful, independent woman. You will make the right decision."

"Thank you Miranda." I'll see you next week.

Chapter 23: Present

Anni

I sit in my car and put my head in my hands. Anni, do you know what you're doing? But I know in my heart I can't move on from Michael without closure. I need to let this play out, and I risk everything. Over two decades I have thought about him so often. I have had several relationships, Ben and Will and what's-his-name, before Jack.

What is it about Michael that makes it so difficult to be emotionally monogamous? Maybe it was because Michael and I had no real beginning or end. When you break up, you get a sense of closure. But we didn't break up. We were never together. When he said he was getting married, that should have been closure for me, right? Taken. Off the market. No more chances Anni. I feel like I will be sick and I think of going back in and talking to Miranda. Telling her I'm canceling my plans. I can't go through with it. This is completely out of character for me. But it's Michael, he makes me do things.

I arrive at the Carriage Motel at 11:00. I pull into the parking lot and think maybe I should have told Michael to meet me at a restaurant. A motel seems a little presumptuous. But I chose this plan because I wanted to lay it all out there. I didn't want to sit in a restaurant and talk about our feelings, or talk about insignificant things. It was now or never. I didn't want to drag it on. It was going to be over this weekend or I was going to be all in.

A sudden thought enters my mind. I didn't check Michael's response. What if he doesn't come? What if he never even saw my message? Or if he was unavailable this weekend? It was a "Meet me at the bell tower at midnight moment...if you don't show up, I know it wasn't meant to be" type message. Like a fairytale. I have a sudden panic attack and look around to see if anyone is watching me hyperventilate in my car.

I start the car back up and I try to convince myself to drive away, back home where I belong. If Michael doesn't show, I can't handle that rejection. But, then again, he's the one that pursued me at the hotel in Beacon and invited me to the bar. And he tried to get me upstairs at the Sands. *Anni, get it together.* I take a deep breath and get out of the car.

I leave my bag so I can make a fast get-away if I need to. I don't want to give the impression that I am willing to jump in the bed and spend the night. Although I am pretty sure that is already assumed. Especially for Michael.

The Carriage Motel is a small building, almost like a bed and breakfast. An old horse carriage decorates the outside of the building. The lobby is quaint and contains many antiques from the area. It is painted a seafoam green with thick dark wooden accents. It is warm and inviting.

"Welcome" says the receptionist. "Are you checking in?"

"Um, yes. Julia Atwood" I say. I hand her cash to pay for the room.

"Can I have your driver's license please?" She says. Anni, you do not have any identification with Julia Atwood on it. I should have thought of this, but, I am a terrible con artist.

"Oh, Um, Julia wasn't able to make it. So, it's just me and uh, my friend." I clear my throat. I am such a bad liar.

"Well, I can't check you in without Ms. Atwood. I'm sorry." She gives me a sad but firm glare.

"Please, can you put the room in my name? I really need to check in." I feel desperate to have this all ironed out before

Michael shows up or it will ruin my plan.

"I'm afraid I can't do that." She says firmly. She bangs her fingers into the keys on the keyboard of her computer and then looks up and smiles "But, I have another room available I can rent to you. It's a suite. Oceanfront. I can give you a discount since it will sit empty, anyway."

"Oh, that would be great. Thank you." I do a little dance in my head and hand her cash.

"Do you have a credit card you can use for security?" She asks. Why is this so difficult, I think to myself? Then I remember the debit card I have in my name. Jack won't get a bill or see I charged anything. And I don't expect breaking or damaging anything in the room. I hand over the debit Visa.

"Thank you...." She glances at the card, "Mrs. Evans." she says and hands me back the card. Mrs. Evans. As in Mrs. Jack Evans. I look down at the floor, ashamed and I swear she is judging me over her reading spectacles and her librarian bun.

She reaches out to hand me the room key and I catch her name tag. Ivy. "Oh, Ivy, I have a friend named Ivy." I say. She smiles and I turn away.

I make my way to the back of the motel where there is a patio facing the ocean. It is a warm fall day, and the air feels comfortable and dry, unlike those hot, humid summer beach days. I sit on a lounge chair and feel the autumn sun bake down on my face and it warms my body. For a moment, I enjoy the peace. The roaring sound of the ocean and the salty smell of the air. The beach is void of crowds and umbrellas and loud music. The lifeguards have gone back to school.

I think of Tyler, seeing him often at his lifeguard post. I think back to the conversation with Maisie and Aiden and realize my daughter is kissing the son of a boy I kissed as a teenager. Funny thing about small towns.

"Hey" a voice says behind me. I freeze and I my throat closes up. I stand up and turn around. Midnight at the bell tower. Michael is standing there, a breeze blowing his dark hair. He squints slightly at the sun in his face. His hands are in the pockets of his jeans, which fall just right on his hips. His collared shirt tucked in, accentuates his broad shoulders. How did I not notice how sexy he looked before?

"Hey" I say back. We are locked in a stare, neither one of us knowing how to proceed. "I, um..." I stutter. "I..."

Michael smiles his signature crooked smile. He takes a step closer and puts his hands on my face and our lips meet. His kiss is filled with urgency and passion. He pulls me tighter to him and puts his hand on the back of my head, grabbing my hair. I stand on my toes to meet him.

Two decades collapse in a moment. Tears well up in my eyes and I struggle to hold them in. I feel like a teenager again. With no responsibilities. No thoughts of kids or laundry or cooking. Please don't cry, Anni I beg of myself. I have not felt anyone's lips but Jack's in 20 years. It felt different. I surrender myself completely in this moment I have dreamed about for decades.

"Wow" I take a step back. Michael smiles and I am speechless.

"So, should we go upstairs?" He says. "That outfit is so sexy, but I really want to get you out it."

"Oh, not much has changed with you." He smiles. If he keeps smiling like that, he may be closer to that goal than he thinks.

"Isn't that why you asked me to meet you here, in a motel. On the beach?" He says. "I'll admit it surprised me at your message."

"Yeah, well, I... I'm not sure, actually." I say. My plans of being cool and confident are flying out the window. I am suddenly unsure of what to do next.

I had not thought this far. My heart pounds and my brain feels fuzzy. I thought we would just meet here and see what happens, but I forgot Michael is like a predator moving in on his prey. He is fast.

"Oh, I am sure" he says. He leans in and kisses me again. I can feel Ivy, the receptionist, judging me through the lobby. Reading Mrs. Evans on my debit card. Knowing something shady was going on. I wonder if Ivy will somehow call Jack and tell him where I am.

"Take me upstairs" he says. Michael picks me up like a child and carries me to the lobby. "Ok, put me down." I demand. "I can walk."

We head through the lobby to the elevator and find the motel room. I put the key in and unlock the door. I feel guilt seep in as I push down on the handle and I try to suppress it.

"Wow, Anni" Michael says. "You sure know how to impress a guy." He jokes looking around at the oceanfront suite. Two bedrooms, a sitting area, jacuzzi tub and private balcony.

"Well, don't be too impressed, Michael. It was a free upgrade." I say.

Michael goes to the sliding glass door that leads to a private balcony. It overlooks the beach which is quiet and serene right now. A lone jogger and his dog trot down along the water's edge. The ocean ebbs and flows, gently folding in on itself as it heads back out to sea.

"I could really use a drink right now." I blurt out, my nerves shot and my thoughts playing games in my head. And, it's only noon.

"Oh, yes, Anni. Let's get you drunk." he laughs. "We need to take the edge off. I'll be right back." Michael walks down to the lobby, presumably to the bar area, while I wait in the room, contemplating my next move.

Michael and I need to talk.

I need to say what needs to be said so I can move on. He returns with a bottle of wine and a bottle of rum and 2 cans of soda.

"Well, I wasn't sure how drunk you wanted to get, so I got wine for casual drinking, or I got rum if you need a fast fix."

"Oh, God, the fast fix is tempting."

"Fast fix it is." He pours rum into a plastic cup and pours the soda over top. "If you prefer, you can have the straight rum".

"No, that is quite alright. I just need to take the edge off."

I sip my rum and coke quickly. I walk over to the slider which is opened, allowing the salty breeze to fill the room. The curtains blow gently into the room and I stare out to the horizon. Michael walks over behind me and puts his arms around me and buries his face in my hair.

"You smell good" he says. It reminds me of how good Michael always smelled of soap and cologne. That smell gave me such a sweet feeling every time.

"Do you know I carried around a department store card with your cologne on it?" I ask.

"That's... stalker level." Michael raises his eyebrows.

"It sounds like that when I say it out loud."

Michael turns me around to face him and kisses my lips, softly.

"Do you know I kept your school picture in my wallet and pretended you were my girlfriend all winter?"

"Ouch" I say. It actually hurts to hear him say that.

"What?"

"You pretended I was your girlfriend." I imagine him showing my picture to his friends at school saying this is the girl I fuck in the summer. Which of course isn't true but also, I wasn't his girlfriend.

"Anni, why can't we reminisce about the past without you getting all fucking psycho? We were kids. Here, have another shot of rum in your coke," I breathe in sharply and exhale, turning back out to look at the ocean.

It's true, I think. It wasn't as big of a deal to him as it was to me. What if I am here, ruining my marriage and my family for a misunderstanding? I let it go. It's too soon to get hysterical, but I have a feeling that I will soon. Michael pours more rum into my drink.

"So, let's change the subject." Michael says. "How'd you get away?"

"Wow. I definitely don't want to talk about that." I say, feeling really guilty. The only person who knows where I am is my barista, Miranda. She wouldn't even know how to get in touch with Jack if something happened.

The rum is going to my head and I'm feeling slightly more loose. I walk a circle around the balcony and rest my glass on the railing. I breathe in the salt air. It reminds me of being on the island in the summers, the motel where I helped my parents, the shops and ice cream stands. And Michael, picking me up in his jeep and driving around town, talking and playing music on the radio. We would grab ice cream sodas and play golf. Late at night we would lie on the balcony at the motel and talk about life. That was before Michael met up with the local guys. That is when our relationship turned unpredictable. Maybe it was the age difference. Three years is a lot when you're a teenager.

"Doug said your husband is a doctor." Michael says.
"I don't want to talk about it." Wait, he talked to Doug about me and my husband.
"I always knew you'd be successful, Anni," he says.
"I'm not successful, Michael, my husband is." I say with a fair degree of annoyance.

"I'm sorry." Michael walks over and embraces me. I am leaning on the balcony and he puts his hands around my waist.
"I don't know what it is you want here. But, I don't want to talk right now. I'm kind of hoping you wanted to get me naked in bed. Because, Jesus Christ, that is what I want to do to you."
"Well, some things will never change." Michael's lips touch mine and his hands find their way under my blouse.

I don't stop him. It all feels so familiar. The salt air, Michael's bad boy attitude, his smell, the touch of his lips and his hands on my skin. I can completely give myself to him. He unbuttons the front of my blouse so my lace bra is exposed. He runs his fingers over the lace and looks me in the eyes. I feel like an awkward teenager again. The last time I felt him touch me like this was in my bedroom at the motel. My parents asleep down the hall. There was the beach, but that was rushed, naked and wet by the ocean. The summer I started college. I want to let him have me, but I know it is wrong. I pull back and pull my blouse closed. Michael tips my chin back and kisses me again. He looks in my eyes and I know he is confused. I walk back into the room and Michael follows me.

"Talk to me, Anni" he says.
"I need a minute." I grab my phone and head into the bathroom.

I sit on the edge of the tub and check to see if Jack or the kids

have texted me. I open Facebook for a distraction. I see a picture of the moms in the mountains in front of a fireplace holding
wine glasses. I scroll down to the comments and see one from
Jack "I guess Anni is in the bathroom, lol. Tell her I miss her and
everything is ok."
My heart sinks. Jack is going to know I am not in the mountains.

   I splash some water on my face and walk back out of the
bathroom. I pour rum into a cup and throw it back. Michael
stares at me, his mouth open.
"Oh, this is getting good," he says.
   I sit on the sofa and Michael sits next to me. He leans over my
body and kisses my neck making his way to my lips. I meet him
with equal passion. I've come this far, I want to enjoy whatever
this is. And I am into kissing Michael. He pulls me into his lap
so I am straddling him. He brings my face down to his and his
hand moves along the smooth skin of my leg. Everywhere he
touches leaves a warm tingly feeling. I'm not sure if it's the rum,
but I can't find the will to stop him. What will the consequences
be if I follow through with this, I think to myself? There you go
again, Anni. Always thinking rationally.
"Let's walk down to the beach," I say.
"No" he says, nuzzling his face in my neck.
"Michael, let's go." I beg. "I want to go down to the beach. My
head is a little woozy from the rum, I want to walk it off".
"That doesn't even make sense, Anni."
"Yes, come on."
Michael takes my hand and we walk down the stairs of the hotel,
through the lobby and on the beach to the water's edge. The sun
is getting low, and the beach feels cooler than before.
"Is everything ok?" He asks.
"Yes" I lie. "I'm sure my husband knows I am not in the moun-
tains like I said I was. I'm so stupid. I should have known."
   Michael pulls me close and presses his lips to mine. He traces
my jawline with soft kisses and I tilt my head back, enjoying
every touch. It feels so familiar. I take a deep breath to smell his

scent.

"Anni, I will not force you into bed with me, even though I really really want to, so fucking bad. But I'm just saying, that you asked me to come here, to a motel, to meet you. You lied to your husband. So, please don't think I'm insensitive when I say this but, what the fuck is going on?"

"Michael" I say. I'm just going to throw it all out there "When you came to visit me at college and said you were getting married, my world collapsed."

Michael clasps his hands and puts them behind his neck, "Seriously, Anni, this is what you want to talk about?" he says. "Please don't tell me you came all this way to rehash this. I've seriously got like 3 fucking condoms in my pocket."

I feel my face flush and I want to forget this whole stupid idea, but no, I will not let him distract me.

"Yes. I have had dreams about your for 20 years. I have been emotionally unfaithful to my husband, not being able to give him 100% of me because of you."

"Well" he smirks, "I guess you're more than emotionally unfaithful" he says. That stings, but I carry on.

"You stole my virginity and...."

"You GAVE me your virginity, if I remember correctly. That purple bikini and the way it clung to your wet body." His eyes drift off in the distance. "You did not stop me."

"It was a game. You tricked me." My voice now loud and grateful for an empty beach.

"It was not a game, I told you that."

"You lied."

"About what?"

"You said you would marry me someday. And then you show up at my dorm and tell me you are marrying someone else," I yell, as the tears flow down my face. "You ruined my relationship with Will."

"How?" Michael's voice is defensive now.

"I couldn't be emotionally available to anyone. He knew it was because of you. He used it against me. My marriage sucks, my husband doesn't know I exist." I am clearly yelling now and the tears are flowing. "On my wedding day I thought, if you showed back up in my life I would leave him for you. On my wedding day, Michael. And then I had a kid and then another kid and each kid made me feel further and further away. And then you show back up in my life and now it's too late. It's too late, Michael."

Michael rubs his hands through my hair and looks in my eyes.

"I loved you," I whisper through my tears.

"I loved you too," he says, pulling me closer.

"Anni" he begins, 'When I met you, we were so young."

"But.." I begin, and Michael holds his finger up to interrupt me.

"Let me finish," he begs "You wore that..."

"Purple bikini." I have heard this a thousand times.

"Something happened. You showed up at my house in these dresses, and your back scratches were, I don't know, different." he says. "And you were so different from my friends. Anni, when you checked out on us that summer with what's his name, I was so bored. I missed you so much. I occupied my time with Scott and Doug."

"I tried to come around," I say, "You wouldn't see me."

"And then, you and that dickhead broke up, and I came over to see you at work, and you..." Michael struggles for the words. "You were just not the old Anni. You were, mature. And I found myself attracted to you. But you were... you."

I listen patiently to his memories. But I don't know what to say.

"And yes, Anni. That fucking purple bikini. And that fucking lifeguard and that lifeguard party. And I couldn't even go out drinking that night. I waited all night for you to get home, praying that little dickhead lifeguard didn't get my girl."

"That was selfish." I say.

"I deserve that," he admits. "But Anni, that night in your room, that wasn't a game. Do you regret losing your virginity to me? I loved you."

"No," I whisper.

"I remember every second of that night, you were so scared.

But you trusted me, you let me touch you and kiss you and lay naked with you."

Hearing Michael talk to me in this way feels like a knife twisting in my back. The pain and agony I felt then resurfaces and I feel like I will vomit. My body jolts with each sob.
"You left me."
"I did what was best for both of us," he says.
"I don't believe that."

I pulled the tin ring out of my pocket and handed it to him. Michael turns the ring over between his fingers and looks at me. He smirks. "Anni, we were kids. What makes you think I would have made you any happier? I was an asshole. I still am an asshole." He hands the ring back and I throw it in the ocean with all the force I can muster. He pulls me close and wipes my face with the palm of his hand and holds me in his arms. I let the emotions flow out and sob into his shirt.

"So, now what?" he asks.
"I need to go back to my family. My husband, Jack, I met him right out of grad school. He was in medical school. We had so much fun together back then. He works so hard to give us everything." I sink to the sandy ground and put my head in my hands. "I have 4 amazing kids. A beautiful home. Yeah, it's stressful sometimes. I gave up my career for them. But they are my world. I need to reconnect with my husband."

"Anni, I'm sorry I hurt you." Michael sits next to me on the sand. I pick up a stick and mindlessly draw. "I could have never given you what you deserved in life. You would have worked so hard and I would be the same immature, free loading guy I always was and still am. I met my... soon to be ex-wife", he chuckles uncomfortably, "at a wedding and I knew she could support me. We got married right away so my mom would stop nagging me to get a job and move out. I tried to start a business, but it doesn't do that well. Things went sour with her, and basically, no one wants an immature guy who will never grow up. We stayed together out of convenience but I'm sure she cheats on me. I don't even fucking care. That's what you missed out on. You deserve more. You went to college, you had dreams and goals. I was nothing." I look at Michael's face, his voice is sincere and sad. "Say something, Anni". He says.

"We could have made it work." I say pressing down the lump in my throat.

"Anni, we were just kids." He says, barely a whisper.

"You were my soulmate." I whimper.

"We still are." Michael stands up and brushes the sand off his pants. He reaches his hand out and pulls me to my feet. He holds me tight and rubs his hands down my hair. He tips my head back with his fingertips and kisses my lips. Then steps back and holds both of my hands in his.

"Anni, soulmates." He says.

"Now, you need to go fix things with your husband. He's a lucky guy." Michael holds me tight in his embrace and I feel his heart beat for the last time.

I know it's over now.

I wipe tears from my eyes as he walks back and gets into his blue convertible and drive away. I watch his taillights until I can't see them anymore. I head back to the hotel room alone, slightly buzzed from the rum. I turn on the water in the shower to have myself one last cry.

The hot water showers over my naked body as I let out the rush of emotions. I feel my gut wrench and my eyes burn with hot tears. I turn the water hotter, nearly scalding my skin, but I make myself stand it. A sob escapes from my voice as my body shakes. I release nearly a lifetime of hurt and longing. Longing for Michael for 20 years.

Thinking I see him in the distance, wondering if he was near as I drove through the city, my heart torn when I pass the dinosaur mini golf or Dustin's Ice Cream. Those night waking up at 2am, dreaming of him holding me, sometimes telling me he loved me, other times out of reach.

∞∞∞

"Anni," Jack shakes my shoulder one night. "You're having a bad dream" he says, as I wake up, my cheeks wet with tears. How am I going to get through this? What about Jack? I have to tell him. He already knows I lied.

Chapter 24: Love

Jack

I sit at the Carriage Motel restaurant stirring my Captain and Coke, around and around, focusing on the ice cubes clinking the side of the glass as it makes contact. My eyes are bloodshot and tired, my face feels flushed. I check my watch and it is 5:00 in the evening. Should be any minute now. My head spins as the rum numbs my nerves.

"You OK?" the bartender asks.

"Yeah."

"Waiting for someone?" he says, looking around.

He arrives on time and takes his seat at the bar next to me. We don't make eye contact, just sit quietly.

"Anni," he says. I shake my head, unable to speak.

Anni

"Ladies night tonight at Rosie's Tavern" Sarah sang and pumped her hands to the air.

"I don't think so, I'm tired. I've been working my butt off waitressing and trying to get out these applications for a new job." I said.

"Oh, come on. It will be great. Just for a bit." She pleaded. "Just two drinks."
"Fine". I conceded.

At Rosie's we took a seat at the bar. Rosie's was one of those hometown bars with pictures of locals, newspaper articles and donated local memorabilia hanging on the wall. The music of a live amateur band was wailing, and the crowd grew as the night went on.

"Two beers please," Sarah said. She handed me a bottle. I took a sip and pressed my back against the bar looking for familiar faces.

"What are you two ladies up to tonight?" Joe, the bartender asked. Joe went to high school with Sarah and me and had been bar tending at Rosie's since then.
"You know, Joe," Sarah said, "having a beer, complaining about life, looking for some company." She nudged his arm.
"Here comes some nice company now," Joe shook his head in the direction behind me.
"Don't turn around, Anni," Sarah said, trying to play it cool.

"Hey, don't I know you?" a tall blond-haired man said. Sarah turned around.
"Um, possibly?" She flipped her brown hair from her shoulder.
"Sarah, right? I'm Adam. I used to work at the radio station. I left right after you were hired."
"Oh, yeah." She recalled, "Hey".
"Hey," he said awkwardly. "Can I buy you a drink?"
"Sure, that'd be nice."
"This is my friend, Jack." Adam pointed to Jack. Jack was tall, thick black hair, cut short with stubbly facial hair. He was dressed in dark blue jeans and a long sleeve button down shirt. He held out his hand to shake Sarah's and then mine. Sarah gave me a glance as if she was giving Jack and claiming Adam for herself.
"This is Anni," Sarah said as she touched my shoulder.

"Hi," I stuttered. Jack looked so familiar but I couldn't place where I have seen him before. His bright blue eyes are mesmerizing and I can't help but have this unexplained sinking feeling. I felt drawn to him though, like an old memory.

Jack sat down on the stool next to me at the bar and turned in my direction. "So, Anni, what are you drinking?" he asked. I held up my bottle of Miller Lite and he pointed to it. "Right," he said. He summoned Joe for two Miller Lites.

I held my bottle out and Jack clinked his bottle to mine. "To beer," he said.

"To beer," I repeated.

I took a few sips of beer before noticing Sarah had vacated her bar stool. I looked around, and I did not see her, and Jack moved over to take her seat.

"So, where are you from?" Jack said, leaning in to my ear so I can hear over the sound of the band.

"Beacon originally. Now I live in Fairway with Sarah."

"How about you?" I asked.

"I summered in Beacon, but I just got an apartment there while I finish school." Perhaps I ran into him somewhere, but I knew he looked familiar.

"Do you dance?" Jack said after some idle conversation.

"Not especially. Do you?"

"Not especially" he smiled. "Do you want to dance?"

I laughed, feeling particularly buzzed at the moment after having more than the two beers I promised Sarah we would stay for. He took my hand, and we headed towards the back room where the band is beginning Brown Eyed Girl and Jack put his hands around my waist. He moved side to side in a cheesy dance move, then put his arms around my neck. I wondered if he would kiss me on the dance floor and I felt nervous. "So" he said "where do you and Sarah live in Fairway? Can I give you a ride home?"

"Oh, I don't think that is necessary. Maybe another time?"

"That's not what I meant, Anni." I felt stupid now for assuming he wanted to take me home to my bed. Sarah distracted me from my thoughts as she and Adam appeared.

"Having fun?" she whispered loudly in my ear. I laughed at her. Neither one of us was clearly sober enough to drive home. Sarah put her hands in the air and bumped me with her hip. She put her arms around my neck and said, "I love you, Anni."
"About that ride?" I said to Jack.

Jack drove us home in his black SUV. I took note at how immaculate the car was inside. Sarah and Adam sat in the back seat and I moved into the passenger's seat. The passing street lights of Main Street made my head spin as we drive. We pulled up to our apartment and I'm sure I could hear Sarah and Adam kissing in the back but I do not want to turn around. I saw Jack glance in the rear-view mirror and then turned to look at me.

"Can I take you out sometime?" Jack said.
"Sure, I'd like that." He kisses my cheek. I cleared my throat to signal to Sarah that it was time to go. She stumbled up the stairs and into the dark apartment.
"Jack seems nice," Sarah said before she collapsed on the couch. I thought so too.

Jack

"Anni," he says again, placing his hand on my shoulder.
"Please talk to me," he begs. "Are you OK?"

"Jack, I was so stupid," I cry. I think about the message I sent to Michael asking him to meet me here. I was so reckless. What is wrong with me? Jack looks around the empty restaurant as we are the only two sitting here.

"Can we go somewhere else?" he asks. I stand up and lead him up to the suite I rented for Michael and me. I open the door and walk out to the balcony where the cool breeze dries my face. The waves are big today, crashing to shore repeatedly, never stopping.

"Jack, I'm sorry, I did something terrible," I begin. "I betrayed your trust."

"Did you sleep with him?" he asks.

"No, Jack, I promise," I say clearly, wiping the back of my hand across my face, realizing how close I came to crossing that line, and how willing I had been.

"It was Michael Carter. I loved him, I thought I still loved him. I never meant to hurt you Jack. I love you so much, you are everything to me, and to the kids."

"Michael Carter?" he repeats. "Michael that played basketball with Doug and his brother?" I nod my head. "Anni, that was high school."

"Yeah, technology is amazing Jack, puts you right back there," I snicker through my hysteria while I smear the tears across my face.

"Jack, remember that day on the beach, the volleyball tournament. You were there with Michael."
"How do you know that?" he asks.

"I was the one that ran after him, that grabbed his arm, begging him to talk to me. I recognized your eyes at Rosie's the night we met."

"Michael's girl? Pinball girl?" Jack looks in my eyes. I laugh at pinball girl. "That's what Doug always called Michael's girl. Michael's girl," he repeats. "Michael's girl was always off limits to the guys. I imagine Doug said that after that last night in Beacon.

"Well, guess you got the last laugh, huh, Jack," I chuckle nervously. "Married Michael's girl."

"Anni, I wasn't like those guys. I just played ball with them." I pull Jack close.

"I know, Jack."

"What about us, Anni?" he asks with hurt in his eyes. "You lied and made plans with Michael. Not just plans, a hotel. That is indicative of your intentions, don't you think?"

"Jack, I know. I'm so sorry. Something is missing," I say, hurt and confused. "I miss you, Jack."

"How do we fix it?" he asks.

"We need to find our way, Jack. We need to remember why

Christine Scarpa

we love each other."

Jack pulls me close, and I let myself go in his broad arms, resting my head on his chest. He kisses my forehead.

"Let's start right now, Anni," he says tipping my head back and kissing my lips.

For the first time in a while my heart is content.

237

Chapter 25

Epilogue

I put my beach chair down on the wet sand as the tide goes out, squishing the sand beneath my toes. Jack takes off his shirt and I admire his amazing muscles. It's been too long since I have appreciated the hours he spends at the gym.

I notice he captures the stares of other women on the beach.

"You still got it, Dr. Evans," I say. Jack winks.
"Let's go, lets go!" Juliette tugs at his hand dragging him into the ocean. He counts to three and swings her in the air jumping over the waves.

Ricky surfs by them on his boogie board.
The air is warm and dry, a perfect beach day. Ivy joins Juliette and Jack to jump waves and my heart swells watching my family enjoy the beach.

My phone buzzes from inside my bag and I reach it and pull up the message.

"Mom, I'm on my way," Maisie texts me. In all these years, this is the first time I will have my entire family together on the beach.

My eyes become wet thinking of the lost time because I couldn't deal with the past. I didn't want to bring my kids here because I was afraid it would open wounds. I put the phone back into my bag and head into the water putting my arm around Jack's waist.

He leans down and kisses me, while holding Juliette in his

arm.

In the distance I spot Maisie walking towards us and I wave my hand in the air to get her attention. Her hot pink bikini stands out in the crowd.

"Hi Maisie, how was work?"

"Good," she says. She walks back to the sand putting her beach bag and chair down. She looks at the lifeguard and waves a little wave, and smiles. I follow her gaze to a skinny blond lifeguard sitting on the stand and he smiles back. Maisie walks to the stand, and he jumps down, embracing her in her hot pink bikini, his bare chest pressing against her bare stomach. He kisses her lips and I turn away.

"Mom, I'm going with Aiden to a lifeguard party tonight," she says. We sit next to each other in our beach chairs, absorbing the warmth of the sun.

I smile at Maisie, "No, darling, you're not."

"Mom," she protests. Of course I'm going to let her go, you can't fight the culture.

Jack emerges from the water, his body wet and his shorts hanging on his hips, accentuating the muscles in his abs. I stand up, pressing my body towards his as our lips meet.

"Ew," Ricky says.

Jack and I sit in our beach chairs, and he takes my hand.

"I love you, Jack," I say.

"I love you, too, Anni." He takes my hand in his, "Here's to making new memories." I look around the beach, my kids, splashing in the surf, talking to the lifeguards, making friends, and my heart swells. New memories.

I notice Jack's gaze fixated on me.

"What?" I ask.

"Is that a new purple bikini?"

The End

About the Author

I grew up in Rio Grande, NJ just over the bridge from the Wildwoods, a popular shore community known for its beaches and boardwalks, and its amusement piers and back bays. While this book is fiction, many memories of my youth went into the story of Anni and Michael. Arcades, namely Ed's Funcade in North Wildwood, where I spent many days playing the Phantom of the Opera pinball game, and Hassle's Ice Cream Parlor and Mini Golf which has the greatest waffles and ice cream you will ever have. Other memories include Morey's Piers, The Sea Serpent roller coaster, Raging Waters and The Kite Shop. All of those places are still there!

I still live at the Jersey Shore area of Cape May County, New Jersey with my husband, Kevin and three children. I love my job teaching Psychology at Atlantic Cape Community College, and I am an active volunteer with the Girl Scouts. I earned my bachelor's degree in Psychology and Criminal Justice at Montclair State University and a Master's Degree in Teaching at Rowan University. One Loose String is my first novel and was inspired by many summers at the beach, especially my family's motel, The Sans Souci, once a landmark in North Wildwood, New Jersey.

The ideas for this book grew out of a collaboration of stories told by people who grew up on the barrier islands of Cape May County, including my husband, Kevin, who grew up in Avalon. And, of course, I throw in some of my own experiences there, but I'll never tell which ones!

Made in the USA
Middletown, DE
20 April 2019